"Dan!" she shouted as she played her flashlight beam in a haphazard fashion over walls and furniture. Was that *more* fake blood? "The prankster got inside again!"

She had to find Bony-Parts. She had enough time to reset this scene and return the manikin to the dining room, but only just, and only if she could locate the skeleton quickly.

There! Behind the sofa. She hurried toward the spot, irritated by the way the bones had been so carelessly dumped.

It was only when Liss bent down to examine the skeleton for damage that she realized she'd gotten it all wrong. She caught a sickening whiff of an odor she'd hoped she'd never have to smell again. The reek of death was both unmistakable . . . and terrifying.

She jerked upright and, for the first time, her flashlight beam shone directly on the face of the manikin.

Bile rose in Liss's throat. Her knees went weak, forcing her to grip the back of the sofa to keep from falling. What lay there was not a manikin. It was a man. A very dead man. The red marks on his neck weren't fake blood. The gore was all too real.

But that wasn't the worst of it.

The worst of it was that she knew him.

Books by Kaitlyn Dunnett

Kilt Dead

Scone Cold Dead

A Wee Christmas Homicide

The Corpse Wore Tartan

Scotched

Bagpipes, Brides, and Homicides

Vampires, Bones, and Treacle Scones

Ho Ho Homicide

Published by Kensington Publishing Corporation

VAMPIRES, BONES, AND TREACLE SCONES

KAITLYN DUNNETT

KENSINGTON BOOKS
www.kensingtonbooks.com

KENSINGTON BOOKS are published by

Kensington Publishing Corp.
119 West 40th Street
New York, NY 10018

All Kensington titles, imprints and distributed lines are available at special quantity discounts for bulk purchases for sales promotion, premiums, fund-raising, educational or institutional use. Special book excerpts or customized printings can also be created to fit specific needs. For details, write or phone the office of the Kensington Special Sales Manager: Kensington Publishing Corp., 119 West 40th Street, New York, NY, 10018. Attn. Special Sales Department. Phone: 1-800-221-2647.

Kensington and the K logo Reg. U.S. Pat. & TM Off.

ISBN-13: 978-0-7582-7268-3
ISBN-10: 0-7582-7268-5
First Kensington Hardcover Edition: August 2013
First Kensington Mass Market Edition: September 2014

eISBN-13: 978-1-61773-610-0
eISBN-10: 1-61773-610-4
First Kensington Electronic Edition: September 2014

10 9 8 7 6 5 4 3 2

Printed in the United States of America

Chapter One

"What do you think?" Liss MacCrimmon Ruskin asked her husband. "Does that look like a haunted house or what?"

Standing beside her at the foot of a steep flight of concrete steps set into an overgrown terrace and flanked by a rusty iron railing, Dan stared up at the old Chadwick mansion with an assessing gaze. "High Victorian architecture. Peeling paint. Ivy run wild on one side of the building. Boarded-up windows. It has potential . . . *if* the structure is sound. The last thing you want is for someone to fall through rotting floor-boards and end up with a broken neck."

Liss gave a theatrical shudder, although she was too much of an optimist to be seriously alarmed. The place would be perfect as part of Moosetookalook, Maine's Halloween festival and fundraiser. It already had the requisite unsavory reputation and its run-down appearance defined *spooky* to a T. Liss especially liked the round windows in the square tower. Lit from behind, they'd look like two glowing eyes.

"All our dead bodies will be department-store

manikins," she assured Dan. "That's why you're going to go through the place today with a fine-tooth comb. We'll have nearly a month and a half to repair any problems you find. If we can't fix something, we'll rope off the problem area to keep the paying public out of danger."

"Uh-huh. As if that ever works. There's always some bozo who takes a KEEP OUT sign as a challenge instead of a warning."

Dan was unenthusiastic about his role as safety inspector. Liss couldn't blame him. He knew the "we" she had designated to make repairs would consist of himself, aided and abetted by his brother Sam. If the house didn't pass muster, the two of them would end up volunteering their labor, as well as donating building materials. The Ruskins all had a strong sense of civic responsibility, and in this case, it was augmented by the fact that Liss, Dan's bride of eight weeks and one day, had been chosen by the Moosetookalook Small Business Association to organize the festival.

"Let's go see how bad it is." Resigned to his fate, he offered his hand and they started to climb.

By the time they mounted the porch steps, Liss was a trifle out of breath. "Thank goodness this isn't the only entrance to the house," she said with a laugh.

The driveway circled the mansion, leading to a small parking area at the back. With the addition of a short ramp, the kitchen door would also allow for handicapped access to the "haunted mansion."

Dan fitted the keys they'd been given into the locks. The last owner had installed three, two of them deadbolts. "And we're in," he announced. The door creaked ominously when he opened it.

Liss took that as a good sign. If all the other doors

in the place were as cooperative, she wouldn't need to use sound equipment to create the same effect. Eyes bright with anticipation, she stepped into the shadow-filled hallway.

There had not been electricity in the house for years. The only light came from the sun outside. It illuminated a rectangle of faded, flowered carpet runner and a swarm of dust motes.

Liss sneezed.

Dan reached into the pocket of his jeans and supplied her with a clean, white handkerchief before removing his backpack and using it to prop the door open. From the pack, he produced two heavy-duty flashlights and handed one to Liss. They turned them on, and she got her first good look at their immediate surroundings.

The hallway was long and narrow, ending in a closed door at the far end. *The kitchen*, she surmised. Two more closed doors flanked her. Before she could decide which one to open first, Dan's low whistle of appreciation distracted her. He had paused just inside the entrance to stare at a large, old-fashioned piece of furniture.

Liss had no idea what to call the object. *Coat rack* seemed inadequate to describe something that stood taller than Dan's six-foot-two. Maybe a hall tree? It had rows of three-inch pegs on either side of a three-quarter-length mirror and five drawers—two on each side and a single one at the center beneath the mirror.

"It's gorgeous," she said.

The streaked and dusty mirror reflected a dark and grainy image of the two of them. Dan's hair didn't show up as sand-colored, but rather a light gray. Her own dark brown locks looked muddy. Her eyes, which ranged from blue to green depending on what she was wearing, appeared in the glass to be murky brown. So did Dan's, although in reality they were the color of molasses. The illusion was nicely eerie, making it seem as if they'd aged several decades in the last few minutes.

"I think I'll keep this just the way it is," Liss murmured. "Being scared by your own reflection is a great way to start a haunted house tour."

Dan wasn't listening. He reached out to run one hand over the smooth wood. "A real craftsman built this."

"It takes one to know one," she said. In addition to his job at Ruskin Construction, Dan was a custom woodworker.

He glanced into the mirror, caught sight of something behind them, and turned to shine the beam of his flashlight on the staircase that curved gently upward from the first floor to the second. "And there's another work of art."

In places, the steps were coated in a layer of dirt thick enough to plant flowers in, but when Dan wiped off a small section on the lowest tread, Liss could make out the gleam of dark, glossy wood beneath the grime.

"Walnut," he said. "Expensive even way back when this place was built."

"To hear the old-timers tell it, the Chadwicks had more money than God. They could afford the best."

"Damned shame the house has been let go like this."

"The family died out." She shrugged. "And the last of them made the mistake of marrying Blackie O'Hare. But sad as it is, all that history makes this place ideal for our haunted house."

"Blackie" O'Hare, notorious gangster and hit man, had come into possession of the mansion through his wife, Alison Chadwick, the granddaughter and only heir of the last family members to actually live in the place year round. The old couple had died before Liss was born, so she'd never known them. Their childless granddaughter's death had followed not long after her marriage to Blackie, who might or might not have later used the mansion as a hideout when things got too hot for him in Boston. Many fanciful stories had sprung up over the years. One had Blackie burying treasure on the property. Another said it wasn't loot but rather dead bodies that he'd hidden in the wooded area surrounding the house. One rumor even claimed he'd murdered Alison and buried her in the basement.

What *was* certain was that Blackie's crimes had eventually caught up with him. He'd been arrested for murder, tried, convicted, and sentenced to life in prison in Massachusetts. During the investigation, a task force had been sent to Moosetookalook to search the mansion and its grounds. They'd hoped to turn up more evidence to use against him, but they'd found neither loot nor bodies. That hadn't stopped the locals from speculating. After all, those out-of-staters might well have missed something. Everyone in Maine knew folks from Massachusetts weren't too bright. Just look at the way they drove their cars!

Blackie had died in prison, stabbed to death by another prisoner. Afterward, no heirs having materialized, the town of Moosetookalook eventually seized the property for back taxes. The housing market being what it was, they'd been stuck with the place ever since.

It hadn't taken much effort on Liss's part to persuade the board of selectmen to let her use the Chadwick mansion for a municipal fundraising effort. Their only condition had been dictated by the liability insurance that covered the town—the house had to pass a safety inspection first.

With that in mind, Liss fished a lined five-by-seven tablet and a felt-tip pen out of Dan's backpack. She'd come prepared to spend the next few hours trailing after him as he checked the place out, noting down everything that needed to be fixed. If there was one thing at which Liss excelled, it was making lists.

They started at the top of the house, climbing to the third floor and then up a steep flight of steps—more like a ladder than stairs—to reach the tower Liss had admired from below. The room at the top was smaller than she'd expected and unfurnished.

"Lights in the windows, yes," Dan said. "Anything else, no. Those stairs are too narrow for safety."

Liss took a moment to admire the view. The leaves had just begun to turn. Spots of brilliant orange, red, and yellow stood out in sharp contrast to the dark greens of balsam, pine, and spruce.

"Five heavily wooded acres," Dan said. "It's a nice piece of property. I'm surprised it hasn't sold."

The trees made an impressive barrier between the house and its neighbors. A long, winding driveway provided yet another layer of isolation. It led to a little-used rural road a quarter mile distant.

The Chadwicks had liked their privacy, and yet the mansion was not all that far from the center of town. From this vantage point, Liss could pick out the top of the memorial to the Civil War dead in the town square and the steeple of the Congregational church beyond. Those were, however, the only visible signs of civilization. If she'd been looking from her own front porch toward the mansion, she wouldn't have known the house was there at all.

The third floor would have been called an attic in most houses. In the Chadwick mansion it was broken up into three bedrooms. They were bare and cheerless with low, sloped ceilings and no heat. Servants' quarters, Liss supposed, back when people could afford live-in help.

The second story also contained three bedrooms, but those were larger and crammed full of furniture. Upon entering each new room, Liss gave a cautious sniff. They all smelled musty—they'd been closed up for a long while—but she detected no hint of mold or mildew. Everywhere they walked, they left footprints in the dust and Liss had to duck more than one cobweb. While Dan did his safety checks, Liss poked around.

Drop cloths protected the contents in one room. In the others, the clutter had been left exposed. There seemed little rhyme or reason in the way items had been deposited. In the second room, two chairs with broken legs shared space with an exquisitely carved bedstead and highboy. Empty picture frames and an old steamer trunk were tucked into the third room between a four-poster and an old-fashioned standing wardrobe, but what instantly caught Liss's attention was the moth-eaten moose head mounted on one wall.

"Yuck," she muttered. "Imagine waking up to the sight of that monstrosity every morning!"

Liss didn't know much about antiques, but some of the furniture and a number of the decorative accessories looked old enough to be valuable. She picked up a lamp in the shape of an owl—brown glass fitted over a bulb. She supposed it was meant to be a night light. The words *art deco* floated through her mind, but she wasn't sure they applied to this piece. Still, it was certainly unusual and therefore collectible. She was surprised the town selectmen hadn't auctioned off the contents of the mansion to defray expenses.

"So far so good," Dan announced. "Ready to go back downstairs?"

"More than ready." She put the lamp back where she'd found it and wiped her fingers on the sides of her jeans to get rid of the grime it had left behind.

Back on the first floor, Dan suggested they start with the kitchen and work their way forward to the front door. Liss half expected to find a nineteenth-century wood stove taking pride of place. Instead, she walked into a scene out of an old black-and-white TV sitcom. It would have been more tolerable *without* color. The cabinets were bright yellow. All the appliances were a sickly avocado green. The dinette set tucked into a corner had chrome legs, a laminate top on the table, and chair seats upholstered in yellow vinyl. The radio on the Formica countertop was big and clunky and made of the same hard black material as the rotary-dial telephone sitting next to it.

"I wonder what Blackie O'Hare thought of this," Liss murmured.

"Hey, this was ultra-modern back in the fifties! The Victorian décor in the rest of the house probably made him more uncomfortable. Assuming, of course, that he ever lived here." Dan crossed the room to examine the back door and the small porch beyond. "Shouldn't be too hard to build a ramp."

"Good."

Liss left him in the kitchen while she began to explore the adjoining formal dining room. Wallpaper had once covered the ceiling, but it had begun to peel away and hung in ragged swaths above a massive sideboard and an equally oversized table and chairs. Liss liked the effect and made a note on her to-do list. She was visualizing an ultra-spooky set piece for the room when Dan called out to her that he was going down to the cellar.

"Let me know if you find Blackie's cache of cash!" she called after him.

His voice was muffled as he descended the stairs to the basement. "If I find buried treasure, you'll be the first to know."

Liss barely registered his answer. Her flashlight beam had come to rest on a painting that hung above the sideboard. Although it was partially obscured by the tattered ceiling paper, she recognized the subject at once. It was a rather famous portrait in Scottish circles—a likeness of the piper of Clan Grant. She had always thought it was an ugly piece. It had been painted, if she remembered right, in the seventeenth or early eighteenth century by a rather mediocre artist. This was a reproduction, of course, but its presence hinted that the Chadwicks had Scottish ancestors. She resolved to find out more when she had the time. Her day job as proprietor of Moosetookalook Scottish Emporium made it good business to make connections to all things Scottish within the local community.

When Dan reappeared, cobwebs caught in his hair and a fresh smudge on one sleeve, they left the dining room by way of the door to the hall. "Back room or front room?"

"Back, then front," Liss decided. "Anything of interest in the cellar?"

"Damp and dirt. I don't recommend letting paying customers go down there."

The back room was a library, although books were outnumbered by knickknacks on the floor-to-ceiling shelves that took up the inner walls. "Hoard much?" Liss murmured.

"The Chadwicks appear to have collected more than their fair share of what the Victorians called curios."

The baubles were displayed on pedestals and tables as well as on the shelves. The walls between boarded-up windows were hung with dozens of framed pictures in all sizes and shapes, so many that the pattern on the flocked wallpaper behind them was all but obscured.

Closed pocket doors led into the front room. Liss supposed that would have been called the parlor back in the day. Another door, also closed, was located directly opposite the one that led to the hall.

"What do you suppose is in here?" Without waiting for Dan to answer, she reached for the doorknob and shone her flashlight into the gloomy interior, expecting more furniture or the ghostly effect of dust covers. Instead, dozens of pairs of eyes stared back at her. A sound embarrassingly like an "eek" escaped before she could stop it and she backed up at warp speed, slamming into Dan's chest.

He grunted and caught her.

A second later, she felt him freeze as he looked past her into the room and saw what she had seen.

"What the—?"

Nothing attacked. No sound issued from the darkness beyond the door. After a moment, common sense returned, and Dan's flashlight beam steadied to reveal that the eyes belonged to a flock of stuffed birds.

"Creepy," Liss muttered, disgusted with herself for having been frightened.

She ventured deeper into what she decided to call the conservatory. Represented were a variety of species. Some stood on pedestals while others were suspended from the ceiling. The room also contained a grand piano with a stuffed pheasant perched on top of it.

"Mr. Chadwick's little hobby, I presume," said Dan.

"Good. This is good." Liss heard the tremor in her voice and ignored it, just as she was ignoring the amused note that had come into Dan's. "Nice and scary. We won't change a thing."

She retreated with more haste than grace, opened the pocket doors, and entered the front room. It *was* a parlor. At least, it contained a parlor organ, together with a sofa and two chairs—one straight backed and one wing—and a couple of end tables. There was also considerable evidence that they were not the first visitors to this particular room. A layer of debris covered the floor, mostly fast food wrappers, empty beer cans, and cigarette butts.

"Teenagers?"

"That would be my guess," Dan agreed. "The house has been standing empty for a long time."

"Looks like they stuck to this one room."

A picture window would have looked out onto the porch if it hadn't been boarded over, but a few shafts of sunlight still managed to make their way in through knotholes and a long crack in a sheet of warped and weathered plywood. That was enough to reveal that one of the sofa cushions had a cigarette burn in its brocade upholstery.

"It's a miracle they didn't burn the place down."

Holding the notepad so he could see the words, Liss wrote *install new lock on back door.*

"That'll help," he agreed.

"So what's the verdict? Is this our haunted house?"

"The whole place is remarkably sound for having been shut up for so long. I didn't find anything that raised a red flag."

Liss pumped her hand in the air. "Yes!"

"But you've got your work cut out for you."

She followed his gaze to the litter on the floor. "This isn't so bad. A thorough sweeping will get rid of the mouse droppings and trash. Then we can pretty much leave the rest of this room as it is. I mean, just look at that chandelier." Suspended from the high ceiling, it was festooned with cobwebs. "Half my decorating is already done if I just keep the lighting fixtures and the peeling wallpaper the way they are."

"So the spiders get to live long and prosper, do they?" Dan slung an arm around her shoulders and joined her in regarding the elaborate glass chandelier above their heads.

Liss leaned back against him, redirecting her gaze from light fixture to husband. He was five inches taller than she, and years of construction work had left him with well-toned muscles and excellent upper body strength. She snuggled closer. At five-foot-nine she wasn't exactly tiny, but Dan was big enough to make her feel delicate and feminine.

"I've got you to protect me, right?" She batted her eyelashes at him and grinned.

He chuckled. "I'd like to see the spider you couldn't handle all by your lonesome."

Liss was about to thank him for the compliment when she heard a whisper of sound from directly above her head. She glanced up in time to catch sight of something that was *not* a cobweb. It was not a piece of twine, either. It twitched. Then it disappeared, only to be replaced by a pair of close-set, predatory eyes—eyes that were *not* made of glass.

She was not particularly fanciful, nor was she squeamish, but the sound of little clawed feet moving over glass pendants gave her the willies. She darted sideways, dragging Dan after her, just as fine particles of dust drifted down over the spot where they had been standing.

"I can handle spiders and mice, but *that* was a rat!"

Since they had already retreated as far as the door to the hallway, Liss kept going. She didn't stop until she was safely outside on the porch. Dan followed more slowly. If he was amused by her sudden panic, he was smart enough not to show it.

"I'll take care of the rodent problem," he promised as he locked the door.

Liss rewarded him with a quick but heartfelt kiss.

By the time they were back in Dan's truck and heading for home, Liss was already adding items to her to-do list. First and foremost, the other members on her committee needed to see the Chadwick mansion for themselves, and the sooner the better. They had a lot to accomplish in just a few weeks. The haunted house, for all that it would be the centerpiece of the event, was only one of the attractions planned for the Moosetookalook All Hallows Festival.

Chapter Two

Lumpkin spat, hissed, and expanded to twice his normal size. Since he was a Maine Coon cat and weighed in at well over fifteen pounds on his slimmest day, he was a formidable sight.

The reason for his ill humor was a dog, Papelbon by name, a black and brown mutt of uncertain ancestry, although it probably included a splash of border collie. He belonged to Dan's brother Sam.

In spite of the unfriendly reception, Papelbon wagged his plume of a tail and tried to touch noses with the outraged feline. Lumpkin took a swipe at the dog and missed. With a yip of surprise, he retreated behind Sam's legs.

"Come out from there you yellow-bellied chicken."

"Daddy!" Sam's daughter Samantha, age nine, knelt beside Papelbon and flung her arms around his furry neck. "Don't be so mean. That nasty old cat scared him."

Papelbon licked her face.

Liss hid a grin as she scooped up the cat and slung

him over her shoulder, thus clearing the way for Sam, Samantha, and Papelbon to enter the house "I'll be right back," she said as she started down the hall. "Make yourselves at home."

Lumpkin growled low in his throat all the way to the kitchen. Liss carried him into the connecting pantry/utility room. "Sorry, sport," she told the cat. "You're confined to quarters for the duration. Live with it." She had to move fast once she put him down, but she managed to shut the door before he could get past her. The unmistakable sound of claws scoring wood made her wince, but didn't surprise her in the least.

Lumpkin was not adjusting well to his new home. He'd lived in the old one longer than Liss had and had not appreciated being uprooted. In retaliation, he'd reverted to one of his old bad habits—biting ankles. Then he'd picked up a new one—chewing on the furniture. Only that morning, Liss had discovered a hole in the upholstery at the back corner of Dan's favorite chair. Ragged tufts of white fill stuck out through the opening and a chunk of fabric was missing in its entirety. Liss worried that Lumpkin had eaten it and that it would make him sick but, aside from bad temper, nothing appeared to be wrong with him.

"Sorry about the dog, Liss," Sam apologized when she returned to the front hall. "Samantha didn't want to leave him at the house alone." Sam's wife June, normally a stay-at-home mom, had been stuck down to Fallstown for the past week, taking care of her mother, who had just gotten out of the hospital following hip surgery.

"Not a problem," Liss assured him. She bent down to pat Papelbon's head.

"I'll keep him with me so he won't disrupt your meeting."

"Sounds good to me."

"If all goes well, we should finish work this afternoon." Sam started up the stairs, Papelbon at his heels.

"That sounds even better."

For the last few weekends, Sam had been helping his brother remodel the attic. When it was done, Liss would have a combination library and at-home office with floor-to-ceiling bookcases on every wall—enough space for all the books she owned with a little left over for future acquisitions. Even though she did sometimes download e-books to her laptop, she still preferred to read the old-fashioned way—curled up in a chair with a printed volume in her lap.

"Would you like some hot chocolate?" she called after Sam. "Or a cup of coffee?"

Man and dog kept going. "I'm good, thanks."

A trifle nervously, Liss turned to face Samantha. She had not spent much time with her newly acquired niece. When it came right down to it, except for her eleven-year-old neighbor Beth Hogencamp, Liss had never had much to do with children.

Samantha watched her through narrowed eyes. Like all the Ruskins, she was tall with sandy brown hair. "You like cats better than dogs." It was an accusation, not a question.

"Apples and oranges," Liss said.

"What does *that* mean?"

The ringing doorbell saved Liss from trying to explain. "Go on into the living room and make yourself comfortable," she told Samantha. "We'll get started as soon as everyone arrives."

It was just after three-thirty in the afternoon on a

Monday, eight days after Liss's first visit to the Chadwick mansion. It had taken that long for everyone on
the Halloween committee to visit the house. Then,
to schedule a meeting, they'd had to find a time
when they were all free. Monday worked because
most of the small businesses clustered around the
town square were closed on that day to make up for
staying open on Saturdays. The time of day was dictated by the school bus schedule. Samantha wasn't
the only young person on Liss's team.

Two people stood on the porch. Liss's close friend,
Sherri Campbell, was dressed for work in the pale blue
uniform of the Moosetookalook Police Department. A
gun rode easily on her hip, despite the fact that in face
and figure she looked far more like a former cheer-
leader than an officer of the law. She had her hand
on the shoulder of a thin, blue-eyed, tow-headed
eight-year-old boy, her son Adam Willett. He was
Liss's youngest recruit.

"Good afternoon, Adam," Liss said. "What did you
think of the haunted house?" He'd been the last
committee member to visit it. The day before, Sherri
and her husband Pete Campbell had taken him out
to the mansion and given him the tour.

His bottom lip crept forward, but he wouldn't
meet Liss's eyes. "Didn't like it," he mumbled.

Taken aback, Liss looked to Sherri for an explanation.

"Scared him," she mouthed, but she was smiling.

"It's just an old house." Liss said in a bracing voice.
"And we're going to fix it up with all kinds of . . . of
magic tricks. They won't really be frightening. This is
just pretend. Like the movies. It'll be fun."

"Magic?" He sounded doubtful.

"Like . . . like Harry Potter." She'd read the books

some time ago and had to struggle to think of an example that would reassure the little boy. "Just think of the most ridiculous thing you can and the scary stuff disappears. Right?"

"Don't want to go back there," Adam said.

"Then you won't have to. You can be in charge of something else for Halloween. Okay?"

"Trick or treating?"

"Sure. Why not?"

He thought it over. "Okay."

They were still standing in the doorway. Sherri gave her son a gentle shove to get him over the threshold. "Just send him to the PD when you're done. I'm on the two-to-ten shift, but he can go up to the library and do his homework until Pete gets off work." Adam's stepfather was a Carrabassett County deputy sheriff.

"Will do." Liss could see the redbrick municipal building from where she stood. In addition to the police department and the public library—the latter took up most of the second floor—it housed the town office and the fire department. It would take Adam less than two minutes to walk there.

Liss had barely settled the little boy on her living room sofa before the doorbell chimed again. On her way to answer it, she glanced around to see what Samantha was up to and found that her niece had unbent far enough to take off her backpack. It sat on the floor beside her as she examined an eight-inch-high Royal Doulton figurine of a nineteenth-century lady, one of the many collectibles displayed around the room.

For just a second, Liss flashed on the clutter at the Chadwick mansion. *This is not the same,* she assured herself. She kept souvenirs and gifts people had

given her, and odds and ends her parents and grand-
parents had passed down to her, or that she'd inherited along with the house she'd lived in until she
married Dan. But there were no stuffed birds or
moose heads!

Liss's treasures ranged from bisque cats—four of
them—and Royal Doulton figurines—an even half
dozen—to majolica-ware cups and saucers and antique bud vases, to small stuffed animals and two
Buffy the Vampire Slayer action figures. Temporarily,
all this bric-a-brac was set out in the living room. As
soon as work was finished in the attic, most of it
would be relocated.

The doorbell sounded as if someone was leaning
on it. Liss increased her pace to a trot, but she'd
barely set foot in the hallway when a dark streak
sailed past her, barreling into the living room. Adam
squealed in delight. Samantha let out a shriek of
alarm.

A moment later, the girl uttered a shrill command. "Papelbon! Down!"

Papelbon woofed happily. Liss had a feeling that
he obeyed about as well as her two cats did. For a
nanosecond, she considered returning to the living
room to help her niece. First things first, she decided, and flung the door open wide to put a stop to
the annoying buzz of the bell.

She found herself face-to-face with a mouthful of
gleaming white teeth—Gloria Weir's wide, friendly,
omnipresent smile. Bright-eyed and ginger-haired,
Gloria was puppy-dog eager to make a place for herself in the tight-knit community of Moosetookalook.
Shortly after she'd opened her hobby and craft store
in the former Locke Insurance building, she'd
joined the Moosetookalook Small Business Associa-

tion. She'd faithfully attended every meeting. When Liss had asked for volunteers for the Halloween committee, Gloria's hand had shot up. She'd all but bounced up and down in her seat in her anxiety to be among the chosen. She hadn't needed to worry about being picked. She'd been the *only* one at the meeting to offer to help.

For a split second, hearing the commotion in the living room, Gloria's smile faltered. "What on earth is going on in there?"

Dan thundered down the stairs, his dark eyes full of laughter. "Papelbon's not so good with *sit* or *stay*," he explained on his way past, "but apparently Samantha did teach him how to open doors."

Sam followed more slowly, looking sheepish. "Sorry, Liss."

Liss and Gloria entered the living room to find chaos. Papelbon danced around his young mistress, ignoring her command to sit, while Dan attempted, unsuccessfully, to catch hold of his collar. Samantha's face scrunched up as if she might burst into tears at any moment. Her mouth opened in an expression of surprise as Glenora, the other cat in the household, emerged from beneath the recliner where she'd apparently been napping.

She was only half the size of Lumpkin, but still impressive—a pure black Maine Coon cat. The second Papelbon caught sight of her, he went into raptures, abandoning Samantha to investigate the newcomer. Glenora arched her back at his approach. She didn't spit or hiss, but neither was she interested in making a new friend. With a fine display of disdain, she turned her back on the dog, flipped her long, luxuriant tail at him, and stalked out of the room.

Before Papelbon could chase after the cat, Sam

grabbed hold of the dog's collar. He sent a wary glance in his daughter's direction and was clearly relieved to discover that she was not crying.

"It wasn't his fault," Samantha insisted.

"I know that, honey, but I'll just take him back upstairs with me now. Okay?"

Samantha sniffled, but nodded, and Sam tugged the reluctant canine out of the room. They'd just started up the steps when someone else knocked on Liss's front door.

"Come on in!" she called out. "Admission to the three-ring circus is free!"

A straight-back wooden chair had been knocked over during the fray. Liss righted it and surveyed the rest of the living room. She couldn't spot any obvious damage and nothing else seemed out of place.

Samantha flopped down on the sofa next to Adam. She held her backpack clutched in front of her like a shield and avoided meeting her aunt's eyes. Liss wondered if she should say something to let the girl know she wasn't angry about the dog. Before she could decide, Beth Hogencamp appeared in the doorway.

Liss had given Beth dance lessons, until a real school of dance opened in town. And they'd shared an adventure or two. Her radiant smile lifted Liss's spirits . . . until she realized the girl was not alone.

A boy slouched into the room behind her. He was tall, skinny, and scowling, and he wore the ill-fitting, strategically ripped clothing that seemed to be the uniform of boys of a certain age.

"This is Boxer," Beth announced. "He's going to help."

The nickname meant nothing to Liss, but a flutter of movement from Samantha's direction caught her eye. She glanced at her niece in time to see the girl's cheeks turn bright pink. Then Samantha ducked her head and stared fixedly at her clasped hands.

She's only nine, Liss thought. *She can't be interested in boys yet!*

Aloud, she welcomed Boxer and invited him to take a seat. Just because he didn't make a great first impression didn't mean he had nothing to contribute. Besides, if he was responsible for Beth's enthusiasm, she could only be grateful. When Liss had first approached her young neighbor, Beth hadn't wanted anything to do with Halloween. She'd argued that she was too old for such a silly holiday and had agreed to help only after Liss promised her that she could invite a friend to serve on the committee with her. That friend, it appeared, was Boxer.

Last to arrive was Stu Burroughs. His business, Stu's Ski Shop, was right next door to Liss's store, Moosetookalook Scottish Emporium. Short, chunky, and graying, Stu was something of a curmudgeon. Liss wasn't surprised when he took exception to Boxer's appearance. He looked the boy up and down, his lips curving into a contemptuous sneer. "You got a last name, kid?"

Boxer's chin jutted out at a belligerent angle. He had a plain, square face but his dark brown eyes were bright with animosity. "It's Snipes. What's it to ya?"

Stu's bushy eyebrows shot up and Liss suppressed a groan. Snipes was a name well-known in Moosetookalook. Several members of the family were . . . disreputable, to say the least. Still, no matter who Boxer's parents were, Liss didn't think it was fair to hold the actions of adults against a child of eleven or twelve.

"Coffee, anyone?" she asked brightly. "Or cocoa?"

"I'll have a beer," Boxer said.

Beth snickered.

"Cocoa all around, then. I'll be right back."

"I'll give you a hand." Stu stomped out of the room and was waiting for Liss in the kitchen when she got there.

"All right, Stu. What's got you on the warpath?" Liss had mugs ready on a tray, a packet of pre-measured hot chocolate mix in each one. All she had to do was add water from the kettle steaming on the stove.

"What's that Snipes boy doing here?"

"Beth brought him."

"I'm pretty sure he tried to shoplift a ski mask out of my store the other day."

"*Pretty* sure?"

"I'm keeping my eye on him."

"You do that, but until you actually catch him walking off with something, you give him the benefit of the doubt. Presumed innocent until proven guilty, right?"

"I don't need proof to know a bad apple when I see one," Stu grumbled under his breath. "Figures he'd be a Snipes."

"Keep your voice down and your opinions to yourself, Stu!" Liss jerked her head toward the doors that opened into the front of the house. One led to the hall and the other to the dining room. Both were open.

"You know what they're like," Stu muttered.

Liss uncovered a plate of assorted cookies, added it to the tray, and started pouring hot water into the mugs. "I don't know any of the Snipes family well. Rodney and Norman were a couple of years behind me in school. Hilary is two or three years older than I am."

"He must be Hilary's kid. Heard she had a boy. She's Cracker's half sister. Quite a bit younger than him, but she's aunt to Rodney and Norman all the same. Works as a checker at the grocery store." Stu made a rude noise. "It's anybody's guess who the kid's father is."

"That's enough, Stu."

Liss kept her voice low, but let her anger show. Boxer was not responsible for anything members of his family had done and he certainly couldn't be blamed for the circumstances of his birth. Besides, there were times when it was a mark of intelligence on the part of an expectant mother to decide that single parenthood was a better choice than marriage to an unsuitable or unstable sperm donor.

Stu looked as if he had more to say, but a noise from the direction of the pantry distracted him. Glenora stood on her hind legs on the kitchen side of the door, batting at the wooden panels with her front paws.

Liss returned the kettle to the stove and handed Stu a spoon. "Would you stir these, please?"

She opened the pantry door just far enough to shove the black cat through. Lumpkin made a gallant attempt at escape, but Liss was too quick for him. She did not intend to put up with any more cat vs. dog confrontations.

When Stu finished the task she'd given him, Liss picked up the tray and handed it to him. Firmness might not work all that well with cats, but sometimes it did with people. She could only hope. "Carry this into the dining room for me, will you, Stu? Just set it on the table and we'll call the meeting to order."

"I should never have let you badger me into joining this committee," he grumbled, but he did as he was told.

Liss rolled her eyes and followed him out of the kitchen.

A few minutes later, everyone was seated at Liss's dining room table and she'd handed around mugs of cocoa, cookies, pads, and pencils.

"What's this for?" Gloria stared at the legal pad in front of her as if she'd never seen lined yellow paper before.

"That's so you can make lists of what has to be done. Lists are always useful." When Gloria continued to look doubtful, Liss turned to the first item on *her* list, the agenda for the meeting. "Has everyone had a chance to look around our haunted house?" She glanced at Boxer.

"Seen it," he mumbled around a mouthful of chocolate-chip cookie.

"Good. Well, then—suggestions? Anyone?"

"How scary do you want to get?" Gloria asked. "A friend of mine was telling me about a play she saw once. One character swept aside a curtain, and there were the heads of the other character's children. Freaked her right out. The heads were wax, or maybe plaster, but they *looked* real. Their eyes were open and kind of bulging out and there was lots of fake blood."

Beth stuck her finger in her mouth and made gagging noises. Adam giggled.

"Have you got a better idea?" Liss asked her young neighbor.

"How about zombies?"

"Oh, nicely gross." Gloria's grin signaled approval. She nibbled delicately at a molasses cookie.

"Do you mean people dressed up as zombies?" Stu asked. "Or manikins?"

For a moment, Beth looked stumped. "Manikins, I guess. But they won't be as scary."

"We don't have a big budget," Liss reminded her. "We can't afford to hire actors. And to make someone look like a zombie, you'd need a lot of make up. Same goes for vampires."

Beth made a face. "Vampires are *so* yesterday!"

Liss just shook her head. Vampires, she could understand . . . sort of. At least there was a long literary tradition of romantic vampire heroes. But zombies? She didn't see anything remotely appealing about animated dead people who were slowly rotting away. After a moment's thought, she decided that she didn't *want* an explanation.

"I realize that the old trick of putting a sheet on a pulley and calling it a ghost is way too tame," she said, moving on, "but we need to keep the blood and gore to a minimum. After all, Moosetookalook's All Hallows Festival is supposed to be family-friendly."

"Can we have spooky sound effects?" Adam asked.

"Definitely. I still have theatrical contacts from my days on the road. I can arrange something without too much trouble." Liss had toured for eight years with a Scottish dance company, until a career-ending knee injury had sent her back to her old home town to heal and regroup.

Stu asked about lighting effects, which led to a discussion about borrowing a generator to supply power to the mansion.

"Candles are way spookier than electric lights," Beth insisted.

"Yes, but open flames are a safety issue." Stu showed more patience than Liss expected of him, although she noticed that he spoke exclusively to Beth and ignored Boxer. "With a generator, you'll have plenty of light while you're setting things up and you can run special lighting effects, too."

"What if we create a poisoning scene in the dining room?" Liss suggested after they'd discussed what to do in the conservatory, the parlor, and the library, and voted to use tour guides to take people around in small groups, rather than let them wander freely through the mansion. They'd also agreed to string a velvet rope across the bottom of the main staircase to discourage people from wandering upstairs on their own. "We can dress manikins in old-fashioned clothing and arrange them around that wonderful antique table. We'll leave the cobwebs and the peeling wallpaper as they are and add platters of fake food. Envision the victims falling facedown onto their plates."

"They *all* die?" Beth asked.

"That's the way the cookie bounces," Boxer said, chomping down on another one of the chocolate-chip variety.

"Balls bounce," Stu muttered in an irritable voice. "Cookies crumble."

Boxer smirked at him. "You sure about that?"

"Yes or no on the poisoning scene?" Liss interrupted.

Everyone voted in favor of the idea except Samantha. She sat with her eyes downcast, concentrating on her mug of cocoa. Her hair fell forward to conceal most of her face. Liss glanced at Boxer and thought she could guess why her niece had yet to contribute anything to the discussion. Liss could remember being just as painfully shy and tongue-tied when she was a young girl . . . and in the same room as a boy she had a crush on. Why Boxer Snipes should appeal to either Beth or Samantha eluded her, but puppy love was rarely logical.

"I think we should hang a body in the stairwell." Gloria's suggestion jerked Liss back to the matter under discussion—decorating the haunted house. "There's just room enough for a rope where the banister curves around at the top."

Liss had no difficulty visualizing the scene. "We could use another manikin for the victim. Or perhaps a dummy made of softer material. More like a scarecrow, so the body won't look so stiff." She'd recently read a mystery by a local author in which the villain left the body in the middle of a cornfield, in place of a scarecrow. Creepy!

"A stiff is supposed to be stiff," Stu said, sotto voce. More loudly, he asked, "Are you sure you don't want blood? What if we cut the body open so the guts hang out?"

"Oh, yes!" Gloria exclaimed. "And we could put up a little sign to tell people that he'd been hanged, drawn, and quartered."

"Um, I don't think they did the last part of that while the body was still *on* the gallows."

"My friend says—"

"The same one who saw that macabre play?" Liss asked.

Gloria nodded.

"Maybe she'd like to join the committee," Stu suggested. "She could take my place."

Liss sent a withering look in his direction. "*Would* she be interested?" Liss asked Gloria. "Not that we can manage without Stu, but there's plenty to do and another pair of hands would be welcome."

A delicate flush stained Gloria's cheeks as she

backpedaled. "Oh, she can't. That is, she'd be un-comfortable . . . oh, dear. The truth is, she's not re-ally a friend. She's my great-aunt, Flo Greeley. She's been my house guest for the last week, but she's re-covering from plastic surgery after an accident and she's very sensitive about her appearance. She wouldn't be at all comfortable meeting strangers. Not at all. Why, I can barely get her to go out into my back yard for a breath of fresh air."

"I understand completely," Liss assured her. "For-get I mentioned it. So, does anyone have any other suggestions to do with the haunted house or shall we move on to the next Halloween activity?"

"How about coffins in the basement?" Stu asked. "Seems like a natural, with or without vampires."

"The cellar is off limits," Liss said. "The stairs are narrow and steep and the floor is dirt. For safety rea-sons, we should keep the cellar door locked during the guided tours."

Next on Liss's agenda was a discussion of games for the community costume party.

"Did you know that Halloween is believed to have originated in Scotland?" she asked, smiling a little in anticipation of being kidded about finding a con-nection to her Scottish heritage. "That's where the name All Hallows came from. That being the case, I thought we could include a few traditional Scottish activities, like bobbing for apples. That's called 'apple dookin' by the Scots. Another Scottish Hal-loween game is 'treacle scones.' "

"Okay." Stu sounded resigned. "I'll bite. What do you do with the scones?"

Liss laughed. "In fact, biting is what you *try* to do. You cover the scones in treacle, tie each one to the end of a piece of twine, and suspend them overhead.

Blindfolded contestants, their hands held behind their backs, attempt to catch hold of a scone with their teeth. The first person to succeed, wins."

Beth giggled.

"What are scones?" Boxer asked.

"The better question is what's treacle?" Stu muttered.

"Scones are . . . biscuits. Treacle is what the British call molasses. We could use anything that's sticky—honey, or maybe maple syrup. The idea is that contestants end up with messy faces and everyone laughs a lot."

Gloria grimaced in distaste. "Messy? I call it disgusting. And think of the germs! The last thing we want is to have festival-goers come down with the flu a week after our fundraiser."

This from the woman who wanted to eviscerate a dummy! With regret, Liss crossed treacle scones off her list of suggestions.

"You forgot the trick-or-treating," Adam piped up.

"Never! Let's talk about that next."

By the time the committee members went their separate ways, they'd set a tentative schedule for Moosetookalook's All Hallows Festival. The thirty-first of October conveniently fell on a Saturday, so the festivities could start early in the day. A corn maze would be open from mid-morning until late afternoon, when tours of the haunted house would start. Meanwhile, a costume parade and contest would take place in the town square. Prizes would also be awarded in various categories for carved pumpkins. Next would come the lighting of the community bonfire. After that, young revelers would go trick-or-treating. They'd reassemble an hour later for a Halloween party. Simultaneously, their parents and other adults would attend their own costume party.

"The meeting went better than I expected," Liss told Dan that evening after supper.

They were in the living room, surrounded by cardboard boxes and bubble wrap. Now that her new library/office was finished, Liss was eager to move in. She chattered cheerfully as they wrapped her bits and bobs, recounting the committee's discussion of blood and gore and ghosts. When everything was packed, they carried the boxes up to the attic.

Liss lost count of how many trips they made, but by the time the living room was empty of cartons, she'd run out of steam. She readily fell in with Dan's suggestion that she call it a day, especially when she recognized the look in his eyes.

They were, after all, still newlyweds.

Chapter Three

Liss's boxes were still unpacked the following afternoon when she put the BACK IN 15 MINUTES sign on the door of Moosetookalook Scottish Emporium and trotted across the town square to the public library.

"I'm looking for information on the Chadwick family," she told the librarian, Dolores Mayfield. "Is there anything in the local history section about them or their house?" Liss was curious as to whether there was a Scottish ancestor in their family tree, but more interested in learning something of the history of the mansion. Who knew? She might even unearth a nice juicy murder somewhere in its past—something to inspire the creation of a resident ghost.

"I suppose I could let you browse through my clippings." Dolores sounded reluctant, but Liss didn't doubt for a moment that she intended to make them available. Dolores liked to be coaxed.

"I didn't know you kept files of clippings."

"I've done it for years. Since before there was an Internet." Dolores gave a small, self-deprecating chuckle as she left her desk and crossed the library to a large vertical file cabinet, rolling up the sleeves of her turtleneck pullover as she went. "Worth their weight in gold sometimes. You never know what information someone will come looking for."

Dolores, as Liss knew to her sorrow, was Moosetookalook's resident snoop. She didn't just collect clippings for the benefit of some future researcher. She clipped items from the newspapers because she liked to know everything about everybody and gossip about them behind their backs.

A bulging file folder labeled CHADWICK emerged from the A-H drawer. Dolores handed it over and stooped to open I-Z. A moment later, she produced a second, equally thick folder. The label on this one read O'HARE, EMMETT (BLACKIE).

"I didn't know Emmett was Blackie O'Hare's real name," Liss said.

"Live and learn. You can look through these files here in the library or check them out for two weeks, same as a book."

A quick glance at the contents of the Chadwick folder told Liss there was way too much material to absorb during a fifteen-minute coffee break. The first three items alone warranted careful reading. They were the obituaries of Alison Chadwick O'Hare, Euphemia Grant Chadwick, and Edgar Chadwick. "I'll just take the Chadwick one for now, Dolores. Thanks."

"Suit yourself." She returned Blackie's file to its proper place. "I hear you're looking for a replacement."

"Excuse me?"

"Stu Burroughs. I hear he's quitting your Halloween committee." Back at the check out desk, Dolores stamped a slip of paper with the due date and tucked it into the Chadwick folder. Her gray eyes were avid behind small, rimless spectacles.

"This is the first I've heard of it." Liss tugged on the file folder, but Dolores still had hold of it.

The last thing she wanted was for Dolores to volunteer to take Stu's place. If he really did resign, she'd ask Sherri to step in. Or Angie Hogencamp, Beth's mother. Even Boxer's mother, Hilary Snipes, would be a better choice than Dolores Mayfield.

"You ought to recruit the gentleman who just moved into Doug Preston's old place," Dolores said, releasing her grip. "He'd be perfect."

Liss told herself to head for the door and not allow herself to be lured in by Dolores's smug expression, but curiosity won out over self-preservation. "How so?"

"Well, I should think that would be obvious. The man is living in a former mortuary."

"A funeral parlor wouldn't be my first choice for a home," Liss conceded. "Sleeping in a house with an embalming room in the basement would give me nightmares. But maybe this newcomer is made of sterner stuff."

Dolores leaned across the wide, highly polished surface of her desk until her face was only inches away from Liss's. She lowered her voice, even though there was no one else in the library to hear them. "I bet he got a real good deal on the price."

No wager, Liss thought, clutching the file folder to her chest and heading for the exit. With Doug out of the picture, Lorelei Preston had packed up all her possessions and her teenaged son, and moved to Portland. She'd have sold out for a song, just to sever her last tie to Moosetookalook.

Liss almost made good her escape, but she couldn't move fast enough to outrun Dolores's voice.

"I think he must be a writer."

Inches from the door, Liss turned back. *Curiosity*, she reminded herself, *killed the cat*, but an old adage was not enough to keep her from wanting to know how Dolores had come to this particular conclusion. "What makes you think so?"

"He unloaded a lot of office equipment from a U-Haul."

"A home office doesn't necessarily equate to a writer."

The absence of solid facts had never kept Dolores Mayfield from jumping to conclusions before. Liss didn't need to ask how she'd come to notice the U-Haul in the first place. The library occupied the second floor of the municipal building. Although row after row of book shelves filled the interior, with a few tables, microform readers, computer terminals, and storage cabinets tucked in among them, there were banks of tall windows along all the exterior walls. They provided an excellent view of the town square and the buildings surrounding it.

Liss made another mental note. *Make sure the bedroom curtains are tightly closed any time Dan and I are in there together!*

"I'm guessing horror writer," Dolores elaborated. "Like Stephen King. Wouldn't that be something?"

"What's the new guy's name?" Liss asked.

"Homer Crane, but I'm sure he writes under a pseudonym. Everyone seems to these days."

"Or maybe our Mr. Crane is a retired sales clerk or a long-distance truck driver or a chicken farmer who decided to buy a former funeral home simply because it was priced for a quick sale."

Dolores dismissed Liss's alternatives with a careless wave of one hand. "If he's not famous, why don't we know more about him? He's kept a very low profile for someone who's been living in this town for a couple of months. He moved in while you and Dan were away on your honeymoon."

I should have kept going when I had the chance, Liss thought. Now that she'd been drawn into the web of Dolores's speculations, she couldn't seem to fight her way out.

"Maybe he's just shy," she suggested.

"He doesn't go off to work every day like someone with a real job. That means he works at home."

"Or he's on vacation."

"He's a loner, too. He hasn't had a single visitor since he moved in."

Liss wondered if Dolores stayed at the library at night to spy on her neighbors, but dismissed the idea as too fanciful. Dolores and Moose Mayfield had a lovely little house out on Upper Lowe Street.

"He hasn't made any attempt to make friends," Dolores continued. "The only time he comes out of that house is to walk to the post office to collect his mail. He gets a lot of mail," she added, a knowing look on her face. "Lots of packages. Manuscripts, I'll bet."

Manuscripts, Liss thought, *would be going the other way if he really is a writer. Or, more likely, be submitted electronically.* She kept that thought to herself. She couldn't spend the entire day debating with Dolores. She'd put that BACK IN 15 MINUTES sign on the shop door fully twenty minutes ago.

"I've really got to get going, Dolores. You have a nice day." Liss thought she'd escaped, but no sooner had she set foot on the pavement outside the municipal building than she heard the unmistakable sound of a window being raised.

Dolores thrust her head out through the opening. "You should stop in and ask him if he wants to be on your committee," she called down. "The house is on your way back to work."

Liss gestured toward the town square on the other side of Main Street from the municipal building. Cutting across it was the most direct route to Moosetookalook Scottish Emporium. The former funeral home was en route only if Liss went the long way around the square.

"It's not as if you have customers beating down the door to get in!" In a huff, Dolores retreated, slamming the window closed for emphasis.

Sadly, her observation was true, even though it was the height of leaf-peeper season. And, if Liss was honest with herself, she had to admit that Dolores's speculations had made her curious about her new neighbor.

There were three buildings on each side of the square. The municipal building was in the center on the north, Main Street. Liss gave the Emporium one last, longing look and turned right. Once she passed Angie's Books, owned and operated by Angie Hogencamp, she had only to hang a left at the corner to reach the former funeral home.

I'm just being friendly, she told herself as she climbed the steps to the porch. Not snoopy. Before she could change her mind, she rang the doorbell. Belated second thoughts immediately assaulted her. What on earth was she going to say to the man when he answered?

Liss shifted her weight from foot to foot as the seconds passed. Make that, *if* he answered. It didn't look as if he was going to. She had just turned to leave when she heard the sound of a deadbolt being released. The door opened only a few inches, just enough for her to glimpse a bulky figure in gray sweats. A man blinked at her from the dimly lit foyer, making her wonder if she'd woken him from a nap.

"Yes?" His voice was very soft, but not obviously unfriendly.

"Uh, hello. I'm one of your neighbors. Liss MacCrimmon. I mean Liss Ruskin." She felt herself blushing. "I only recently got married. Sometimes I forget my own name."

Liss's flustered explanation seemed to have a positive effect. The door eased open another inch. "My name is Homer Crane. How may I help you?"

"I'm your neighbor," she repeated, and gestured toward the south side of the square. "My shop, Moosetookalook Scottish Emporium, is over there and my husband and I live almost directly across from you on Birch Street. I just wanted to introduce myself and, well, I imagine you'll think me silly, but I'm also the chair of Moosetookalook's Halloween committee and we're working on ideas for a festival and fundraiser. In particular, we're turning an old mansion on the outskirts of town into a haunted house, and someone suggested that you might have some, um, expertise in the area of ghosties and ghoulies and things that go bump in the night."

Very fair eyebrows lifted all the way to what appeared to be a receding hairline—it was hard to tell between the shadows and the hoodie he was wearing—and his tone of voice sharpened. "Who told you that?"

Liss took an involuntary step back. "Our town librarian. She's convinced that you write horror novels. Under another name."

"Another—? She's wrong." He closed the door in Liss's face, but not before she caught a glimpse of alarm on his face.

"Sorry to have bothered you," she called through the solid wooden barrier.

His only reply was to reengage the deadbolt with a decisive click.

Since it was on her way around the square, and since there was still no line of potential customers waiting in front of the Emporium, Liss stopped in at the post office before she returned to work. Julie Simpson handed over two envelopes—bills, unfortunately—and a magazine.

"What do you know about Homer Crane?" Liss blurted.

"Odd duck," the postmaster declared in a loud, nasal voice that betrayed her New York origins.

"Dolores thinks he's a writer."

"Artist," Julie said. "At least that's what he told me. He said he designs video games. Said he does the artwork on a computer. Not the story lines, though. Said he's not clever enough to write those."

"I'm surprised he was so chatty."

Julie's brassy laugh bounced off the walls of the small post office. "Not so's you'd notice. One of his packages was damaged when it got here, so I got a look at what was inside. On top was this really disgusting picture of a dead body. Lots of blood. He told me it was research for the artwork he's doing for a vampire story. I got a feeling the vampires he draws aren't the sexy kind."

"Maybe it's just as well I couldn't persuade him to help us design spooky sets for the haunted house."

"He said no?"

Liss nodded. "He made it pretty clear he wanted to be left alone." Like most Mainers, Liss had been taught to oblige folks who wanted to keep themselves to themselves.

"Good luck with that if Dolores has him in her sights."

"I don't think she's been able to see much, although she did say the only time he leaves his house is to come here and pick up his mail."

"She doesn't know everything." Julie snorted. "And she'd need x-ray vision to see through Angie's place and take a gander at the old funeral home parking lot and that big garage Doug Preston built for his hearse."

"Meaning Crane *does* go out?" Somehow that relieved Liss's mind.

"Oh, sure. I can just see the corner of Elm Street from here. He heads out that way, so he avoids circling the square. No idea where he goes, but I've seen him three or four times. He drives a black Toyota."

Arms filled with the bulging Chadwick file and her mail, Liss returned to work. She put the odd little man living in the former mortuary out of her mind. She intended to spend the rest of the afternoon reading clippings, but she'd barely started on Alison O'Hare's obituary when a tour bus pulled up in front of the Emporium. Two dozen leaf peepers poured out, intent on visiting the quaint little shops of Moosetookalook, Maine. Online promotion, it seemed, was paying off.

Fixing a "friendly shopkeeper" smile on her face,

Liss stashed the file folder beneath the sales counter and concentrated on helping potential customers find souvenirs of their trip to view Maine's fall foliage.

Moosetookalook Scottish Emporium sold everything from figurines of pipers to clan crest pins to canned haggis. Kilts and tartan skirts filled two large clothing racks, and she stocked scarves and hats, too. An item she'd recently added—a small pewter figure in a kilt standing next to a large pewter moose—seemed to tickle the fancy of the tourists. She sold four of them, along with several other, less expensive items.

More than two hours later, just as the last shopper was leaving, the phone rang. The bell over the door fell silent as Liss answered.

By the time she hung up, the good mood created by a successful afternoon of selling merchandise had evaporated. Dan wasn't going to make it home for supper. He was on his way to Three Cities to hunt for a particular brass drawer pull a customer had decided she had to have on her kitchen cabinets. Since Ruskin Construction was trying to finish that job by the weekend, he didn't want to wait around for a mail-order delivery.

Liss thought about seeing if any of her friends were free. She considered mooching a meal off Aunt Margaret, who lived above the Emporium, but Margaret hadn't come home from work yet. Deciding she wasn't really in the mood for company, Liss closed up and walked home, the Chadwick file tucked under one arm.

At the house, a quick check of the refrigerator, freezer, and kitchen cabinets revealed nothing that appealed to her. She fed Lumpkin and Glenora, then stood in the center of the room, thinking. Fruit, she decided. She was in the mood for fresh fruit, something her new husband ate only when forced into it.

Grabbing her lightweight fall jacket, she headed out again. It was only a short walk to the High Street Market. Liss ordinarily did her food shopping once a week at the Hannaford in Fallstown, but the small mom-and-pop store served as backup for everyone in Moosetookalook. If you ran out of milk, or beer, or cat food, you stopped by the local grocery store to pick some up. Like as not, you came home with a few other goodies, as well.

It was already getting dark outside by the time Liss entered the store. The bright lights inside momentarily blinded her. They seemed particularly glaring over the produce bins, but she was glad to see that the selection of fresh fruit was all she could have hoped for. She took her time over melons and oranges, apples and grapes. She added a bunch of bananas, thinking they'd be good sliced on cereal, too.

Her selections made, Liss carried her bright red plastic shopping basket to the cashier. There was no line. She wasn't even sure there were any other shoppers in the market. After she unloaded the fruit onto the counter, she shifted her attention to the woman standing on the other side.

"Hilary?" she asked.

Liss wouldn't have recognized Boxer's mother if Stu hadn't mentioned that she worked at the market. Hilary Snipes had never been a great beauty, and Liss remembered her from high school as having a "boyish" figure. Worn down by life, she was downright skinny and looked far older than her early thirties. She wore her mousy brown hair scraped back into a thin ponytail. Her eyes, the same brown as her son's, were dull with fatigue. Liss struggled to conceal the burst of pity she felt for the other woman as, with slow, listless movements, Hilary rang up the items Liss had selected and stuffed them into a paper sack.

"It *is* Hilary Snipes, isn't it?"

The woman didn't meet her eyes. Her voice was scarcely more than a whisper. "Hello, Liss. It's been a while."

Liss had to strain to catch the words. "Yes. Yes, it has been. I, uh, met your son the other day."

Hilary's hand tightened on the green plastic bag holding two large Cortland apples. Her gaze collided with Liss's for just a moment, long enough to reveal that her expression was no longer blank. Her eyes had narrowed in sudden suspicion. "Where did *you* run into my Teddy?"

At first Liss thought she must have misunderstood. "Maybe we're not talking about the same kid. The one I know goes by Boxer."

"He doesn't like his real name," Hilary mumbled, and told Liss how much she owed for the groceries.

Teddy? Liss thought first of President Teddy Roosevelt. Teddy was short for Theodore. She could understand why the boy wouldn't want to be stuck with that moniker. The only other Theodore who came to mind belonged to Alvin and the Chipmunks.

As Liss paid up, she debated whether to say more. Hilary didn't seem happy to hear that her son had been fraternizing with Liss. That didn't bode well for Boxer staying on the committee. Then again, she'd talked to all the other parents before recruiting their kids. She owed the same, somewhat belated courtesy to Hilary Snipes.

"I hope it's okay with you that your son volunteered to help out with the Halloween festival. Several of the village young people are working on ideas for activities—trick or treating, a corn maze, a haunted house. They're quite enthusiastic. I'm surprised Boxer, er, Teddy hasn't mentioned what we're planning."

Hilary handed over her change. "You looking for my permission?"

"Yes, I am," Liss said brightly. "We held our first organizational meeting yesterday. There will be several more and then, of course, the actual work of setting up for Halloween."

Hilary thrust the paper sack full of fruit into Liss's arms. "Teddy's old enough to do what he likes. He will anyway."

"Okay then. Thank you." Unable to think of anything else to say, Liss left the market and walked home.

Chapter Four

On Friday—just four weeks and one day before Halloween—Liss opened the Emporium in a cheerful frame of mind. Plans for the Moose-tookalook All Hallows Festival had been moving smoothly forward, especially after the addition of her aunt, Margaret MacCrimmon Boyd, to the committee. Margaret was events coordinator at The Spruces, the luxury hotel on the hill above the town. In short order, she'd located a volunteer to create the corn maze, booked rooms in the hotel for the two costume parties, and arranged for ads in all the local papers and online.

Liss booted up her laptop and the cash register to the accompaniment of saws whining and hammers banging. Renovations had begun on the house next door, the one in which Liss had lived before her marriage to Dan. The first floor was being converted into a display room and store for Dan's custom wood-working business and they were installing an apartment on the second floor. Sherri, Pete, and Adam, who currently lived in a much smaller place above the post office, intended to move in as soon as it was ready.

It hadn't been easy to decide which house to live in and which to convert. Liss had liked living right next door to her shop. She'd inherited the property shortly after her return to Moosetookalook—after ten years of total independence, eight of them traveling with an itinerant dance troupe—and had lived in it for the best part of two years.

During those years, she'd worked at the Emporium, first as an employee, then as a partner with Aunt Margaret, and finally as sole proprietor. She'd increased their online and mail order business since she'd taken over, but the shop itself was much as it had always been. Scottish items, many of them imported, were displayed in cabinets and on shelves and tables. Liss gave the stock a lick and a promise with a feather duster every day and polished the furniture with lemon-scented wax once a week. Margaret approved, which was a relief to Liss, especially since her aunt still owned the building and continued to live in the apartment above the store.

As if she'd conjured Margaret up by thinking about her, Liss heard the clatter of high heels on the stairs. "I didn't realize you were still at home," Liss said when Margaret came bustling through the private entrance to the showroom. She usually left well before eight to make the ten minute drive to The Spruces.

Although she was in her early sixties, Margaret Boyd had as much energy as a woman half her age, and the most consistently cheerful disposition of anyone Liss had ever met. She looked trim and well-groomed in tailored slacks and a tunic top.

"I was tied up at the hotel until nearly midnight

last night," she explained. "Not that I have to worry about the boss firing me for being late. My hours are pretty flexible."

That boss was Dan's father, Joe Ruskin, and he knew full well what a gem he had in Margaret. He wouldn't bat an eye if she decided not to come in until noon every day of the week.

"Do you have time for coffee?" Liss asked.

Margaret glanced at her watch. "Why not? I want to give you an update anyway. The manikins you arranged to borrow for the haunted house are going to be delivered this afternoon."

The pot of coffee Liss had started brewing in the stockroom as soon as she arrived at work was ready to pour. She picked up the bakery bag with a half dozen blueberry muffins from Patsy's Coffee House, and Margaret carried their gently steaming mugs to the area of the store furnished with comfortable chairs and a coffee table and designated as the "cozy corner." They were still on their feet when the bell over the door jangled.

"Sorry! Not a customer," Sherri Campbell called out as she entered the shop.

"Hey, Sherri. Coffee?"

"No time."

Margaret was already on her way back to the stockroom to fill a third ceramic mug. "You can spare a few minutes to take on fuel," she sang out as she went.

"I just stopped by to ask if you'd installed any of the scary stuff at the Chadwick mansion yet," Sherri said.

Liss registered the serious expression on her friend's face and the fact that she was in uniform. That meant she was on the six-to-two shift, and *that* meant that she'd already been on duty for more than four hours. "What's wrong?"

"We had a report of suspicious flickering lights at the mansion last night. I'm on my way out to investigate. I thought I'd better check in with you first. Make sure it wasn't just some sort of early promotion for the haunted house."

"None of my doing," Liss said. "We don't have anything rigged up yet, not even the generator we've arranged to borrow."

"Most likely it was just kids exploring the place on a dare." Margaret pushed a mug of coffee, already doctored the way she knew Sherri liked it, into Sherri's hand.

Sherri gave in and took a sip, but she remained standing.

"Muffin?" Liss offered the bakery bag.

"I'm good." Sherri inhaled the fresh-baked scent, a rapturous expression on her face, and finally cracked a smile.

"I remember back when Ned was in middle school." Margaret, seated opposite Liss, had a faraway look in her eyes. "He and his friends were fascinated by the rumors they'd heard about Blackie O'Hare."

Liss and Sherri exchanged wary glances. Aunt Margaret almost never talked about her son, Liss's cousin, not since he'd been sentenced to five years in the state correctional facility for manslaughter.

"They were certain there was loot from a bank robbery buried in the basement." If Margaret sensed the sudden tension in the air, she chose to ignore it. "The boys went out there more than once, even though they were told not to. I don't think they ever managed to get inside, but I'm sure it wasn't for lack of trying."

Liss took a sip of coffee and considered the current situation. Margaret was probably right. Teenagers were the most likely culprits, just as they were probably responsible for the cigarette butts and beer cans she and Dan had cleared out of the parlor. "Who reported seeing lights?"

"Dolores Mayfield."

Liss swallowed wrong and coughed. Tears filled her eyes by the time she recovered.

"I know." Sherri heaved a resigned sigh. "But I still have to follow up."

"What was she doing out there in the first place? The Chadwick house isn't exactly on her way home from the library. It's not on the way to *anywhere*."

"Who knows? All she told me was that she drove by there last night and noticed a light shining through the trees. When she stopped the car to take a better look, it blinked out, but she saw it again in her rearview mirror as she was leaving. She says she thought about those lights all night long and decided she'd better report the sighting."

"How virtuous of her. I'm surprised she didn't go tromping in there on her own to check it out." Liss had to smile at the mental image that suddenly popped into her head—Dolores Mayfield, wearing the traditional white flowing Victorian nightwear of a Gothic heroine, looking over her shoulder at the tower of the Chadwick mansion as she fled through the woods, pursued by some unknown terror.

"She probably would have," Sherri said, "if it had been broad daylight. Even Dolores has sense enough to avoid an isolated and deserted house in the dead of night." She gulped down the rest of her coffee. "I'll let you know what I find."

"Dan put a new lock on the back door. Do you need a copy of the key?"

Sherri shook her head. "I borrowed the duplicates for the front door from the town office."

Left alone with her aunt, Liss returned to the subject of Margaret's son. "Do you know how Ned is doing?"

Margaret's shoulders sagged. For a moment, she looked years older than she was. "He still won't see me. I write to him, but he doesn't answer."

"I'm sorry."

Margaret met her eyes. "It's not your fault. I spoiled him when he was growing up. Everyone said so. It made him selfish and unfeeling."

"*You're* not to blame, either." Liss leaned across the coffee table to put her hand on her aunt's forearm and squeezed.

"I know that." Margaret pulled away, stood, and busied herself clearing the table. "It took me nearly a year to believe it, but I know it's true. Still, I bitterly regret what happened. I will until my dying day."

When she disappeared into the stockroom, Liss didn't follow. A few minutes later, she heard the back door open and close and then the sound of Margaret's car pulling out of the driveway.

Less than half an hour later, Sherri returned to the Emporium.

"Nothing. Nada. Zip," she reported. "As far as I can tell, no one's been inside the mansion since you and Dan were there to sweep the floors, install that lock, and put out the traps for the rats."

Liss paused in mid sweep with her feather duster and frowned. She'd heard an odd note in her friend's voice. "But?"

Sherri shrugged blue-clad shoulders. "It looked to

me like someone *tried* to break in. There were scratch marks all over that pretty new deadbolt."

Liss went out to the Chadwick mansion that afternoon after work to see for herself. Stu Burroughs went with her.

"How did you hear about the lights?" Liss asked him as she examined the lock. "Village grapevine?"

"Direct from Dolores. She thought I ought to be informed, as she put it, since I'm on the Halloween committee."

"Funny. She didn't bother to give me a call."

"You didn't report back to her on your visit to the so-called famous writer."

Liss laughed. "Take a look at this, will you, Stu. These scratches don't seem particularly ominous to me. The keyhole plate at the Emporium looks worse."

"Faulty aim with a key is pretty common," Stu agreed.

"Especially when you're trying to juggle packages or the mail or too many tote bags." There had been times, Liss recalled, when it had taken her four or five tries to jam her key home. "So—kids were out here again and tried to get in and were foiled by the new deadbolt?"

"Looks that way to me. I wonder if Boxer Snipes was one of them."

"Give the kid a break, Stu," Liss chided him as she unlocked the door and stepped into the kitchen. She didn't plan to stay long, but she wanted to drop off two Coleman lanterns. They'd be a help until the generator arrived. The days were getting shorter and the interior of the house was gloomy even on sunny days.

"Two of his cousins are serving time in the youth center."

"So? My cousin is serving time in state prison. Does that make me dishonest? Boxer hasn't caused a bit of trouble. In fact, he's made several good suggestions. And yesterday he stopped by the Emporium after school and volunteered to help cut the paths in the corn maze—that's more than I hear you doing!"

"I've got a bad back," Stu mumbled. "Are we going to take a look around, or what?"

Using flashlights, they went through the house from top to bottom, but found no evidence that anyone had been inside since Liss's last visit.

"How can you tell?" Stu grumbled. "Between the clutter and the shadows, an army could be hiding in here."

Liss ignored him, locked up, and went home.

Three days later, on Monday when the Emporium was closed, she was back. This time she was on her own. She'd spent the weekend thinking about the house. She'd gone through the file folder from the library. The items it contained had been interesting, but hadn't given her any new ideas for Halloween.

She'd also mapped out detailed plans for all the set pieces she planned to create in the haunted house. They'd be simple enough to put together, but each one required a good deal of advance preparation. The first step was to take careful measurements.

Shrugging out of the lightweight, pale blue jacket she wore only a few weeks each year, in the spring and again in the fall, Liss hung the garment on the back of a chair, then lit one of the Coleman lanterns.

The hiss of propane sounded abnormally loud in the stillness. She wondered where the other lantern had gotten to, but supposed that Dan or Sherri had used it and left it elsewhere. Both had been in the house at one time or other since Friday.

It was eerily quiet in the mansion as Liss, lantern in one hand and tape measure and small, spiral-bound notebook in the other, headed for the dining room. No power meant the absence of all the familiar house sounds—no hum of a refrigerator; no dripping faucet. Only the occasional gust of wind provided a soundtrack, rattling the window frames and shaking leaves off the trees.

Dan had removed a few of the boards from the windows. A little natural light filtered through the grime on the glass, but wasn't much help in illuminating the room. Glad of the lantern, Liss set it down on the sideboard and got to work.

I can bring the manikins out any time, she thought as she wrote down the dimensions of the table. *And the prop food, too.* She'd titled the scene in this room "Death by Poison" and would display an entire meal spread out in front of her "victims." When she finished taking measurements, she jammed pencil and notebook into the back pocket of her jeans and stood at the head of the table, trying to visualize the final display.

Out of the corner of her eye, Liss saw a sudden movement on the far side of the window. She started, then felt like a fool when she peered through the dirt-streaked panes. No one was out there. She'd only imagined there was. Or maybe it had been a bird flying past.

"Overactive imagination," she muttered under

her breath. She hadn't thought it would bother her to spend time in this spooky old house alone, but maybe her subconscious hadn't gotten the memo.

Liss picked up the lantern and walked across the hall to the parlor. She cast a wary glance at the chandelier even though Dan had assured her the house was now rat free. When nothing moved and she heard no scurry of little feet, she breathed a sigh of relief.

The parlor's set piece would make use of the skeleton she'd borrowed from the theater department at the University of Maine at Fallstown. She made a note to herself to bring a three-step stepladder with her the next time she came out to the mansion. She'd need it to reach the molding to install a hook. Her in-house expert on all things to do with the construction of houses would know how to manage it without damaging the woodwork. Then, if they laid out "Mr. Bones," as young Adam had dubbed him, on the sofa, they could use very thin wire, invisible to the naked eye, and a pulley arrangement to hoist him upright every time the door to the hallway opened to admit another group of eager-to-be-scared tourists.

Liss gave a nod of satisfaction. The effect would not be difficult to implement. She just needed to work out the logistics. She was holding her lantern high and running her gaze along the length of a strip of ornate molding, considering the best location for a hook, when she heard a loud thump. Momentarily startled, Liss froze. The hairs on the back of her neck prickled. Had the sound really come from the second floor?

"Idiot," she muttered. She was alone in the house.

Of course she was. She'd locked the door behind her when she came in.

Like that would stop a ghost!

"Shut up," she told the little voice in her head. *There are no ghosts on the premises. And no burglars, either.*

She slowly lowered the lantern, wishing she was armed with a supersize Maglite instead. Oh, for a generator, pouring bright light into every room!

Moving quietly, she made her way back into the hallway and peered up the staircase. She couldn't see much except shadows, but as far as she could tell, nothing moved. She heard nothing, either. The house was silent as a tomb.

Squaring her shoulders, Liss reminded herself that she was responsible for the Chadwick mansion until the first of November. Undoubtedly, there was a simple explanation for that odd noise. Maybe a small animal had gotten in—hopefully not another rat! Or one of the windows had been broken by a branch blown into it by the rising wind. The day was certainly gusty enough. *That's it,* she told herself. *The wind blew in through a broken window and knocked something off a table and onto the floor.*

She climbed the stairs to the second floor. Straight ahead of her was a linen closet, the door closed. Three bedrooms and a bath opened off the hall. Their doors were open, as they had been on Liss's last visit. She poked her head into each room, shining the lantern around.

Every corner was filled with ominous shadows. When she passed too close to a chair protected by a dust cover, the fabric stirred, lifted by the current of air she generated as she sidled past. It was only her over-active imagination that made it seem as if the yellowed, once white cloth was trying to follow her. And that the eyes in the portrait on the wall of the master bedroom were watching her.

Nothing accounted for the sound she'd thought she heard. She found no broken windows and no intruders. There weren't even any new droppings to indicate that the rodent population of the house had returned.

"Next you'll be imagining vampires," she muttered under her breath as she left the last of the bedrooms and returned to the hallway. "Except that it's daylight."

But sunshine, she recalled, only stopped vampires from moving around during the day in *some* versions of vampire lore. Other writers came up with varied scenarios that allowed these "creatures of the night" to be awake and biting twenty-four/seven.

Fiction, Liss. There are no such things as vampires in real life. Or ghosts.

Annoyed that she'd allowed the house to spook her, Liss stomped back downstairs. If there was anything in the Chadwick mansion more dangerous than an overly aggressive spider, she'd dress up as a vampire herself on Halloween, right down to the phony fangs.

Liss had just reached the foot of the stairs when the front door slammed open. She gasped. Her eyes went wide with shock. The figure looming in the opening came straight out of a horror movie. A slouch hat, pulled low, hid most of his face. His long, dark coat resembled nothing so much as Count Dracula's cloak. When he spoke, it was in a deep, sepulchral voice that chilled her right down to the bone.

"I've been looking for you," the apparition said.

* * *

The man sitting opposite Liss in one of the three booths in Patsy's Coffee House was no vampire, although he had been known to suck the life right out of innocent victims. His "killings," however, had all been in the realm of real estate. In person, he was depressingly human—not overweight, exactly, but getting flabby. What had started life as a strong, jutting jaw was well on its way to becoming a double chin.

"I thought you'd seen me through the window," Jason Graye said for the fourth time since he'd scared Liss out of ten years' growth. "I never intended to frighten you."

Liss didn't believe him any more than she had the last three times he'd apologized.

As soon as she'd recognized the intruder, her heart had resumed its normal slow and steady rhythm. Graye had wanted to come in, but she'd had enough of the Chadwick mansion for one day. Over his strenuous objections, she'd insisted they go elsewhere to talk.

"Meet me at Patsy's in fifteen minutes," she'd told him.

Taking only enough time to extinguish her lantern, she'd herded him onto the front porch and followed him out, locking the door behind them. She hadn't given him any opportunity to argue. Leaving him to descend the terrace steps to his car, she'd circled the mansion to the small parking lot at the back to retrieve her own vehicle.

Patsy's small restaurant and bake shop was situated right next door to the municipal building and was a popular meeting place, but at the moment, they had it to themselves. The other booths, the two tables, and the five stools at the counter were all empty. Patsy was in the kitchen, whence wafted the good smells of that morning's baking. Liss inhaled yeast, chocolate, cinnamon, and another aroma she couldn't quite identify. The cumulative effect was soothing—exactly what she needed after the scare Jason Graye had given her.

"Who'd have thought Liss MacCrimmon would be such a nervous Nellie," Graye marveled. "Why, I always thought you had nerves of steel." He took a huge bite out of the homemade fudge brownie he'd ordered.

His mocking tone raised Liss's hackles. She didn't know what game he was playing, but she didn't trust him and never had. She took a taste of her choice, a generous wedge of apple pie, before she replied. "Anybody would be a little jumpy if someone came barging in like that through a door that was *supposed* to be locked. In fact, I'm sure it *was* locked. Have you taken up breaking and entering?"

Graye bristled at the accusation. "I'll have you know that I borrowed the keys to the front door from the town office. No one had any objection. They know I'm interested in buying the place."

On the surface, his explanation was reasonable. He *was* a real estate agent and he occasionally bought properties and then resold them. But he also had a long history of using questionable methods to lower a seller's asking price. As far as Liss knew, he'd never broken any laws, but he'd certainly skated close to the line. She couldn't help wondering what would have happened if she hadn't already been at the mansion. She wouldn't put it past him to walk off with a Victorian curio or two. Nor would she have been shocked to hear that a water heater or an oil tank had sprung a leak just after he'd "inspected" them, thus lowering the asking price for the property.

"Kind of sudden, this interest," she drawled. "The town has owned that house for a couple of years. Why haven't you taken a look at it before this?"

Graye's smile looked forced. "Conflict of interest," he said in an offhand manner that instantly made Liss more suspicious. "I was one of the town selectmen during most of that time."

True enough, Liss thought. He hadn't been voted out of office until the last town meeting. Still, he'd have been one of the first to know when the Chadwick property was seized for back taxes. Conflict of interest or not, she was surprised he hadn't found a way to purchase the place a long time ago. Perhaps he'd been biding his time, waiting for the price to drop. She wondered how he'd managed to keep other realtors from stepping in. She was certain he'd had a hand in keeping them away. That was just how Jason Graye did business.

As these thoughts churned around in her head, Liss continued to eat her pie. It really was delicious. She reached for her coffee cup and sipped appreciatively. Patsy made good coffee, too.

Graye muttered something under his breath.

"What was that? I didn't quite catch what you said."

"I said I came out to the house to volunteer my assistance with the All Hallows Festival. Surely you can use another pair of hands."

Liss had to bite back a laugh. "Do you really expect me to believe that?" Jason Graye wasn't altruistic enough to do anything for free. He always had an ulterior motive.

"Now, Liss, is that any way to treat a generous offer? It's not as if I don't already have a great many demands on my time." He sent a thin-lipped, smarmy, completely insincere smile her way before taking another swallow of tea.

"Exactly what are you volunteering for?" Liss asked. "The role of resident ghoul?"

She couldn't quite figure his angle but was sure he had one. Perhaps it was a ploy to get a look at the inside of the mansion. That possibility made her wonder if Graye might have been responsible for the lights Dolores Mayfield had seen. Maybe for those scratches on the kitchen door lock, too. Had he attempted to get inside the house that night, thinking no one would be around to see him?

"I'm suggesting that I join your little committee," Graye said through clenched teeth.

"Well, thank you for the gracious offer, but my committee already has exactly the number of members it needs. Now, should you want a tour of the house, that can be arranged."

"Oh, yes?" He couldn't quite keep the eagerness out of his voice.

"But you'll have to wait until Halloween and pay your admission fee like everybody else. Until then, the place is my responsibility and I don't want any unauthorized personnel on the premises. That being the case, why don't I just return that set of keys to the town office for you?" She held out a hand and waited.

To her surprise, he gave up the duplicates without an argument. Then he smirked at her. "I can borrow them again any time I like, you know. I have a legitimate reason for wanting to look at the house." He stood, tossed a ten dollar bill on the table, and left her sitting there with her rapidly cooling coffee.

Patsy emerged from the kitchen, carafe in hand, and refilled Liss's cup without being asked. "I'd hang on to that second set of keys until after the festival if I were you," the pale, cadaverously thin baker advised.

Clearly, she'd heard every word Liss and Jason Graye had exchanged. Liss wasn't surprised, and Patsy's eavesdropping didn't bother her in the least. "I was planning to ask the town clerk not to loan them out again," she admitted. "To anybody."

"That might not be enough. I wouldn't put it past that sneaky snake in the grass to wait until Francine's back is turned and swipe them."

"He *says* he wants to buy the place." Liss took a sip of the steaming brew and awaited Patsy's response with interest. When it came to knowing what was going on in Moosetookalook, the coffee shop owner ran a close third after the librarian and the postmaster. Betsy Twining at the Clip and Curl came in a distant fourth. Most of the truly interesting people in town either went to Fallstown to have their hair done or didn't bother with old-style beauty parlors at all. Then, too, since the shop was situated in the back half of the building that housed the post office, Betsy didn't have much of a view.

"Maybe he does," Patsy said, "but my money's on the obvious. He thinks there's buried treasure on the property, just like everybody else in town has thought for the last twenty-plus years."

Chapter Five

The All Hallows Festival committee met at four that afternoon in the stockroom of Moose-tookalook Scottish Emporium, where Liss had temporarily stored the skeleton, a half dozen manikins, and other assorted stage props. She already knew how she wanted to arrange them at the mansion, but a responsible committee chairperson listened to suggestions at every stage of a project.

"Hi, Mr. Bones!" Adam sang out as he entered by the side door.

Boxer, slouching through right behind him, eyed the skeleton suspended from the ceiling. "Calling him Mr. Bones isn't classy enough for my man here."

"What do you suggest we name him?" Liss asked.

"How about Napoleon Bony-parts?"

Liss was still chuckling when Beth and Samantha arrived.

Gloria came in a few minutes later. "I've been thinking," she said even before the door swung shut behind her.

Liss suppressed a groan. So far, Gloria's ideas had

all been far too gory for a family-oriented festival. She had a lurid imagination . . . or else her Aunt Flo did.

"Instead of a dummy," Gloria continued, "I think we should hang the skeleton in the stairwell. It would give visitors a huge scare if it swung down from the second floor just as they were starting to climb up."

"First of all, no one's going upstairs," Liss reminded her.

"And the knife in the ribs won't work with a skeleton," Boxer pointed out. "Nothing to stick it into."

"We wouldn't be able to use the blood either," Beth chimed in. "Skeletons can't bleed."

Adam nodded solemnly. "No blood."

Samantha said nothing. She stood by the table where Liss packaged items from the Emporium for shipment, her arms rigid at her sides, as if she was trying to keep herself from touching anything.

Instead of the usual bubble wrap, cardboard boxes, and tape dispensers, the surface of the worktable was littered with an assortment of fake food. Liss had ordered a complete banquet from a theatrical supply company. They'd sent everything from a bowl of mashed potatoes to a pumpkin pie. The main course was a roast turkey with all the trimmings. Adam poked at the bird with his finger and laughed.

"What do you think, Samantha?" Liss asked.

"Nothing!" Samantha glanced sideways at Liss, then averted her gaze and wouldn't meet her aunt's eyes again. "I don't have any ideas," she mumbled.

Although Liss wondered what on earth was wrong with her niece, she didn't hassle the girl. The last thing she wanted was to embarrass her. Besides, the other young people more than made up for her silence, coming up with ideas for tweaking the set pieces at the haunted house and sharing their thoughts about the costume parade.

It was some time before Gloria glanced at her watch and asked where Margaret and Stu were.

"Margaret can't make it today. Something came up at the hotel."

"She hasn't attended any of our meetings so far," Gloria complained.

Liss shrugged. "Her schedule isn't as regular as ours. That doesn't make her input any less valuable. But Stu should have been here by now."

The ski shop was right next door to the Emporium. Like the rest of the town square shops, it was closed on Mondays, but Stu lived in the apartment above his store. Liss tried phoning, but there was no answer at either number. He was still a no show when the meeting broke up, making Liss wonder if he'd finally lived up to Dolores's predictions and quit the team. If he had, she wished he'd at least had the courtesy to resign in person.

Irritated, Liss stopped at his place on her way home. No one answered her knock and there were no lights showing anywhere in the building. She tried to tell herself that he'd just forgotten about their meeting, but it wasn't like Stu to miss an appointment. By the time she let herself into her own house, she was seriously worried. She dug out the address book she kept in the drawer of the phone stand and hunted up Stu's cell phone number. It rang eight times before he answered.

"What?" He sounded grouchy and out of sorts.

"Uh, Stu, it's Liss. I was just checking to—"

"This is all your fault!"

Liss held the phone away from her ear. Dan, who had just come in, raised his eyebrows in a question. He could hear Stu ranting from the far side of their living room.

The gist of the tirade was that Stu had gone out to the Chadwick mansion, thinking that the committee was meeting there, and had taken a fall. He'd injured his ankle and was not a happy camper. Neither was the emergency room nurse who came on the line to tell Liss that cell phones had to be turned off inside the hospital. Then she disconnected the call.

"Do you think we should drive down there?" Liss asked.

Dan shook his head. "If he got himself to Fallstown to have that ankle looked at, he can get himself back." Then he noticed the expression on Liss's face. "What?"

"How did Stu get inside the house? I'm the only one who has keys."

"The town office—"

She shook her head. "I have that set, too." She explained how she'd confiscated them from Jason Graye earlier that day and why she'd kept them.

Dan drove her to the Chadwick mansion to make sure the house was locked. When they had assured themselves that it was, Liss insisted that they make the twenty minute trip to the hospital in Fallstown. Stu had some questions to answer. If he'd had a duplicate set made of the keys to the mansion, she meant to read him the riot act.

They arrived just in time to catch Stu hobbling through the parking lot on crutches. He'd almost reached his car when Liss hopped out of hers to confront him. He tried to ignore her, but she was persistent.

"I'm sorry you misunderstood about the meeting. And I'm sorry you got hurt. Is your ankle broken?"

"Just a sprain, but it's a bad one."

She winced in sympathy, but moved to block his driver's side door with her body.

"You want to get out of my way, Liss? The only good thing about this fiasco is that it's my *left* ankle. I can still drive. Right now all I want to do is go home, put my feet up, and take the pain pills the doctor gave me."

"I'll drive you home. Dan can bring your car. You have to fill a prescription for more pills, right? Dan can do that for you, too."

Stu wavered, grumbling and looking sour. "You *do* owe me." He handed over his car keys.

In less than five minutes, Stu had been settled in the passenger seat with his crutches in the back and they were on their way home. "So, do you want to tell me what happened?"

"Damned if I know. I was just taking a look around, waiting for the rest of you to show up, and I tripped over a duffle bag somebody left right in the middle of the hallway."

Liss was so startled that she momentarily took her eyes off the road to stare at him. "A *what?*"

"A duffle bag. You know, one of those—"

"I know what a duffle bag is." She forced her attention back to her driving. "What I don't know is how one got inside the mansion. There was no such thing there earlier today."

"It *was* there at four. I ought to know."

"Don't get surly on me, Stu Burroughs. And while we're on the subject, how did you get inside that house in the first place?"

"What do you mean, how did I get inside? I opened the front door and walked through it."

Her hands tightened on the steering wheel. "Are you telling me the Chadwick mansion was unlocked?"

"Well, yeah. That's why I thought you were already there, even though I didn't see your car. I called your name, then headed down the hall toward the kitchen. I figured you'd parked around back and came in that way. I was about halfway there when I tripped over the duffle bag. You know how dark it is in that place. I didn't see the damned thing until I fell on top of it." He frowned. "I guess I didn't really see it then, either. I felt what it was when I was trying to get back to my feet."

"Then what?"

"What do you mean, then what? I had to go back down all those stone steps in the terrace on my butt because I couldn't put weight on my ankle. And then I had to drive myself to the emergency room."

Liss supposed he had a right to be cranky, and she was sorry he'd been hurt. Trying to sound conciliatory, she said, "I appreciate your taking the time to throw the deadbolts before you left."

His reply was as terse as it was startling. "I didn't. Hell, I'm not even sure I closed the door behind me."

"How can you not remem—"

"I have a low threshold for pain," he defended himself.

They rode in silence for a few minutes before Liss ventured another question. "Did you *hear* anything before you tripped? Any sounds from upstairs? Or from the back of the house?"

"No." Now he was sulking.

"Look, Stu, here's the thing—no one should have been able to get inside that house. Somebody obviously did, and that person left a duffle bag lying around for you to trip over. We need to find out who he is, especially if he's still there. Because somebody locked up *after* you left." She wished that she and Dan had gone inside the mansion, but all they'd done was check to be sure the doors were locked. Then they'd headed for Fallstown in search of Stu.

"*I'm* certainly not going back out there tonight," Stu muttered. "And if you're smart, you won't, either."

"I won't go alone," Liss said. Beyond that, she made no promises.

As it turned out, she didn't go at all. When Dan heard Stu's story, he called the Moosetookalook Police Department for backup. Sherri wasn't on duty, but the officer on the two-to-ten shift went with him to investigate. Liss was not invited to accompany them. She stayed home with the cats. To add injury to insult, Lumpkin bit her on the ankle.

"No sign of any duffle bag," Dan reported when he returned home. "And thanks to the thorough floor-sweeping you gave the place the other day, there weren't any footprints in the dust. Best guess is that a vagrant got in, planning to sleep there, and was scared off when Stu turned up."

"And this mysterious homeless person considerately locked the doors when he left the house?" Liss, seated at the vanity in their bedroom while she brushed her hair, met Dan's eyes in the mirror.

"Your guess is as good as mine." He came up behind her and put his hands on her shoulders, still holding her gaze. "Will you promise me something, Liss? Promise me you won't go out to the Chadwick mansion alone, not even in broad daylight. It's just too damned isolated out there."

Remembering the scare Jason Graye had given her, Liss promised.

Dan looked relieved. He planted a kiss on the top of her head, then began efficiently stripping off clothes in preparation for turning in for the night.

"Just one question—how did an intruder get in? I know I locked all the doors before I left there earlier today. And I kept *all* the keys." She abandoned her brushing to swivel around on the vanity stool.

"I wish I knew. We checked the doors and all the windows. Nothing was unlocked or open. I couldn't find any signs that someone had broken in. Maybe our mysterious visitor had a set of cat burglar tools and knew how to use them."

"As opposed to whoever had the light Dolores saw out there the other night?"

"Take your pick," Dan said, straight-faced. "Homeless person with housebreaking skills . . . or vampire."

In spite of herself, Liss smiled. She'd always been a fan of comic relief and they were badly in need of some. "Why vampire? I thought zombies were the paranormal soup de jour."

"It's vampires that can change themselves into bats, right?" He climbed into bed and patted the space next to him, an invitation in his eyes. "I figure a bat might just be small enough to find a way inside the house."

"There's only one thing wrong with your logic." She turned off the bedside lamp, plunging the room into semidarkness. A streetlamp provided enough illumination to make out Dan's familiar shape.

"Only one?"

She ignored his sarcastic tone of voice. "It was still daytime when Stu was at the mansion. Vampires don't do well in daylight." She crawled in next to him.

His arm came around her and he nuzzled her ear. "Okay, then, what's your explanation?"

"Shape shifter," she said promptly. "A creature who can change at will into a mouse, or a squirrel . . . or maybe a black fly."

He laughed. "Shape shifter it is."

His next suggestion had nothing whatsoever to do with haunted houses.

Two days later, early in the morning before the Emporium was due to open at ten, Liss went back out to the mansion. True to her promise, she did not go alone. Margaret Boyd rode shotgun.

"I'll only be a minute," Liss said as she unlocked the kitchen door. "I just want to see if I left my jacket here the other day." She had a vague memory of hanging it over the back of one of the kitchen chairs and then forgetting all about it when Jason Graye made his unexpected appearance.

Aunt Margaret came in right behind her. "An escort at all times," Margaret reminded her. "That's what you promised Dan."

"And a royal pain it's going to be, but I'll keep my word." Liss frowned, staring at the dinette set in the corner. The pale blue jacket wasn't there. "Maybe I took it off in the dining room."

There were no lanterns in the kitchen. Liss remembered leaving the one she'd used on Monday at the foot of the stairs. She still wasn't sure where the other one had gotten to. But once Margaret turned on the flashlight she'd brought with her, Liss dismissed all thought of any other source of light from her mind.

Her jacket was not in the dining room either. "I could have sworn. . . ."

"Getting forgetful in your old age, Liss?" Margaret kidded her.

"I guess so. Oh, well, I imagine it will turn up somewhere. Maybe I left it at Patsy's."

"Anything else you need to do here?"

"Shine your light up and down the hallway, will you? Who knows? Maybe the mysterious duffle bag has reappeared."

It hadn't. Nor was the lantern where Liss remembered leaving it.

"I sure hope Dan moved it," she told her aunt. "Otherwise I'm going to start worrying about short-term memory loss."

Margaret laughed. "You're too young. And I'm sure there's a perfectly logical explanation for everything."

"Like what? Ghosts?"

Margaret ignored the sarcasm. "Do you want to go through the entire house?"

"I suppose we'd better. I *am* responsible for it."

She found one lantern in the parlor, but the other never did turn up. Neither did Liss's jacket, convincing her that she must have left it at the coffee shop. They had returned to the kitchen and were about to leave when Margaret glanced through the small window in the back door and frowned.

"Who is that skulking about at the tree line?" she asked.

Liss took a quick look, expecting to see Jason Graye. Instead, she recognized Boxer Snipes. "That's the youngster I told you about, Beth's friend Boxer." Although Margaret was on the Halloween committee, she had not yet made it to a meeting, nor had she and Boxer met. Margaret's frown deepened. "He looks familiar."

"You've probably seen him around town." Liss sincerely hoped her aunt didn't know him because she'd caught him shoplifting at the Emporium. Liss wanted to discount Stu's accusation, but it continued to linger at the back of her mind.

"Isn't this a school day?" Margaret asked.

Liss opened the door and stepped out onto the back stoop. "Boxer!" she shouted. "Come here at once!"

He froze like a deer in the headlights, staring at her in shock and dismay. For a moment, Liss thought he might bolt, but he apparently thought better of it. With slow, reluctant steps, wary as a dog expecting punishment for messing on the rug, he approached the house.

"Boxer, I'd like you to meet my aunt, Margaret Boyd. She's on the Halloween committee, too, but she's had to be at work when we've held our meetings."

Head lowered, Boxer mumbled a hello. Margaret seemed equally uneasy with him and retreated a little to let Liss talk to the boy in private.

"What are you doing out here, Boxer?" Liss asked.

He met her eyes at last. The look in his was sly. "I'm guarding the place. I heard about poor old Stu."

Liss bit back a laugh. "Poor old Stu would blow a gasket if he heard you call him that."

"Yeah." Boxer grinned at the thought. Then he slapped the back of his neck. "Shoot! Bug just bit me!" His fingers moved over the spot. "Still there."

"Let me see."

He stood still while she lifted his hair and deftly plucked the tick from a spot an inch below his ear. Fishing a tissue out of her pocket, she squished it to make sure it was dead.

"I'm doomed," Boxer said.

Liss's eyebrows lifted in a question.

"Well, yeah. That was a deer tick, right? Now I'm gonna get Dutch elm disease and die."

Liss couldn't contain a snort of laughter. "It was a *dog* tick." Deer ticks were much smaller. "And it's *Lyme* disease."

"You're sure it's not lemon?"

"I'm absolutely certain."

"Well, *that's* embarrassing."

"What? You getting a word wrong?" She'd already realized that he used malapropisms deliberately, most often when he wanted to change the subject.

"Color me mortified," Boxer quipped. "I'm going to go live in a cave and be a helmet."

He'd already put some distance between them. Too much for her to grab hold of him. "Hey, Boxer," she called as he continued his steady retreat toward the woods.

"Yeah?"

"You know I could report you for playing hooky, right?"

"Aw, you wouldn't do that to me. You *like* me."

Liss bit back another laugh. Encouraging him to skip school was *not* a good idea. "Just don't do it again, okay? If you get good grades, you can be anything you want to be. Go anywhere you want to go. No one and nothing can hold you back."

"What a load of crap," Boxer said, and took off into the forest.

Several times during the next few weeks, the Moosetookalook Police Department received reports of mysterious lights in the wooded area surrounding the Chadwick mansion. An officer investigated each complaint, but never found anyone suspicious in the vicinity or anything to indicate that someone had broken into the house. Sherri was of the opinion that kids were playing pranks. Stu immediately leaped to the conclusion that Boxer Snipes was involved. Liss maintained that the boy was innocent, although she did encourage Sherri to check on his attendance record at the middle school. She was relieved to learn that he had not played hooky again.

True to her promise to Dan, Liss continued to take someone with her every time she went out to the mansion. On the Monday before Halloween, it was Aunt Margaret again. They took Dan's truck, intending to pick up the two large wooden tubs for the "apple dookin"—bobbing for apples—that Liss had been storing in the mansion's kitchen until Margaret was ready for them at the hotel.

"So you still have no idea who's haunting the place?" Margaret asked as Liss pulled into the parking area at the rear of the house.

"Not a clue." Liss backed as close as she could to the ramp they'd installed for handicapped access via the back door.

"You know, there are some folks in town who think the Halloween committee is responsible." She met Liss's startled look with equanimity. "It's a draw—*real* ghosts in the haunted house and all that."

"I can think of better ways to generate publicity than risking arrest for filing a false report with the police." Liss unlocked the back door, tucked the key into the pocket of her jeans, and ushered her aunt inside.

"Speaking of generating, when will the lights be hooked up?"

"Tomorrow, I hope." Liss was looking forward to having power. "It's been a real pain stumbling around in the shadows to arrange the set pieces. At least we have more sunlight here in the kitchen now. I had Dan remove the boards from all the windows in this room." She made a beeline for the first tub. "Help me with this?"

"Liss?" Margaret's voice sounded peculiar. "Where's the second one?"

"It's right—" Liss broke off to stare in disbelief at the empty spot on the cracked linoleum where the other wooden tub should have been. "Okay, this is weird. They were both right here two days ago when Gloria and I came out after work to add the china and cutlery to the Death by Poison scene." They'd arranged the turkey on a flow blue platter, a prop carving knife and Liss's good two-tined fork lying next to it.

"Could someone else on the committee have moved it?" Margaret asked.

Liss shook her head. "No one can get into the house without asking me for a key."

"I suppose we'd better search the place. Again!"

"This is getting old fast," Liss grumbled, but didn't see that they had much choice in the matter.

Together, Liss and Margaret went through the mansion from attic to cellar. The latter smelled slightly damp. In common with many Maine homes, it had a dirt floor. There were even boulders sticking up here and there, since the house was built on bedrock. Upstairs, everything looked the same. In the conservatory, the stuffed birds still sat on their perches, staring glassily at all who entered their domain. They found no trace of the large wooden tub and only in the front parlor did any sense that something was out of place tickle at Liss's subconscious.

"Where could it have gone?" Margaret wondered aloud when they returned to the kitchen.

"It's probably in the same place as my three-step stepladder," Liss said, finally putting her finger on what it was that had been missing from the parlor.

"Dan has the extra set of keys. Maybe he took the tub."

Liss shook her head. "He'd have no reason to. And he'd tell me if he had."

After they'd carried the remaining tub outside and deposited it in the back of the truck, Liss double-checked to make sure the house was secure. She shook her head as she tried the lock one final time. Did it really do any good to bolt the doors? She was beginning to think it was a wasted effort.

She dropped Aunt Margaret and her cargo off at the hotel and then drove straight to Dan's current construction site, an addition on a house on the Fallstown road. She wasn't surprised to hear him deny all knowledge of the apple dookin tub and the three-step stepladder.

"Somehow, someone's getting inside the mansion and playing tricks on you," he said. "Simple as that."

"But why take the tub? And why the ladder? I hate to mention it, but I still haven't found that second

Coleman lantern or my good fall jacket. I wore it out to the mansion on the day Jason Graye gave me such a scare. I thought for awhile that I'd left it at Patsy's and I assumed that someone walked off with it, but the more I think about it, the more convinced I am that it was hanging over the back of a chair in the kitchen at the Chadwick house the last time I saw it."

"There was no jacket there that night when I went out to look for whoever left the duffle bag."

"I know."

"Maybe our mysterious homeless person took it. Or maybe you did leave it somewhere else and it will turn up again when you least expect it."

"And maybe it was stolen by a vampire or a shape shifter or a ghost!" Liss had stopped finding such suggestions amusing.

As frustrated as she was, Dan scraped his fingers through his hair. "I don't know what to tell you, Liss. The ladder and tub should have been in the mansion. So should a hammer that went missing on me the other day. I thought at the time that I'd just mislaid it, but now. . . ."

Liss took a deep breath and reached for her supply of common sense. "This is ridiculous. I'm making a mountain out of a molehill. You're right. I've been busy lately. I've just forgotten where I left my jacket and you could have misplaced your hammer anywhere. It happens all the time—losing track of things." She gave a short, self-deprecating laugh. "It's not just at the mansion, either. When I unpacked the Royal Doulton figurines and the little bisque cats that came to me from Mrs. Norris so I could set them out in my new office in the attic, I discovered that I'm one short."

Liss was certain the missing figurine would even-

tually turn up, no doubt in the same place Dan
thought she'd find her jacket—wherever she least
expected it.

"And the apple dookin tub?" Now Dan was the
one who sounded skeptical.

"That's a mystery all right," Liss admitted. "That
sucker is just too darned big to misplace!"

Chapter Six

The following day, Liss and Dan went out to the Chadwick mansion after work to inspect the generator that had been installed that afternoon. After firing it up, they went from room to room, turning on all the lamps and overhead fixtures. Some bulbs had burned out, but most worked just fine. The first thing Liss saw when she flipped the switch for the chandelier in the front parlor was the three-step stepladder.

"That was not there yesterday."

"You're sure?"

"Dan, it's standing directly in front of the window. I couldn't have missed it even if I was searching by the light of a single candle."

When he didn't answer, she turned to find him staring at the parlor organ. On top of it, precisely centered, lay a hammer.

"Yours?"

He nodded. "Shall we see if we can find your jacket?"

There was no trace of Liss's pale blue coat. Nor

did they come across the big wooden tub. But in the dining room, Liss made another discovery. "One of the manikins is missing." She gestured toward the empty place at the head of the table. "The one dressed as a fashionable matron from the early 1900s."

"There has to be a hidden entrance to the house. That's the only possible explanation."

"I thought I was the one with the overactive imagination."

"You are." Dan managed a half-hearted smile. "But first thing tomorrow I'm going to do a little digging at the town office and see if I can come up with a set of builders' plans for this place."

"You think there are blueprints?"

"It's a possibility. It depends on what the town fathers required for permits back in the day."

"Jason Graye is interested in buying the mansion," Liss said slowly. "I wonder if he might already have found something like that."

"What if he did? Why would he want the place to get a reputation for being haunted?"

"It might lower the town's asking price."

"It would also lower the resale price."

Liss grimaced. "Darn. He would have been such a perfect villain!"

But Dan was right. If people became convinced that the mansion really was haunted, Graye would not be able to sell it at a profit. That pretty much killed his motive for playing childish tricks.

They left the mansion and drove to Graziano's, their favorite pizza place. Since they'd called ahead with their order, Dan went in to pick it up while Liss waited in the car. She was staring through the windshield, looking at nothing in particular, when a flurry of activity in front of the High Street Market caught her attention. The grocery store was only two doors down from the pizza parlor, giving her an unobstructed view of two people squaring off, prepared to do bodily harm to each other. One was Hilary Snipes. The other was her older brother.

"Cracker" Snipes hadn't changed a bit since the last time Liss had encountered him. In fact, she thought he might be wearing the same pair of ratty old sweatpants he'd had on when she'd seen him the previous January. Most people would at least change into jeans to make a beer run—she could see the shape of a six-pack under one arm, tucked in against rolls of belly fat—but not Cracker.

Hilary lunged for the cans, trying to take them away from him, making Liss think that Cracker must have taken the beer without paying for it. He probably thought Hilary should let him get away with it, or put her own money into the till to cover the cost.

You go, girl, Liss thought . . . just as Cracker casually cuffed his sister across the face and walked away.

Liss reached for the car's door handle, then stopped herself. Hilary had already bolted back inside the store. She wasn't badly hurt and Liss doubted she'd appreciate knowing there had been a witness to her brother's bullying. It wasn't as if she'd press charges. Liss knew the statistics as well as anyone. Domestic abuse most often went unpunished because the victims had been taught to think getting beat up was their own fault.

Dismal thoughts consumed her. The tendency of men to mistreat and bully women descended from one generation to the next. Boys learned by example. Cracker's oldest son, Rodney, who was only a few years younger than Liss, had been the kind of boy who delighted in pulling girls' hair and shooting people with water pistols. Liss knew for a fact that he had no respect for his mother, the only hard-working member of the family. So what did that mean for young Boxer?

When Liss realized how very little she really knew about the boy, she resolved to try to find out more. She couldn't help herself. He'd been right—she liked him.

"I'm hoping you can fill me in on Boxer Snipes," Liss said.

"Why would I know anything?" Angie Hogencamp's voice was muffled. The bookstore had closed hours ago, but she was still hard at work. She'd just unpacked a new shipment of books and was rearranging her shelves to make room for them. Volumes at the end of one shelf had to go down to the next. Between the bending and the lifting, she was out of breath and her face was pink with exertion.

"I thought Beth must have talked to you about him."

Angie straightened so abruptly that a cloud of packing peanuts rose with her. Her voice went dangerously soft. "And just why would my daughter do that?"

Uh-oh, Liss thought. *Cat. Bag.* But it was too late to retreat. Under her friend's glare, she stammered out an explanation.

"Let me get this straight," Angie said when Liss had stumbled into silence. "My Beth brought that boy with her to the first Halloween committee meeting?"

"I assumed you knew they were friends."

Angie glared at her. Liss threw up her hands, palms out.

"Okay. Okay. I shouldn't have jumped to any conclusions. But really, Angie, where's the harm in it? I admit Boxer doesn't make a great initial impression, but he's been a real hard worker on the committee."

"Checked your silverware lately?"

"What is it with everyone in this town? Give the kid a break. He's not a convicted felon. He's not even a juvenile offender. He—"

"How do you know?"

"What?"

"How do you know he hasn't got a record? They keep information on kids who commit crimes confidential."

"Not from the police who arrest them." Liss was sure Sherri would have told her if Boxer had actually been caught and convicted of any crime. "As far as I can tell, the only count against that young man is that he had the misfortune to be born with the last name Snipes."

Liss sighed deeply. The possibility that Angie might be right about Boxer had to be considered, even though the very thought that he'd been deceiving her generated a sick feeling in the pit of her stomach. The prejudice against the boy was horribly unfair. If you expected someone to turn out badly, they often did. It was called a self-fulfilling prophecy! But had Theodore "Boxer" Snipes really defied the odds? Or was she just deluding herself because she wanted him to be what he seemed?

"I've got no proof," Angie admitted, a grudging expression on her face, "but I just don't trust that kid. Not since he started hanging around here last summer."

"Flirting with Beth?"

Angie barked a laugh. "Messing with the stock. I can't count how many books he pulled off the shelves to look at."

"Angie, you own a bookstore. You're supposed to encourage people to examine the merchandise."

"That doesn't mean I want them to stand there and read half the book, then put it back without buying it."

"Maybe he didn't have any money."

"And maybe the next step would have been to steal what he couldn't afford to buy. If I hadn't kept a close eye on him, I shudder to think how much inventory I might have lost."

There were several replies Liss might have made. Wisely, she held her tongue. She had to admit to her own suspicions of Boxer. That was why she was at Angie's in the first place. "Do you mind if I talk to Beth for a moment?"

"Committee business?" Sarcasm tinged Angie's question.

"In a way. Okay. Yes, I want to ask her about Boxer Snipes. Unlike some people, I'm investigating *before* I leap to any conclusions about the boy."

Angie stalked to the door that led to the stairwell, opened it, and yelled Beth's name. "Get down here!" she added before she went back to her shelving.

The upstairs apartment door banged open a moment later. Liss heard the sound of canned TV laughter before Beth closed it behind her and pounded down the stairs. She burst into the bookstore, eyes wide with alarm. "What's wrong?"

She checked when she saw Liss. The second glance she gave her mother was even more wary.

"Hi, Beth," Liss said. "Got a minute?"

The girl nodded, but Liss sensed a certain reserve.

"I just want to ask you about a couple of things. To get them straight in my own mind. Okay?"

"I guess."

"It's about that Boxer Snipes," Angie interrupted. "I didn't realize he was such a good friend of yours, Beth."

The angry look Beth sent Liss's way before she answered her mother made Liss feel like the worst kind of traitor.

"He's okay," Beth said, feigning nonchalance, but not doing a very convincing job of it.

"He's older than you are," her mother said.

"So?"

"Don't use that tone with me, young lady."

"Sorry," Beth mumbled.

Liss cleared her throat. "I'm not trying to cause trouble, Beth."

Angie opened her mouth to say more, but Liss caught her eye and scowled at her until she subsided.

Liss leaned closer to Beth and put one hand on the girl's thin shoulder. "Was Boxer the friend you had in mind when we first talked about the Halloween committee?"

Liss remembered that day well. She'd asked Beth to join the committee. Beth had been insulted. "I'm too old for Halloween," she'd said. "Trick or treating is for babies."

"And you don't have to do any," Liss had assured her.

She hadn't anticipated that it would take more than a few minutes to get Beth to agree, especially since she'd already secured Angie's approval. Beth, however, had hung her head, scraped one toe back and forth on the hardwood floor, and avoided Liss's eyes.

Much as she was doing now.

"It might be fun," Angie had said then.

Beth hadn't been so sure. Liss could remember having exactly the same reaction when *her* mother wanted her to do something that she thought was stupid. She'd asked Beth if bribery would help.

Beth had considered the proposition, her expression solemn. She had her mother's big brown eyes, but where Angie's always looked a little sad, Beth had a naturally optimistic disposition. She'd tossed her head, making her dark, wavy hair bounce on her shoulders, and announced that she had conditions.

Liss had been prepared to negotiate.

Condition one was that Beth's little brother *not* to be on the committee.

Condition number two was that she could ask someone else to join with her.

"I don't see why not," Liss had said. She could remember thinking *if it will convince you to agree, I'm all for it!*

Beth hadn't given her a name. Instead, claiming she had homework to do, she'd taken off up the stairs to the apartment above the bookstore. Liss and Angie had agreed that she'd probably gone to send a text to whomever she had in mind.

I should have asked more questions up front, Liss thought. Hindsight was always 20/20.

Beth stopped waxing the floor with her toe and lifted her head to meet Liss's eyes. "I wasn't thinking of Boxer. I asked my friend Luanne, but she didn't want to do it. I was trying to talk her into it at school and Boxer overheard."

Caught by surprise, Liss blinked at her. "So . . . it was *Boxer's* idea that he join the committee?"

Beth nodded and once more averted her gaze.

"Told you he was up to no good," Angie mouthed, but she didn't say the words out loud.

"Beth? Why did you agree? You could have told him you couldn't invite him without my approval."

The thin shoulders rose and fell in a shrug that told Liss absolutely nothing.

"Are you . . . friends with him?"

"He's okay."

"Beth, this is like pulling teeth. You must have had a reason for agreeing to bring Boxer to that first meeting."

The crimson tide climbing Beth's neck into her face was an answer in itself. Liss took it as proof that she'd guessed correctly at the start—Beth had a major-league crush on the boy.

"Sweetie, he's not in any trouble and neither are you. I'm just trying to get a handle on things. Has Boxer said anything to you about the haunted house, other than talking about the plans we all made together?"

"He said his cousins used to hang out there. They broke in 'cuz they needed a place to smoke cigarettes and drink beer."

"The cousins who are at the youth center now?"

Beth nodded. "Boxer doesn't even like them. Honest. And *he* didn't break in. Or steal stuff. Or anything."

"Steal stuff? Is that what his cousins did?"

Beth nodded. "They took snowmobiles into closed-up camps off-season and broke in. They mostly took liquor. They're both morons. And bullies. Nobody likes them."

"And Boxer?"

"What about him?"

Again with the pulling teeth! "Is he a moron?"

"No!"

"A bully?" *Like his Uncle Cracker?*

"Of course not."

"Honest?"

"Yes!"

"What do the other kids think of Boxer?"

Another shrug. "How would I know?"

"You'd know. Come on, Beth. Do they think he's a troublemaker? Or is he cool?"

Beth gave her an incredulous look. "*Cool?* What century are *you* from?"

"Be glad I didn't ask you if he was wicked good. Thumbs up or thumbs down from most of your class-mates?" Liss made the appropriate gestures.

A smile made Beth's lips twitch as she held her own thumb in the UP position.

"Ah. Well, I guess that means we can't feed him to the lions."

To her relief, Beth laughed out loud. Liss left the bookstore feeling much more optimistic about her team of young helpers.

On Wednesday, when Liss went out to the mansion with Sherri for company, they found the missing apple dookin tub sitting in the middle of the kitchen, right where it should have been in the first place. The manikin that had vanished was stuffed inside it.

Liss's first thought was to wonder if Beth had warned Boxer that she was asking questions about him. Her second was to remind herself that even if the boy had been responsible for the pranks, they were still just that—pranks. No harm, no foul. Least said, soonest mended.

She amused herself coming up with other clichés while she restored the Death by Poison scene to its former state. When she was done, she solemnly crossed her fingers, hoping everything would still be where she'd put it the next time she checked.

She and Sherri were about to lock up and leave when Dan drove in. He hopped out of the truck, a grin splitting his face from ear to ear as he bounded up the back steps to meet them on the stoop.

"What are you so happy about?" Liss demanded.

"I found it!" He thrust a thick roll of paper at her.

"Found what?" Liss took it gingerly, seeing how old it was.

"An architect's drawings of the house and grounds. Let's go back inside so I can show you."

The edges of the drawings flaked a bit when Dan unrolled them. There were four floor plans, labeled First Story, Second Story, Third Story or Attic, and Basement. It was the latter that he wanted them to examine closely.

"Huh," Sherri said, studying the diagram. "The original kitchen was in the cellar."

"And look what else was." Dan pointed to what at first glance seemed to be a long narrow room jutting out to the east of the main house.

Liss started to laugh. "Good grief. It's a secret tunnel."

"That's what it looks like to me," Dan said. "Let's go see if we can find the entrance." Instead of heading for the cellar steps, he went back outside to circle the mansion to the east. He stopped halfway along that side of the building and cocked his head toward the nearby woods. "Hear that?"

Sherri answered. "Running water. Ten Mile Stream, I'm guessing."

They set off for the tree line, following the murmur of sound. Less than a hundred yards from the house, they came out into the open again at the top of a steep embankment. Directly below was a rocky shoreline. The stream was sluggish at this time of year, dotted with boulders and no more than twenty feet wide.

"I wonder how much the course has changed in the last hundred and fifty years," Dan mused as he picked his way down the bank, blazing a trail for Liss and Sherri. At the bottom, he stared intently at the overgrown underbrush along the bottom of the embankment.

"What are you looking for?" Liss asked.

"Any anomaly. Ah! Look there."

Liss had to squint to see what he had spotted. Branches had been carefully arranged to conceal a very old wooden door.

The latch was rusty and in places the wood had rotted away. Dan gave one good tug and, hinges groaning, the door flew open. A musty passageway yawned before them, black as pitch.

Sherri produced her police-issue Maglite.

"I liked it better dark," Liss muttered when the

beam revealed broken spider webs and evidence of a partial collapse.

"This was probably built as a way to unload supplies from a boat directly into the house," Dan speculated. "I'm guessing the stream was wider and deeper back when this place was built."

"And it may explain how the Chadwicks got so wealthy," Sherri said. "Smuggling paid well back in the good old days."

"Even before Blackie O'Hare came into the picture?" Liss asked.

"Didn't you ever wonder how Alison Chadwick met him in the first place?"

"Food for thought," Liss agreed.

Dan took charge of the flashlight, playing it over the support beams. "Looks like most of these are still intact. It's probably safe enough to go inside."

"Probably?" Liss didn't think that was good enough, but before she could stop him, Dan had stepped over the door sill, ducking to avoid hitting his head on the lintel.

Liss tried to go after him, but Sherri caught her arm and pulled her back. "If the tunnel collapses, someone needs to be on the outside to mount a rescue."

"Oh, that makes me feel *so* much better!" But she stayed put.

Five long minutes passed as Dan's slow, cautious footsteps faded into the distance. Then they stopped altogether. A moment later, Liss heard a horrific screech. Her heart leaped into her throat even as she belatedly recognized the sound as another door with rusty hinges being opened.

"Meet me in the basement!" Dan's voice was muffled by distance and dirt walls, but the words were clear enough to understand.

The door from the tunnel into the cellar was all but invisible so long as it was closed. Liss examined the area in front of it with considerable curiosity. At some point, it had served as a coal bin. By the time the Chadwicks installed an oil burner, they'd probably forgotten that any tunnel ever existed.

"I found footprints in there," Dan said, gesturing back the way he'd come. "Going in both directions. This has to be how our ghost got into the house."

"Can you board up the entrance?" Sherri asked. "That ought to put an end to the trespassing."

Dan agreed that it should and spent the next hour making certain no one else could sneak into the Chadwick mansion from the entrance by the stream. He nailed sturdy two-by-fours into place across the cellar end to keep the old door closed and intruders out.

All was well at the mansion the following day. Liss hoped that meant their troubles were over, but when she and Dan went out again on Friday, the eve of Halloween, to make a final check before the big day, they discovered that the fuel tank for the generator was empty.

"*Another* prank?"

"Maybe," Dan sounded disgruntled. "Or maybe just an opportunistic thief. We had to set up the generator outdoors for safety reasons. It's easy to get at with a siphon."

When Dan had refilled the generator with gas—the same kind used by cars—Liss ran a final test of the special effects she'd installed. This time *she* was the one responsible for the flickering lights and eerie sounds. Thumps, moans, and even a distant scream echoed through the deserted house. Lightning flashed. In the parlor, a sickly green glow surrounded the bones lying on the sofa.

"Pretty effective," Dan said approvingly.

"Why, thank you kind sir. I do my best." He'd been in the basement, checking on the door to the tunnel. "Everything okay?"

"Still safely sealed off."

"Good."

Liss shut everything down. Dan turned off the generator. Then they checked all the locks one last time, including the new one Dan had just installed on the gas cap.

Halloween dawned clear and crisp—a perfect fall day—at a little past six in the morning. Sunset would occur around four-thirty. Later there would be a full moon.

The corn maze was an immediate success, drawing patrons from towns within a hundred mile radius. Many of them made their way to the town square to watch the preparations for the bonfire, register for the costume contest, and visit the specialty shops for which Moosetookalook was becoming famous.

In addition to Moosetookalook Scottish Emporium, Stu's Ski Shop, Angie's Books, and Gloria Weir's craft and hobby shop, there was also a jewelry store that specialized in original designs made with Maine gemstones. On the other side of the municipal building from the bookstore, Patsy's Coffee House offered shoppers a break with gourmet coffee blends and homemade baked goods.

An hour before the haunted house was scheduled

to open, Liss left the Emporium in the capable hands of a college student who sometimes worked part-time for her and headed out to the mansion to serve as one of the "guides." She was already in costume, as she had been all day, tricked out as a gypsy fortuneteller in a long, colorful skirt, a peasant blouse, a flowered shawl, and a long, black wig.

Dan went with her. He'd put on his hard hat and called it good. If anyone asked, he was dressed as a construction worker. He powered up the generator while Liss unlocked the back door and stepped into the kitchen.

"I want to run one more check of the effects," she called over her shoulder as she flicked the switches that would activate them.

Without waiting for Dan to join her, Liss headed for the parlor, which was designated as the first stop on the tour. The skeleton had worked perfectly the previous day, but the key to a successful performance was attention to detail. Check and double check— that had been the rule the stage manager of her former dance company had lived by. That simple philosophy had prevented theatrical disaster on more than one occasion.

"Showtime," she whispered as she opened the door from the hall.

The eerie greenish illumination she'd installed came on as it was designed, to, but the skeleton failed to sit up. Napoleon Bony-Parts remained in an immobile heap.

Liss squinted in the murky glow, unable to make out much more than a vague shape lying on the sofa. She wondered why the plaster bones weren't reflecting the green light. They weren't fluorescent, but they ought to show up better than they were.

Glad she'd brought a flashlight with her, she switched it on and at once swung the beam upward to check on the pulley. One end of the wire hung down, unattached and useless. Liss swore under her breath. "Damn mice."

She redirected the beam, aiming it at the sofa, and gasped.

The skeleton was gone. In its place was one of the manikins. It lay sprawled in an ungainly pose on the sofa and someone had painted two bloody puncture marks on its neck, turning it into a "vampire victim." Fake blood had even been dribbled down the side of the brocade cushions to puddle on the floor.

Annoyed that someone had messed with her set piece, Liss's first thought was that she needed to search the room for the skeleton. The eerie, pulsing green lighting effect made it difficult for her to identify even the most common objects. The parlor organ looked positively sinister.

"Dan!" she shouted as she played her flashlight beam in a haphazard fashion over walls and furniture. Was that *more* fake blood? "The prankster got inside again!"

She had to find Bony-Parts. She had enough time to reset this scene and return the manikin to the dining room, but only just, and only if she could locate the skeleton quickly.

There! Behind the sofa. She hurried toward the spot, irritated by the way the bones had been so carelessly dumped.

It was only when Liss bent down to examine the skeleton for damage that she realized she'd gotten it all wrong. She caught a sickening whiff of an odor she'd hoped she'd never have to smell again. The reek of death was both unmistakable . . . and terrifying.

She jerked upright and, for the first time, her flashlight beam shone directly on the face of the manikin.

Bile rose in Liss's throat. Her knees went weak, forcing her to grip the back of the sofa to keep from falling. What lay there was not a manikin. It was a man. A very dead man. The red marks on his neck weren't fake blood. The gore was all too real.

But that wasn't the worst of it.

The worst of it was that she knew him.

Chapter Seven

"Ned Boyd? Son of a gun! I thought he was still in jail!"

Feeling oddly detached from reality, Liss listened to Chief of Police Jeff Thibodeau exclaim over the body she'd found. She sat at the kitchen table in the Chadwick mansion, her back to the doors that led to the rest of the house. She clutched the cap from a thermos in both hands. She didn't know who had given it to her—the place seemed to be full of people, some of them in uniform and some not—but it contained hot coffee and she felt chilled to the bone. She gulped it down, grimacing only slightly at the strength of the brew. The taste lingered on her tongue, making her feel slightly ill.

"You should go home," someone said. "You don't need to stay here."

Liss turned her head to look at the person sitting next to her and recognized her with a vague sense of surprise. "Sherri? Where did you come from?"

"You've had a shock," Sherri said, "finding your

cousin like that." She relieved Liss of the empty thermos cap. "Good Lord! Your fingers are like icicles."

She set the cap on the table and grabbed both of Liss's hands. As she rubbed them between her own, warmth and circulation slowly returned. Along with feeling came increased awareness of her surroundings. The awful truth Liss had been trying to block out crashed through her defenses. The tears she'd been holding back streamed down her face.

"How am I going to tell Aunt Margaret?" she choked out between sobs. "Ned wasn't much of a person, but he was the only son she had."

"You don't have to be the one to tell her." Dan's voice was so close that Liss jumped. She hadn't heard him enter the kitchen.

"She's my aunt," Liss said without glancing his way. "He was my cousin."

"Gordon Tandy's here now. Let him break the bad news." Dan pulled out a chair on the opposite side of the table and sat down, reaching across the laminate surface to pass her a clean, white handkerchief.

As if from a great distance, Liss heard the sounds of the state police forensics team at work in the parlor. Gordon Tandy would be the trooper in charge of the investigation. This was his patch. And it *was* murder. She dabbed at her eyes and blew her nose. The world came back into focus.

First she'd screamed, Liss remembered. Then Dan had come running. He'd taken one look at poor Ned and hustled her out of the room. He'd used his cell phone to call the police. Then he'd tried to get her to leave the house, but she'd refused. "Someone has to stay with the body," she'd said.

After that, things got fuzzy. She didn't remember seeing Sherri arrive. Or Jeff, who was Sherri's boss.

Or George Henderson, the local ME, although Liss was sure he'd been called out. Or Gordon.

That meant all kinds of official vehicles were parked in the driveway. And anyone who'd showed up to tour the haunted house had been turned away. Liss had no idea how much time had passed since she'd made her grisly discovery, but she was sure that everyone in town knew a crime had been committed up to the old Chadwick place.

"Aunt Margaret believes Ned's still in prison," she said aloud, "but if she can't find me at the Halloween party, she'll worry that I'm the one in trouble."

"All the more reason for us to go home." Dan said. "She'll likely phone there and you can reassure her that you're fine."

"I'm not going to lie to her, and you don't break news like this to someone over the phone. I have to tell her in person. I—" She broke off at the sound of heavy footsteps clumping toward the kitchen from the front of the house. She stood up, her fingers tightening spasmodically on the handkerchief. She half expected to see two men enter carrying a body bag and breathed a sigh of relief when only one person, Gordon Tandy, came through the doorway.

The state police officer topped six feet by an inch or two and was solidly built. He had a military bearing and wore his reddish-brown hair short to go with it, but no matter what he did, he couldn't overcome perpetually youthful features. He was in his early forties and still looked like a fresh-faced kid. That he was frowning made no difference.

"What are you still doing here, Liss?" Gordon directed a glare at Dan, who spread his hands in a gesture of helplessness.

"What was *Ned* doing here? He was supposed to be

in jail, Gordon. If he was in jail he wouldn't be dead." Aware that her voice had risen steadily during this harangue, Liss abruptly stopped speaking.

"I'd like to know what he was doing in this house myself." Gordon spoke with irritating calmness. "You had no idea he'd been released early?"

"He'd been released early?" Dan repeated the words, but gave them a far different inflection. Slowly he got to his feet, his hands balled into fists at his sides.

Liss winced. She heard in Dan's voice what Gordon and Sherri clearly did not. She alone knew what Dan must be remembering—that he'd arrived on the scene too late to help her on that dreadful day when Ned had tried to kill her. That she'd managed to save herself had been a near thing, and although Dan had gone along with her wishes, he had not approved of her decision to keep that part of the story from the police.

As a result of Liss's reluctance to cause her beloved Aunt Margaret still more grief, Ned had never been charged with attempted murder, only with manslaughter. That death, he'd insisted in court, had been an accident. It had occurred during the commission of a burglary and should have earned him a longer sentence, but the judge had been taken in by Ned's apparent contrition. He'd been sentenced to a mere five years for taking the life of another human being.

Liss closed the distance between herself and Gordon. She wanted to be able to see his face clearly. That way she'd know if he was holding anything back.

"Ned should have had another three years to serve. Why did they let him out ahead of schedule?"

Gordon hesitated, then shrugged. He made no attempt to avoid meeting her eyes. "I don't know, Liss, and that's God's honest truth. Maybe he got time off for good behavior. Maybe it had more to do with overcrowded conditions at the correctional facility. I'll find out tomorrow."

"If he was out of jail, why wasn't anyone in the family notified?" Dan joined them to sling an arm around Liss's shoulders.

If she'd had energy to spare, Liss would have protested the not-very-subtle staking of his claim on her. Now that they were married, Dan was going to have to stop thinking of Gordon as his rival for her affections. Liss knew for a fact that *Gordon* had moved on.

"There's no law that says relatives have to be informed," Gordon said. "Or anyone else, either, except the local probation officer. It was up to Ned himself to contact his mother. Are you sure he didn't?"

"She'd have told me if he had." Liss frowned. "When she mentioned him the other day, she said he refused to see her or answer her letters."

"Margaret talked about him?"

Liss could understand Dan's surprise. It had been the first time she knew of in more than a year that Margaret had so much as spoken her son's name. "We were discussing this house and she said that Ned used to come up here when he was a boy. That he was fascinated by the place. There's supposed to be buried loot on the property, you know," she added for Gordon's benefit. He was a native of Carrabassett County but lived a good hour's drive from Moosetookalook, in the equally rural village of Waycross Springs.

"That's right." Sherri had remained at the table,

watching the little drama play out in the mansion kitchen. She joined the others to confirm the part of the conversation with Margaret she'd been privy to and to summarize the pranks that had plagued the Chadwick mansion. She finished with an account of Dan's discovery of the tunnel.

"Have there been any more incidents since?" Gordon asked.

"Someone siphoned gas out of the generator." Dan was about to elaborate when Liss interrupted.

"When did Ned get out of jail?"

Gordon consulted his notes. "September fifteenth."

"A couple weeks before Dolores Mayfield noticed flickering lights at the mansion," Sherri murmured. "I wonder how many times he was in and out? And how he got in again after Dan blocked the tunnel entrance to the basement?"

"I don't think he *was* in and out." Liss was remembering the mysterious thump she'd heard above her head on the day Jason Graye had given her such a scare and with sudden clarity she understood its source. "I think he was living here. If I were you, Gordon, I'd look for a panic room."

Telling Aunt Margaret that her son had been murdered was the hardest thing Liss had ever had to do. She put her arms around her aunt when Margaret dissolved into tears and sat with her on the love seat in Margaret's office at the hotel, but there was nothing she could do or say to alleviate the older woman's suffering. What comfort did anyone have to offer a parent who'd lost her only child? It didn't matter what Ned's failings had been. Once he'd been an innocent baby in his mother's arms.

Margaret was still in shock when Liss and Dan bundled her into the car and drove her home. It wasn't until they reached Margaret's apartment that Liss was struck by the fact that she was still in her fortuneteller costume. Margaret was dressed as a witch. She'd even used food coloring to dye her hair green. The image was incongruous with grief, but it didn't make Margaret's suffering any less real.

Since it seemed to help her aunt to talk, Liss sent Dan home and stayed to listen. Margaret had hundreds of fond memories to offset the disillusionment she'd suffered on that terrible day two years ago when she'd learned that Ned had confessed to the crime of manslaughter.

For that matter, so did Liss. She and Ned had never been close, but they'd grown up together. Lacking siblings and any other first cousins, the bond between them, while not particularly loving, had been unique. She was sorry he was dead . . . and she was furious at his killer.

It was not just that Ned's death ended any hope that he might have made amends for his past failings. Liss's anger also stemmed from the hurt the murder of her cousin was inflicting on her aunt. Margaret's agonizing loss was made even worse by the intensity of her regret over not having done more to force a reconciliation with Ned before he died.

"I should have *made* him talk to me," Margaret said in a choked whisper. "I should have kept going back to that prison until he agreed to see me."

She'd said the same thing a half dozen times already and Liss repeated the answer she'd been giving right along. "You tried your best. It's not your fault that Ned didn't want anyone to visit him."

No one could force a prisoner to entertain family on visiting day. It was one of the few rights a convicted felon retained after he went to prison.

"Why didn't he call me when he got out? *Why*, Liss? He had to know I'd help him get settled."

"Maybe he wanted to prove he could start over on his own." But even as Liss uttered these platitudes, she doubted they were true.

Unless Ned had changed a great deal while he was in prison, he wasn't the altruistic type. He'd mooched off his mother for years and "self-centered" had been his middle name.

Abruptly, Margaret pulled away from Liss and stood. She gathered up scattered tissues and deposited them in the wastepaper basket on her way to the bathroom. Liss heard water running and guessed that her aunt was splashing it on her face.

Liss braced herself. Once Margaret got a grip on her emotions, she'd start asking pointed questions. Liss dreaded the inquisition. She didn't want to remember finding Ned's body and she knew next to nothing about anything else.

Margaret emerged from the bathroom wearing a robe. She'd hidden the green hair with a towel. Liss couldn't tell if she'd washed the color out or just covered it up. Liss had pulled on a cardigan over her peasant blouse and buttoned it up to the neck. She'd left the black wig in the car. Ignoring Liss, Margaret went straight to the kitchen. It was not until she'd brewed a pot of soothing chamomile tea and poured a cup for each of them that she again addressed her niece directly. "Do you suppose Ned was here in town all along? Ever since he got out, I mean."

Liss shook her head. "I don't know. No one saw him. I'm sure of that much." Given the effectiveness of the local grapevine, word should have reached them within an hour of any such sighting.

"Gordon Tandy is in charge of the investigation, I suppose."

It wasn't a question, but Liss nodded anyway. She and her aunt had taken seats opposite each other on two of the stools arranged around a center island. Liss took a sip of the herbal brew Margaret had placed in front of her and grimaced. She'd never been fond of chamomile, but if it had a calming effect on her aunt, she was all for it.

"Tomorrow is going to be hellish," Liss said after a long silence. "The news media will have picked up on the story. The Halloween angle is too good to ignore." They'd probably make the national news, God help them!

"I know."

It made sense that she had already considered that particular problem, Liss realized. Margaret's job involved public relations and she was good at it, but it worried her that Margaret was staring vacantly into the dregs of her herbal tea. She wondered if she should suggest that her aunt take a sleeping pill and send her off to bed. Or would it be better to get her to reminisce about Ned? Liss wasn't sure she could stomach hearing too many more of Margaret's fond memories of her son. For years, she'd remained blind to Ned's many faults. He'd been a good liar and his mother had been willing to be deceived.

Liss's thoughts drifted as she waited for her aunt

to give some hint of what she wanted to do. Exhaustion crept up on her as she considered what a very long day it had been even before she'd found Ned's body. She was unable to hold back a jaw-popping yawn.

"Go home, Liss," Margaret said. "I'll be all right. You don't need to stay and babysit me."

"I hate to leave you alone."

"I've been coping with life alone for years." Margaret's lips twisted into a rueful half smile. "And to be honest with you, I lost Ned a long time ago."

"But—"

"Don't worry about me. Go."

Liss went.

The next day was every bit as bad as Liss had expected, made worse because she hadn't gotten much rest the night before. Nightmares had haunted her sleep. Although she couldn't remember much about them this morning, she was certain there had been vampires.

With the dawn, camera crews had arrived in droves. Reporters swarmed the Emporium, fortunately closed on a Sunday, and climbed the external stairs to bang on the outside entrance to Margaret's apartment. She sent Liss an e-mail to say she was fine, but that she'd unplugged her phone, closed the blinds, and was going back to bed.

Having failed to interview her aunt, the slavering horde descended on Dan and Liss's house. They knocked on the door and rang the bell, annoying Lumpkin so much that he chewed a hole in the footrest of Dan's recliner. The phone jangled constantly until Dan followed Margaret's example and unplugged it. Eventually, however, the siege lifted. The state police issued an extremely vague statement. And then Gloria Weir turned up in the town square to announce that she, too, would talk to the press . . . speaking on behalf of the Moosetookalook All Hallows Festival committee.

"Who elected her queen?" Liss muttered, peering out through the front window of her new attic library/office to watch Gloria's performance. The hobby shop owner stood in the center of the gazebo in the middle of the town square, surrounded by representatives of all three local network affiliates and a bevy of print reporters.

"Someone needed to talk to the press." When Dan came up behind her, Liss leaned against his chest, taking comfort in the warmth and strength of him. "Better her than you, me, or Margaret."

"I suppose you're right. I just wish I had some idea what she's saying."

"Tune in at six."

Liss snorted. "I guess I'll have to. Did you talk to Stu?" She felt Dan nod.

"The good news is that everything except the haunted house went off as planned last night. It looks as if the festival may even have made a profit."

Surprised, Liss turned in his arms to look up into his face. "Don't get me wrong. I'm delighted to hear it. But how on earth did the police manage to keep things quiet that long?"

"You'll *love* this—it was Jason Graye's doing. I don't know how he got involved, but apparently he stationed himself at the foot of the Chadwick driveway and turned people away. He told everyone the

haunted house attraction had to be scrapped because of an electrical problem. Most people didn't
hear any different until this morning."

It was three in the afternoon before the news
hounds dispersed. Liss watched the town square for
another hour, sitting by the window with Glenora on
her lap to make sure they'd really gone. Finally satisfied, she transferred the black cat to the seat of the
chair she'd just vacated and went downstairs. She
found Dan in front of the TV, a bowl of microwave
popcorn beside him and Lumpkin stretched out
across the back of the chair.

"Is he okay?" she asked, indicating the cat.

"Much better since he threw up."

"Sorry."

"Not your fault." She had only half his attention.
The rest was on the football game on the screen. The
Patriots had a bye week, but Dan liked the Bills, too.

"It's safe to go out now," Liss told him, "and I need
a breath of fresh air. I'm going to go check on Aunt
Margaret."

"Do you want me to come with you?" Dan even
reached for the remote.

"Thanks, but no thanks. One person at a time is
probably all Margaret will want to deal with"

She found her aunt almost exactly as she'd left
her—seated at the kitchen counter and staring into a
china cup. Now she wore a nightgown and bathrobe.
The empty cup had contained coffee, not tea. If it
had been mid-morning instead of late afternoon,
Liss wouldn't have been concerned. As it was, she
tread warily.

Margaret looked up and spotted Liss hesitating in

the kitchen doorway. "Tell me again how Ned got out of prison," she demanded.

Liss repeated what Gordon had said. "He told me he'd know more today," she added.

"But will he tell us?"

"Probably not. Has he talked to you yet?"

Margaret shook her head. "Not yet, but he will. I want to speak with Ned's probation officer, too."

Demanding answers from anyone in law enforcement was bound to be frustrating. Liss knew the type—they didn't like to tell civilians anything. Above all else, she was determined to spare her aunt any further distress. "Why don't you let me talk to the probation officer for you?"

Margaret's bleak expression broke her heart. "Don't you think I'm up to it?"

"You're one of the strongest women I know," Liss told her truthfully, "but why put yourself through what's certain to be a wrenching interview when I can handle it in your stead?"

"Will you yell at him for me? Because right now I am very angry with him, whoever he is. What right did he have to turn Ned loose without *telling* me? Ned was my *son!*"

Liss hoisted herself up onto the stool next to her aunt's. "I don't think the probation officer is the one who decided to let Ned go. From what Gordon told me, he wouldn't have had any choice about whether or not to notify family members, either."

"I don't see why not. Victims of violent offenders are given advance warning when the criminals complete their sentences. I read that in the newspaper just a few weeks ago. That case down to Three Cities, I think."

"And sometimes victims of violent offenders can

argue against a felon's early release," Liss agreed, "but that wasn't the situation with Ned."

The irony wasn't lost on her. If she'd pressed charges, she *would* have been advised beforehand when Ned was about to be set free. She might even have been asked for input ahead of time, to help the powers that be decide if he was truly rehabilitated and no longer a danger to her. But what good did it do to speculate? She wasn't really sure how such things worked and what did it matter now anyway? Ned *had* been let out of jail. Then someone had killed him. Nothing could change those two facts.

"I'll find out everything I can about where Ned went after his release and what he was up to," Liss promised. If it would help Margaret come to terms with her son's death, that was the least she could do for her.

Margaret folded her hand over Liss's as if Liss was the one who needed comfort. They sat that way for a few moments in silence. Liss watched her aunt's face. Margaret's eyes were unfocused at first, but after a bit she pulled herself together. She looked down at her empty cup, then up at the kitchen clock.

"I should get going," she murmured. As she slid off the stool, her gaze roved over the rest of the kitchen. Without warning, she froze, staring at the door that was the back entrance to the apartment.

Alarmed, Liss swiveled in that direction. Someone was standing just on the other side, on the small landing at the top of the flight of stairs that ran up the outside of the building. All Liss could see clearly were eyes shaded by gloved hands and a nose pressed right up against the glass. Moving fast, she crossed the kitchen and tried to jerk open the door. Unfortunately, it was locked. By the time she twisted the deadbolt, the peeping Tom had reached ground level and was sprinting away. Liss watched him until he was out of sight. There was no need to give chase. She knew where to find him.

"Was that a reporter?" In her robe and slippers, Margaret lacked her accustomed air of self-confidence. Her graying hair hung in scraggly clumps. Her hands were trembling.

"No. No, it was just . . . it was nobody." Liss shut the door firmly and once more engaged the lock.

Margaret inhaled deeply. Then she did it again. "I don't know what's wrong with me. I'm not usually like this."

"You've had a terrible shock. You're entitled to be off your game."

"The only thing I'm *entitled* to is information."

That sounded more like the Margaret Mac-Crimmon Boyd Liss knew and loved. "And you'll get it. Only I don't think we'll have any luck getting hold of a state employee on a Sunday. First thing tomorrow, though—"

"That's not what I meant." Aunt Margaret was sounding more and more like herself. She crossed the kitchen to peer out through the small window in the door. "Who was that, Liss? Most of my neighbors would have stuck around until you had the door open and then come in for a minute or two."

"Not this neighbor," Liss muttered.

"Liss. . . ."

"Okay. Okay. It was Boxer Snipes."

For a moment Margaret looked blank. Then her lower lip began to tremble. "That boy? That boy I met out at the Chadwick mansion? The one who was playing hooky?"

"Right."

"I . . . I didn't realize he was a Snipes."

"Oh, not you, too! Just because his cousins are troublemakers, it doesn't necessarily follow that—"

Margaret held up a hand to halt Liss's automatic defense of the boy, her expression closed. "I didn't mean that."

Liss had no idea what she was thinking.

"Is he Hilary's son?"

Liss nodded and waited for her aunt to say more. When she didn't, Liss asked, "Is that why you thought he looked familiar?" She imagined that Margaret had seen Boxer around town with his mother.

Margaret busied herself measuring coffee into the pot. "Yes, I suppose it is." Her movements were uncharacteristically clumsy, but when Liss offered to help, Margaret shooed her away. "Go home to Dan. And first thing tomorrow, you go down to Fallstown and talk to that probation officer."

Liss gave her aunt a mock salute, but it did not produce the hoped-for smile. Discouraged, she exited through the outer door, descending slowly so that she could scan the surrounding area.

Boxer was sitting on the steps that led to the front porch of her old house. Without comment, she joined him there. Together they stared out across the town square. It was quiet, now. All signs of the bonfire had been cleared away. There was no longer any trace of Gloria's press conference, either.

"So what did you want with my aunt?" she asked after a while.

"I just wanted to make sure the old lady was okay. It was her son that got killed, right?"

Old lady? Well, Liss supposed, someone in her early sixties *was* old to a boy of twelve.

"That's right. Did you ever see Ned Boyd out at

the mansion, Boxer?" She slanted a glance sideways, but he had his head down. She couldn't make out his facial expression.

"I didn't see nothin' at all," he mumbled. "Dead guy's got nothin' to do with me."

"Well, that's that then." She made a production of looking at her watch. "It's getting on toward supper-time. I've got to go. You'd better head home, too."

Boxer got reluctantly to his feet. Liss had the feeling there might be more he wanted to say to her.

"I don't know where you live," she said aloud. "Do you need a ride?"

"Naw. It's not far." Now he seemed anxious to be off, and before Liss could think of a way to coax him into divulging more information, he bolted.

She stared after him, puzzled, then shrugged. One mystery at a time.

Liss entered the town square. Instead of veering right to go home to Dan and the meal she'd left simmering in the slow cooker, she went straight, which took her to the municipal building. Circling it, she entered through the back entrance, the one directly outside Moosetookalook's police department.

Chapter Eight

The office at the Moosetookalook Police Department was a single inner room containing the bare necessities—two desks, chairs, filing cabinets, and the computer, printer, and other electronic gadgets essential to modern law enforcement. Sherri, seated in a creaky wooden swivel chair, glanced up when she heard Liss enter the waiting room from the hallway. Under her steady gaze, Liss covered the rest of the distance at a fast clip and plunked herself down in the bright red plastic chair reserved for visitors. It had never been intended to be comfortable, but rather to encourage those with complaints not to linger.

"I want to talk to Ned's probation officer," Liss announced.

"I'm not sure that's such a good idea."

"Better me than Aunt Margaret."

"No argument there, but no matter who talks to him, you won't get any answers. Under the law, a probation officer can only give a civilian, even a relative, information that's already part of the public record.

That pretty much amounts to telling you when Ned went to prison and why and when he got out. Nothing else."

"I know I'll be beating my head against a stone wall," Liss admitted, "but if I don't talk to him, then Aunt Margaret will insist on confronting him herself. At the very least, she wants to give him a piece of her mind for letting Ned go free without telling her."

Before Sherri could get a word in, Liss went on. "I know. I know. Not his call. I told her that, too. But I promised I'd try to find out everything I could. I get that a civilian isn't going to learn anything from a probation officer, but what if the person asking for information is a duly appointed officer of the law?"

Sherri sighed. "You'd still have the same problem. Assuming he'd even answer me, I'm not supposed to repeat anything I learn from Chase Forster."

"Forster's the probation officer?"

Sherri nodded. "He's a good man. He's been in the job for what seems like forever and, believe me, he would have been keeping an eye on Ned. He holds regular reporting days, when everyone on his caseload has to go in to Chase's office in Fallstown and tell him what they've been up to, where they're living, and whether or not they've got a job. If there are conditions of probation, like no drinking or no contact with minors, then the probation officer also makes spot checks at the client's home."

"Client?"

"That's the PC term for it. You don't need to know the others."

"So, this Chase Forster would have known where Ned was living?" Liss slid forward in her chair to lean her elbows on Sherri's desk.

"Ned would have given him an address, which

might not be the same thing. He'd only been free for a short time. Chase probably hadn't paid him a home visit yet. Huh."

"What?"

"Probably nothing. I just remembered something that makes me wonder if Ned ever did report in."

"Wouldn't some action have been taken if he hadn't?"

"Oh, sure. He'd end up back in jail . . . *if* he was caught. That's the thing. There was this other guy on probation with Chase, back maybe six or eight months ago. He *didn't* show up when he was supposed to. That's how I met Chase. He stopped by to leave a copy of the warrant, so we could make an arrest if we spotted his missing man. I imagine he supplied the same information to every department in the county."

"But you didn't get a warrant for Ned?" Liss asked, wanting to bring the conversation back where it belonged.

"No. But maybe it's just too soon. In any case, it gives me a legitimate question to ask Chase."

"You'll call him?" At Sherri's nod, Liss leaned back in the uncomfortable chair. "Great. And will you ask him what address Ned gave him? Please, Sherri. I think it may be important. Ned didn't come home to his family, but he must have gone somewhere after he got out of prison."

"Liss, I don't—"

Liss talked right over her protest. "The more I think about this, the more likely it seems to me that Ned was up to no good. Why else would he keep his release from prison a secret? And if he was the 'ghost' at the Chadwick mansion—"

"Why would Ned haunt the place?" Sherri gave her head a decisive shake. "It makes no sense. It has to be mere coincidence that he was released at around the same time the lights and other pranks started."

"Are you listening to yourself?" Liss was back to perching on the edge of the red plastic seat. "That's a pretty darned big coincidence!"

Sherri heaved a deep sigh. "Okay. Okay. You're right. Ned was probably up to something shady."

"And he must have had an accomplice. Or, at the least, someone to drive him as far as Moosetookalook. Can you ask his probation officer about that, too?"

"I'll ask. But I still won't be able to repeat anything Chase tells me." Having looked up the number while they were talking, Sherri reached for the phone.

Liss watched her friend punch in the digits for a call to Fallstown. When she heard the phone begin to ring, she leaned across the desk and pushed the button to activate the speaker. Sherri either didn't notice or pretended not to.

On the second ring, somewhat belatedly, Liss remembered that it was still Sunday. Not only that, but it was close to suppertime. "You're calling him at home?"

"Probation officers are on call twenty-four seven." Sherri gestured toward Moosetookalook's single closet-sized holding cell, currently empty. "If I arrest someone on Chase's caseload, I'm supposed to contact him ASAP so he can give instructions about whether to hold the guy on a probation violation or not. If he puts a hold on someone, that someone stays put until Chase gives the okay to allow bail. Sometimes the guy gets out again. Sometimes he doesn't." She grinned. "Don't you watch the news? Half the people law enforcement arrests for major crimes in this state are already in jail on probation violations."

An answering machine picked up on the sixth ring.

"He screens calls," Sherri said while Chase's brief message ran. It consisted of little more than confirmation of his phone number and instructions to wait until after the beep to leave a message.

Sherri identified herself to the machine. "I just have a quick question," she continued. "I'd appreciate a callback when you—"

"Hold on a sec." The voice that cut Sherri off was decidedly feminine. "Chase will be right with you."

In the background, Liss heard the sounds of a football game on TV, probably the same one Dan was watching. She quashed any feelings of guilt over disturbing the probation officer at home. It wasn't as if the Pats were playing.

Speaking in a deep, pleasant voice, Chase Forster came on the line. "Officer Campbell? You're with the Moosetookalook PD?"

"That's right," Sherri said. "We met briefly a few months ago. I was in the office when you stopped by to talk to Jeff Thibodeau."

"You're married to *Deputy* Campbell, right?" The county jail and sheriff's office were located in Fallstown, as were the county courthouse and Chase Forster's office. "What can I do for you?"

"It's about Ned—that is, Edward—Boyd. I assume the state police have already contacted you about his death?"

"They have." He didn't volunteer more and Liss understood why. Once the state police took over a murder investigation, local law enforcement personnel were generally left out of the loop.

"I'd really appreciate it if you could provide me with a few more details," Sherri said into the phone. "None of his family even knew he was out of prison. As you can imagine, his murder has been a terrible shock to them. To the whole community, really. I do understand that everything not in the public record is confidential, but—"

"That's right," Chase interrupted. "The rest is not for public consumption."

"I understand that," Sherri repeated, careful to avoid meeting Liss's eyes, "but it would really help me out if I knew how he got back to town in the first place."

"No idea. Sorry. Boyd only reported to me once. During that initial meeting, I took his photo for my files, gave him the standard lecture, and told him to come in or phone me, without fail, the second Tuesday of every month."

Sherri flipped her desk calendar back to October. "So that was on the fourteenth?"

"Right."

"He'd been out of prison almost a month by then," Sherri observed. "What about an address? He must have told you how to reach him. Where was he living? By rights, it should have been at his mother's place on Pine Street here in Moosetookalook."

"Hold on a sec." Liss heard the faint clatter of keys on a laptop. "Well, he had moved back to Moosetookalook, but the street address I have is 134 Raglan Road."

"The Chadwick mansion," Liss murmured.

"That's where he was killed," Sherri said into the phone, "but no one was supposed to be living there. It's an old, abandoned house."

After a few more keystroke sounds, Chase Forster

said, "He gave the same address as his destination when he was released."

"Doesn't anyone check these things?"

"Not so you'd notice," Chase muttered, sounding as disgruntled as Liss felt.

After Sherri thanked Chase and disconnected, she and Liss sat in silence for a few minutes. The probation officer hadn't told them anything new, except that Ned *planned* on living in the Chadwick mansion. Or rather on *hiding* in the house.

"Did Gordon find a panic room?" Liss asked.

Sherri shook her head. "Not that I've heard."

"Did he even look? Or did he just decide that the whole idea of an old fashioned priest hole was too reminiscent of a third-rate Gothic novel to be real? You'd think that after we told Gordon about the tunnel into the basement, he'd realize it wouldn't be all that far-fetched to think the mansion might also have a hidden room."

Sherri spread her hands wide. "You'll have to ask him that."

"Then I will." Before she could think better of it, Liss grabbed the phone and punched in Gordon's cell number. In the not-so-distant past, she'd had occasion to memorize it. There had been a time when she'd thought Gordon might even ask her to marry him.

He sounded distracted when he answered, but Liss plowed ahead. "Have you found a panic room yet?"

Silence answered her.

She waited. He knew who she was and why she was asking. If he hung up on her, she'd just call him back. He knew that, too.

"We had a few other things to do that took priority," Gordon finally said.

"Ned had to be hiding somewhere."

"It's a big house. Maybe he just stayed ahead of you. Or was up in the attic. And just who is supposed to have built this panic room? That's a pretty modern concept for an old house."

"Blackie O'Hare's house," Liss reminded him. She had the feeling he counted to ten before he answered her.

"Let me do my job, Liss. We'll be back out there tomorrow. We will look for more secret passages and, yes, for hidden rooms, too. Bad enough that the victim's wounds made everyone who saw them think of vampires," he grumbled as an aside.

Liss felt the color drain from her face. She'd been trying to avoid remembering that particularly gruesome detail. Her hand clenched on the phone and her voice no longer sounded like her own. "What *did* cause those puncture marks?"

"Liss, you know I can't tell you that."

"I . . . I think I might sleep a little better at night if I was sure it *wasn't* a vampire." Was that nervous laughter really coming out of her mouth? Liss throttled back and ended up making a sound eerily like a sob. "Sorry. I'm sorry, Gordon. I know it's none of my business. But you know what an active imagination I have."

Trying to make light of it made her feel even more of a fool. She was about to break the connection when Gordon spoke.

"Two-tined fork."

"What?"

"The murder weapon. It was a two-tined fork taken from the display in the dining room."

"Oh, my God."

"That's privileged information, Liss. We're not re-leasing it to the press. If one hint of what I just told you appears in the newspapers, online, or on TV, I'll know who leaked it."

"I . . . I . . . don't worry." She swallowed convul-sively. "It's my fork, Gordon. I supplied all the cutlery for Death by Poison."

His voice gentled ever so slightly. "I figured. We al-ready identified your fingerprints on it, since we had them on record. Can you think of anyone else who would have had reason to touch it?"

For a moment, Liss couldn't think at all. Then she rattled off the names of everyone who belonged to her Halloween committee. "Gloria Weir is the most likely. She was with me when I set the table. Does that help?"

"It will allow us to eliminate suspects, so yes. But, Liss?"

"Yes."

"Don't help anymore, okay?"

Liss meant her promise when she gave it, but by the time she returned home, her thoughts had re-turned to the conviction that there had to be a hid-ing place somewhere in the mansion. She found Dan in the living room. Now Lumpkin was in his lap and Glenora occupied the back of the recliner. All three of them appeared to be riveted to the football game on TV.

"What did you do with those blueprints?" she asked.

He started to speak, then just shook his head. Dislodging Lumpkin, he left the room and returned a few minutes later with the roll of floor plans.

"Once you found the tunnel, we forgot all about the rest of the house," Liss said as she separated the pages. She sat cross-legged on the floor and spread the plans out on the carpet in a half circle around her.

"I looked them over pretty thoroughly. There's nothing labeled SECRET ROOM on these plans."

Liss ignored the sarcasm and continued to pour over the drawings, comparing the rooms represented on paper to the real ones she'd seen. It didn't take long to spot a discrepancy on the second floor. "This shows four bedrooms." She tapped the page, which indicated that there was an entrance to a fourth room just at the top of the stairs. "This isn't a bedroom. It's a linen closet. And it's nowhere near as deep as these blueprints say it is."

Dan knelt beside her for a closer look, the game forgotten. "Could be they converted it at some point." He traced a line down the center of the missing bedroom. "If you put a wall here, the bedrooms on either side would gain a good-sized clothes closet."

"But that would cut this window right in two." She tapped it lightly. "Don't you think that would be a little odd? Besides, I don't remember any big closets in either of those two bedrooms, just little ones at the inside corners." She indicated their location on the floor plan with her index finger. "Here and here, as shown."

"So, you think your cousin got in through the tunnel, then hid out in a secret room behind the linen closet? How did he know about either one?" Dan shoved Lumpkin aside when the big cat tried to walk across the blueprints.

"As a kid, Ned was fascinated by the mansion. Aunt Margaret said so. Maybe he found them both way back then."

"Okay, let's say he did. Why decide to hide out there now?"

"How do I know? He wouldn't allow any contact with anyone in the family after he went to prison. Maybe he'd been plotting revenge the whole time he was locked up." This time it was Liss's turn to catch hold of the cat. She pulled him into her lap and stroked his long fur, soothing both of them.

"Really stupid way to get it," Dan muttered.

"Then maybe he was hiding from some lowlife he met while he was incarcerated."

"I'd find it easier to believe he was hunting for Blackie O'Hare's loot."

"Maybe he was," Liss shot back.

"Then how does taking my hammer and the ladder and your jacket and that big wooden tub and the manikin, and then putting them back again fit in with his plans?" Dan leaned against the sofa, arms folded across his chest.

"Maybe the pranks were meant to scare us away. Maybe he didn't know we were planning to use the house for a Halloween attraction." Liss spotted the flaw in her logic before Dan could point it out to her. "No. He *had* to know. He would have overheard us talking when we were in the house. And he must have seen the set pieces, too."

"At least the disappearance of the lantern and the fact that the generator ran out of gas make sense now. It hasn't been the coldest October on record, but I bet it got mighty nippy in that old house at

night. And dark, too." Dan heaved himself to his feet
and bent to retrieve the blueprints. "I'll take these to
Gordon Tandy tomorrow, and that will be the end of
it as far as you and I are concerned. It's Tandy's job
to figure out what Ned was up to and find whoever
killed him. *Your* job is to be there for your aunt."

Liss didn't argue. Dan was right. They had a funeral to plan. Family would be coming into town—
her parents, at the least. There was nothing more
she could do for Ned that the police couldn't do better. Tomorrow she'd tell Margaret that, and mean it,
too.

If the state police had a suspect in Ned Boyd's
murder, they didn't share that information with his
family. Liss's aunt grieved for her son, but after she
buried him, she went on with her life. She took only
two days off from work.

Thanksgiving, Christmas, and New Year's were
busy times at The Spruces and Liss suspected that
Margaret was relieved to have her duties as events coordinator to distract her. But at the beginning of
February came a lull. Most of the hotel's guests were
skiers who saw to their own entertainment. No cor-
porate dinners or anniversary parties or weddings
were scheduled for the first thirteen days of the
month, not until the flurry of activity that always surrounded Valentine's Day. That left Margaret Mac-
Crimmon Boyd with way too much time on her
hands—time to dwell on what had been done to her
only child.

Dusting snow off the sleeves of her heavy winter
coat, Liss hurried into the lobby of The Spruces.
Light, fluffy flakes had been falling all morning, too

little to make driving dangerous and just enough to cover the ugly brown patches along the side of the road. Maine at its prettiest, Liss thought.

She had pulled off her wool mittens and stuffed them into her pockets before she realized that she was not the only one Aunt Margaret had summoned to the hotel for a meeting. Sherri Campbell had been watching the entrance from the comfort of one of several armchairs drawn up beside the huge lobby fireplace with its tile-lined hearth and Victorian mantel and mirror above. Flames crackled invitingly, sending welcome warmth out into the room. The hotel burned apple wood and the scent was both pleasant and soothing.

Sherri rose as soon as she spotted Liss. They met at the entrance to the wide hallway that led to the hotel dining room.

"You, too?" Liss slipped out of her coat and tucked her wooly hat into one sleeve so she wouldn't lose it.

"Looks that way. I guess Margaret got tired of phoning the PD." Sherri was out of uniform, dressed much as Liss was in jeans and a sweater.

"You don't have to tell her anything, you know. She can't badger you the way she can a blood relative."

"Don't kid yourself. I worked part-time in the Emporium when Margaret was running it. She gave me a break when not everyone would have, including my own parents. I owe her."

At the end of the wide hallway was a vestibule, where a smiling hotel employee waited to show guests to their tables, but Liss and Sherri didn't need to go that far. They took the first door to their left, the one marked PRIVATE. The area beyond contained several offices, a conference room, a room for the copier, and a bathroom. Margaret's office was straight ahead of them, but although she'd left the door open for them, Liss didn't immediately see her aunt. Then she heard the soft clink of china—cups and saucers and a teapot being set out on a serving tray.

"I know you're out there," Margaret called. "Come on in. The tea will be ready in a minute."

"Green tea means she wants us alert," Liss muttered under her breath. "Herbal means she knows we're not going to like what she's up to and she wants to lull us into a false sense of security before she drops the bomb."

Sherri chuckled as she waved Liss into Margaret's office ahead of her.

It was a welcoming room, designed to put clients at ease. The walls were painted a pretty pale green and decorated with Carrabassett County landscapes by local artists. At first glance, Margaret looked no different than she had before Ned's death. Dressed in office casual—Maine people never went in for too much dressing up—she finished preparing the tea with her usual quiet efficiency and set the tray on the glass-topped coffee table in front of a loveseat upholstered in a bright floral print.

"Well, come on. Sit. Drink up."

They sat, and Margaret took the small lady's chair facing them, where the light from a nearby floor lamp fell on her face. She'd made a noble attempt to hide the ravages of grief with a careful application of makeup, but nothing could completely disguise the dark circles under her eyes and a lifetime of smiling had not created the lines that seamed her face. Sorrow and sleepless nights had done that, and in an appallingly short amount of time. Two weeks earlier, Liss had insisted Margaret see her doctor. He'd prescribed antidepressants and regular exercise. If there had been any improvement since, Liss couldn't spot it.

"I want to know what the police are doing to find my son's murderer," Margaret said when she'd taken a few sips of her tea.

It was black and strong. Liss wasn't sure what that meant.

"You know already, Margaret." Sherri managed to keep the pity out of her voice, but Liss saw it in her eyes. "They never close a murder case. They follow up leads. They pursue inquiries. They—"

"In other words, there has been no progress whatsoever."

"If they have any answers, they haven't shared them with me, either," Sherri admitted. "But then, they wouldn't. You'd be more likely to hear something than I would. Honestly, Margaret, they're doing their best. They just don't have much to go on."

"What about the duffle bag they found? That was Ned's, wasn't it?"

Sherri spread her hands in a gesture of helplessness. "I don't know enough to answer that question, Margaret, but I think we can assume that it was. The state police did discover it in that hidden room."

Liss drank her tea and kept her mouth shut. Gordon Tandy had been willing to tell them little more than that he'd located a nearly invisible door at the back of the linen closet. Beyond was a small room. Inside, he'd found a duffle bag, presumably the one that had caused Stu's fall.

"How do I get the police to hand over that bag

and its contents?" Margaret asked. "I'm Ned's only living relative. I should have his belongings."

"They're holding whatever they found as evidence," Sherri reminded her.

"Can't they at least give me a list of what was inside the duffle bag?" Margaret turned to Liss, desperation in her eyes. "You're supposed to be good at finding things out. Why don't *you* know what he was up to? Someone must have an idea why he was hiding out in that house instead of coming home to me."

Alarmed by the way her aunt's voice was rising, Liss tried to keep her own as soothing as possible. "Margaret, I'm not a detective."

"But you've been so clever in the past. Surely you can uncover something."

"I can't interfere in a police investigation. If whoever did this terrible thing is to be caught and punished, I have to stay out of it. I could compromise their entire case if I blunder in looking for clues."

Liss understood Margaret's frustration. She felt the same way. But aside from the fact that both Dan and Gordon had strong objections to her meddling, Liss had no idea what she *could* do to help, or where to begin.

"Liss, I'm begging you. The police aren't doing anything. You're my only hope."

As much as she wanted to resist, Liss heard herself agree, once again, to look into Ned's activities between the time he got out of prison and the day she'd found him in the old Chadwick mansion. Surely, she couldn't do any harm by investigating that angle. Besides, although she knew and accepted all the arguments against getting involved, there was one

important one in favor of taking action. It was Aunt
Margaret who was asking her to.

Sherri kept her opinion to herself until they were
back in the lobby. "I hope you know what you're
doing," she said then.

"It will make her feel better to think I'm taking an
active role. That's the least I can do for her."

"Does that mean you're not really going to poke
your nose in where it doesn't belong?"

Liss shrugged back into her coat and avoided
meeting Sherri's eyes. "Pretty much," she mumbled.

Sherri huffed out a frustrated sigh as she pulled
on her own outerwear. "What are you going to do?"

Liss stared off into space for a moment before she
answered. "I'd like to take another look at the house.
I want to see that secret room for myself. The mansion is no longer off limits as a crime scene, right?"

The Moosetookalook grapevine had been prompt
to report it when the state police had finally taken
down the yellow tape and returned the house keys to
the town office. From that source, more specifically
from Dolores Mayfield, Angie Hogencamp, and Julie
Simpson, as verified by Patsy of Patsy's Coffee House,
Dan's sister Mary, and Stu Burroughs. Liss had also
heard that Jason Graye's efforts to buy the place had
been put on hold. She wasn't sure why. She'd been
offered a variety of reasons, everything from the fact
that he thought the place was haunted to a more
likely rumor that the current town selectmen were
refusing to sell for the pittance Graye had offered.

"Do you want company?" Sherri asked. "I still have
an hour or two free before Adam gets home from
school."

"You mean to go out there *now*?" After the grisly

discovery she'd made the last time she'd entered the Chadwick mansion, Liss was not all *that* eager to revisit the place.

"Why not? Let's get it over with. We'll find nothing. You'll tell Margaret you tried. Bingo! We're both off the hook."

"If only it were that simple."

Chapter Nine

A short time later, Liss pushed the starter button on the generator. Nothing happened on the first try, but on the second she was rewarded with a steady hum.

"How come this generator is still here?" Sherri asked.

"The guy we borrowed it from is in Florida until April. He said to leave it where it was until he gets back and he'd pick it up then."

The moment Liss unlocked the back door and stepped inside, she reached for the light switch. She wished she could turn on the heat, too, but the aged furnace hadn't passed inspection. She didn't even know if there was fuel left in the oil tank. It didn't matter, she told herself. They weren't staying long.

From the kitchen, she went straight down the hallway to the stairs, flipping every light switch she came to. She avoided looking toward the dining room or the parlor. The police had long since released the manikins and the skeleton so that she could return them to their owners. Except for the two-tined fork, her cutlery and china had also been restored to her. She imagined that the forensics team had kept other items, as well—like the sofa Ned had been lying on— but she felt no urge to verify that hunch.

The linen closet door at the top of the staircase stood open, exposing empty shelves that ran from floor to ceiling. It looked exactly as it had on Liss's first visit to the house. Although the overhead light in the hall was fairly bright, it failed to reveal any sign of an entrance to the room behind the closet.

"Do you know how to get in?" Liss asked.

"No, but how hard can it be?" Sherri peered into the cramped space. "We *know* there's a door here. That's half the battle. I wonder if we need to remove this shelving first."

"I don't think so. It wouldn't be much of a secret hiding place if you had to leave a stack of shelves on the floor outside." Hesitantly, knowing she was likely to come in contact with spider webs or mouse droppings, Liss raised her arm and felt with her fingertips along the back of the top shelf. Nothing happened.

Sherri examined the narrow strip of wall between door and shelves. "No levers. No indentations. No button marked PUSH ME TO GET IN."

"Oh, for a wall sconce on the wall outside the door. Something with a candle in it." Liss couldn't help smiling as she recalled the classic scene from Mel Brooks's *Young Frankenstein*.

" 'Put the candle back,' " Sherri quoted, sharing the memory. "Oh! Wait. I've got an idea. I saw this on a TV show."

Easing Liss aside, she stepped up close to the shelves and, one by one, lifted each by gripping the front and raising it slightly. She worked from top to bottom. The lowest shelf was the key. As soon as she pulled up on it, the entire back wall started to swivel.

It stopped when she let go.

"All right, Sherri!" Liss stooped to take hold of the edge of the shelf. When she lifted it high enough, a distinct click sounded, loud as a pistol shot.

The entire back wall of the closet swung toward them, forcing Liss and Sherri to step smartly out of the way. It stopped moving on its own. At a right angle to its former position, was an opening on the back side of the shelving wide enough for a slender person to slip through.

"This is almost as good as the fireplace in *Indiana Jones and the Last Crusade*," Sherri marveled.

"I was thinking Nancy Drew and *The Hidden Staircase*," Liss replied, but neither of them moved any closer to the opening. The room beyond was shrouded in darkness.

"Are we going in?" Sherri asked.

"Sure. Of course. This is what we came for, right?"

Liss switched on the flashlight she'd brought with her and stepped through the opening. Sherri followed with her Maglite, but Liss felt a tremendous surge of relief when she found a light switch, flicked it, and was rewarded with additional illumination from an overhead fixture.

The hidden chamber was smaller than the other second floor bedrooms. It was furnished with a twin bed, a nightstand with a lamp, and a dresser with a mirror. A rag rug covered the wooden floor beside the bed. A brand new electric space heater was plugged into a wall outlet.

"Why did I assume the room would be empty?" Liss asked of no one in particular.

"Maybe because Gordon implied that they didn't find anything in here except Ned's duffle bag?" Sherri headed for the dresser and started going through the drawers.

"And why am I *not* surprised that he wanted us to jump to that conclusion?"

"The state boys hate to share information with anyone, even other police departments." The drawers were all empty, but to be thorough, Sherri took each one out, flipped it over, then felt in the empty space in case anything had been hidden there.

Liss opened a door and discovered a closet. Two wire coat hangers dangled from the clothes rod. She wondered if Ned had hung her lightweight fall jacket on one of them, and if the police had it now. Except for that, all the other missing items were accounted for.

She searched the nightstand with as much care as Sherri had used on the dresser and with as little to show for it.

Sherri checked under the bed. "Nothing but dust bunnies," she reported.

Liss crossed to the small room's one window. Heavy fabric had been nailed in front of it.

"A makeshift blackout curtain," Sherri observed.

"Well, at least that gives us one answer. This is why Ned borrowed Dan's hammer and my three-step stepladder—so he could block off the window. He wanted to be able to turn on the overhead light in this room without having to worry about it being seen from outside."

"That doesn't explain what he wanted with the other stuff that went missing."

"No, it doesn't." Liss sat down on the bed and surveyed the room from that angle, but nothing new popped out at her. "Ned must have been responsible for the thump I heard the day Jason Graye gave me such a scare. He was living here even then. But he can't have been trying to frighten me away."

"If he had been," Sherri agreed, "he'd have done a better job of it."

"It makes more sense to assume that he meant to stay hidden until after Halloween. Once we were out of his hair, he'd have the place to himself."

"But *why* was he hiding out?" Sherri asked.

"That's the question, isn't it? And I have no idea what the answer is." Convinced that there was nothing left to see in the hidden room, Liss rose from her perch on the bed. "Ready to go?"

Sherri turned off the lights, Liss closed the hidden door behind them, and they stepped back into the upstairs hall.

"Anything else you want to see before we leave?" Sherri asked.

Liss shook her head. "I've spent enough time in this haunted house to last me a lifetime. Today's visit was a waste of time. The state police took everything that might have been of interest." She started down the stairs, once again averting her eyes as she passed the door to the parlor.

"If no one knows what Ned was doing here, how would they know what's important and what isn't?" Sherri frowned. "Did what I just said make any sense at all?"

"It made as much sense as anything about this situation. Ned must have come to this house for a reason. Even though he hid from his family, he didn't try to keep his presence here a complete secret. He gave this address to his probation officer."

"It looks to me as if he didn't want anyone *in town*

to know he was here," Sherri said as they entered the kitchen once more, "but he didn't care otherwise. That's very peculiar, and not just because the Ned I remember would have gone straight home to mama so he could mooch off her."

"That part troubles me, too. Even though Ned refused to see any visitors while he was locked up, he knew Margaret still loved him and that she'd welcome him home. She was horrified by what he'd done, but she helped pay for his lawyer. And I know she wrote to him all the while he was in prison, even though he refused to let her visit. Since the letters didn't come back, he must have received them."

"What about you?" Sherri asked. "Would you have welcomed him home with open arms?"

"I'm a lot less forgiving than my aunt. Aside from the reason he was in jail in the first place, and a few other things he did that I did not share with the police, I saw how badly his actions hurt Margaret. It took her the best part of a year to come to terms with what happened and begin to rebuild her life. It wasn't until after she went to work at The Spruces that she really got over the shock of what Ned did. Now his murder has shattered her peace of mind all over again."

Liss had her hand on the light switch, ready to plunge the kitchen into semidarkness, lock up, and go home when she noticed, out of the corner of her eye, that the cellar door was slightly ajar. She froze.

"What?" Instantly, Sherri went on alert.

For a moment, Liss wished her friend was in uniform . . . and armed. "It's probably nothing, but shouldn't the door to the basement be closed and locked?"

Sherri stared at it. "No one's supposed to have been inside this house since the state police left."

"Maybe they were the ones who left the door open." Liss did *not* want to investigate.

"And maybe someone has opened the tunnel entrance again."

"What if they're down there right this minute?"

With a resigned sigh, Sherri took the lead, Maglite at the ready. "Trained police officer," she snapped when Liss started to object.

"Fine! You go first." Liss flipped the stairwell light switch. One low-wattage bulb illuminated the way down. Below, she remembered, more bare bulbs hung at intervals throughout the cellar, but the corners were in deep shadow.

Cautiously, the two women descended the steep wooden steps, Liss following close on Sherri's heels. The air temperature dropped as they went down, making Liss shiver, but spooked or not, she wasn't about to let her friend face danger alone.

Liss shone her flashlight beam over the furnace and oil tank, searching for the remains of the old coal bin. Even from the foot of the stairwell she could see that the boards Dan had nailed across the door to the tunnel were still in place. At once, she breathed a little easier. "False alarm."

"Maybe not." Sherri had her Maglite trained on the dirt floor. "Someone has been digging holes down here."

The police took over the Chadwick mansion. Again. This time, the local PD had jurisdiction.

"There's no need to call in the state boys," Sherri informed Liss when she stopped by Moosetookalook

Scottish Emporium at mid-afternoon the next day. "We can handle a vandalism case on our own."

"Find any clues?" The clipboard Liss carried held a printout listing every item in her inventory. She put a check mark next to "pewter piper figurine, 2" and set the clipboard down on the shelf so she could give Sherri her full attention.

"There was a broken window in the room with all the stuffed birds. That's how they got in."

"What were they digging for?"

Sherri laughed. "Buried loot, I suppose. What else? Everyone in town has heard those old rumors."

"You don't believe it exists?"

"I might, if all the stories were the same. But no one agrees on just what Blackie O'Hare is supposed to have hidden. In some versions it's bank loot. In others it's gold. Or jewels. Or uncut gems. Or rare stamps." Her grin widened. "Your guess is as good as mine."

"I've always preferred the cache of cash. It has such a nice ring to it. So, you're telling me that you're not going to search the rest of the cellar?"

"You mean dig the whole thing up? Not a chance. That dirt is packed solid as a rock. You have to admire the industry of whoever took a crack at it, even if he didn't show much common sense."

"If you excavated and found nothing, it would put an end to the treasure hunting."

Sherri was shaking her head. "There would always be some damn fool who was sure we missed the mother lode by inches. No, the best thing we can do is put the boards back over the windows in the conservatory, make sure all the doors stay locked, and keep that tunnel entrance blocked off. Selling the place would be even better. Then it wouldn't be the town's responsibility any longer."

"I'm surprised the selectmen don't just accept Jason Graye's offer and be done with it."

Sherri glanced around to make sure no one else was in the shop. "You know my mother-in-law is still on the board of selectmen, right?"

Liss nodded. Thea Campbell had served in that capacity for years.

"Let's just say she really doesn't want to do Jason Graye any favors, even if it means cutting off her nose to spite her face."

"Don't you just love small town feuds?" Liss murmured. "So who do *you* think broke into the Chadwick mansion?"

Sherri's hesitation spoke volumes. So did the way she avoided meeting Liss's eyes. "Kids. Probably."

Liss's fingers tightened on the pencil she still held. "Any particular kid?"

"Look, Liss, I know you like the boy, but Boxer Snipes comes from a long line of troublemakers. You remember the Snipes boys we went to school with. Rodney and Norman were bad enough, but those teenaged cousins of Boxer's are even worse. They're almost certainly the culprits who were using the mansion as a place to drink and smoke."

"But you can't tar Boxer with the same brush. And may I just point out that the kids who were partying out there before we started planning for Halloween were *not* looking for Blackie O'Hare's loot."

"That's probably because they hadn't heard about it yet. They aren't the brightest bulbs."

"Wait a minute. I thought those cousins were currently enjoying the hospitality of the state at the youth center."

"They are," Sherri admitted, "but that still leaves us with Boxer."

"Do you have any proof he's involved?"

"You put two and two together and you get four. There are all sorts of small, portable antiques in the Chadwick house. It's hard to tell if anything's gone missing, but Boxer's mother just bought herself a new supersize flat screen HD TV." Sherri rolled her eyes. "That raises questions about her common sense as well as her honesty. Hilary and Boxer live in a beat up old trailer out on the Owl Road. She drives a rust bucket that's older than she is. If I were in her shoes and came into some extra cash, I could find much better uses for the money."

Liss seized her clipboard and started counting ceramic Loch Ness monsters. She didn't like what she was thinking, but a new TV *was* the kind of thing a twelve year old might buy as a present for his mother, if he suddenly came into some money. Blackie's loot? Or cash from fencing stolen goods? She didn't care for either possibility.

Aloud she said only, "I won't condemn someone simply because he has some bad apples on his family tree. If you're going to use that logic, then I should be a suspect, too. After all, Ned was *my* cousin."

"Now, Liss, you know that's not what—"

"Yes, it is."

"Why are you so sure he's innocent?" Sherri kept her expression bland, but Liss heard the annoyance in her friend's voice.

She answered without thinking. "Because I *like* the kid. Beth likes him, too," she added, and knew she sounded way too defensive.

"And we all know what good judges of character eleven-year-old girls with crushes are!"

Liss grimaced. "I know. The bad boy is always more appealing. But I don't think she'd hang out with him if she suspected he was doing something illegal. Angie brought her up right."

Sherri's snort told Liss what she thought of that.

Liss glared at her. She hesitated, then asked, "Has he been in trouble with the law in the past?"

"Not as far as I know," Sherri admitted. "Juvenile records are more tightly guarded than those of adults. I haven't been able to find out for sure. Kids even have their own probation officers, separate from adult caseworkers. Layers upon layers of protection, whether they deserve it or not."

"Why don't you just ask Boxer?"

"I can't do that, either. Not officially. Because, again, he's a *juvenile*." Sherri's exasperation was showing, warning Liss to tread carefully. "I'd need more than speculation to interrogate a kid and you're right. I have no proof—only theories based on the fact that in a small town people talk about their neighbors."

After Sherri left, Liss continued taking inventory, but her heart wasn't in it. What if she had been wrong about young Boxer? Worse, what if he'd involved Beth in criminal activity? Or Samantha?

Liss remembered what she had been like at their age. She'd been enough of a daredevil that the idea of sneaking into a deserted mansion to hunt for treasure would have appealed to her. She might even have been tempted to appropriate a knickknack or two that had seemingly been abandoned, especially if there had been peer pressure involved.

She paused, her fingers clenched hard on the edge of her clipboard. Her gaze was fixed on what was visible of the town square through the display window, but she saw nothing of what was there. If Sherri's suspicions were correct, then she, Liss, was responsible. She was the one who'd brought those three young people together. Even though Beth and Samantha had already known Boxer from school, she had made it possible for those two innocent young girls to spend a great deal of time in his company, much of it unsupervised. She'd often seen the three of them with their heads together. She'd assumed they were debating new ideas for the Halloween committee. But what if they'd been plotting something less innocuous? What if those two little girls had been lured into committing a crime because they'd been eager to impress Boxer Snipes?

Liss blinked and came back to reality. She was jumping to conclusions. It was too early to shoulder blame. How could she feel guilty when she didn't even know if anything untoward had happened? She needed to find out more—*much* more—before she condemned anyone, even herself.

Sam and June Ruskin weren't any happier than Angie had been at the revelation that their daughter had been fraternizing with a member of the Snipes family.

"Really, Liss, what were you thinking?" Lips pursed in disapproval, June nervously twined one long lock of honey-blond hair through her fingers.

Next to her on the couch, Sam looked uncomfortable. Dan stood, propping up a wall with one shoulder and watching his brother, sister-in-law, and wife through narrowed eyes.

"Honestly? I was thinking I'd give the kid a chance. That's what I'm *still* trying to do. Do you actually know anything about the boy, good or bad? All I've heard so far are stories about his cousins, his uncles, and his mother."

"Don't forget his Great Grandpa Harry, the bootlegger," Sam said.

They all turned to stare at him.

Sam shrugged. "Cracker Snipes used to brag about old Harry when he'd had a few beers."

"Any connection to Blackie O'Hare?" Liss asked.

"Not that I know of."

"Good. Now, the reason I came to you at all, and will speak with Angie next, is because I want to give Boxer a chance to refute this suspicion and I think it would help to have Beth and Samantha there when I talk to him about it."

"What?" The volume of June's shriek made Liss wince.

"Why?" Sam demanded. "My daughter has nothing to do with digging up the cellar at the old Chadwick place."

"But she may know something about it." Liss managed to keep her own voice level, but it was not easy. "Assuming there's anything *to* know."

Sam pounced. "So you *do* think Boxer is guilty."

"I think he may be a legitimate suspect for some of the pranks played before Halloween and for the digging after. But so is just about any other Moosetookalook kid with a bike and enough endurance to pedal out to the mansion. Beth and Samantha are bright girls. At the very least, they may have heard rumors that haven't made it to the adult grapevine."

"What are you going to do?" June asked. "If you ask the boy straight out and he denies it, how will you be able to tell if he's lying or not?"

That was the question, Liss thought, that had plagued parents for generations. She'd done her own fair share of fibbing when she'd been caught doing things she shouldn't. Probably every kid ever born had lied about something to his or her parents. The old instinct for self-preservation kicked in and you said the first words that came to mind. *It wasn't me. It must have been somebody who looked like me. The dog ate my homework.*

"I was thinking along the lines of a traditional mystery ploy—gathering all the suspects together and dazzling them with my brilliant deductions." She shrugged. "We're not dealing with sophisticated criminals here, even if one of them may have broken into the mansion. They're kids. And they're *probably* completely innocent. All of them. This is just a way to make sure of it."

Liss chose her new attic home office/library as the venue. Neutral territory.

"Are you sure you want to do it this way?" Dan asked her as they waited for Boxer, Beth, and Samantha to arrive. Adam had not been invited.

"Do you have any better ideas? If I just try to be friendly Auntie Liss and they do have something to hide, they're not going to confide in me. This way, I'll look like their best hope of getting off the hook."

They'd been over this ground before. Liss fervently hoped no one would confess, but she wanted the truth. She needed to solve at least one of the mysteries surrounding the old Chadwick house.

When Dan left to answer the doorbell, Liss realized she was nervous. Doubts swamped her. Maybe this wasn't such a good idea, after all. She started to go downstairs and call the whole thing off, but the sound of footsteps coming up stopped her. What could it hurt to talk to them?

A moment later, Boxer, Samantha, and Beth trooped in.

Liss sent a bright smile their way. "Sit down. Please." She gestured toward assorted seating options, but remained on her feet. "This won't take long. We just have a few loose ends to clear up—leftovers from Halloween."

"Candy?" Boxer flashed his trademark smirk and slouched over to her reading chair. It was already occupied by a large Maine Coon cat. "Shove over, Fatty," Boxer told him.

Lumpkin opened one baleful eye.

"Careful," Samantha warned. "He bites."

"Oh, he does not," Liss said, and rushed in to scoop up the cat before he could make a liar of her. He was no lightweight. She had to get both forearms under his bulk before she could carry him across the room to the door. "Be somewhere else," she whispered when she set him down again.

Lumpkin stalked off in a huff . . . but not before he sank his sharp little teeth into her ankle.

Liss bit back a yelp and sent a guilty look in Boxer's direction, but he wasn't looking her way. Neither were Beth or Samantha. They were too busy checking out her bookshelves.

"If we could get started?" She suspected that her carefully laid plans had already gone awry.

Boxer wandered back to the well-upholstered reading chair next to the floor lamp. He sprawled rather than sitting. Samantha selected a straight-back wooden chair, one of a pair that Liss had chosen more for appearance than for comfort. Beth perched on one corner of Liss's desk.

"If it's not candy you want to talk about, it must be dead bodies," Boxer said. "Did you find a new one?"

Liss took a deep, calming breath. Trust the boy to try and rattle her. "No, there are no new bodies. But there has been more trouble out at the Chadwick mansion. I've called you together in the hope of getting to the bottom of things. Let's start with what's been going on in the cellar of our haunted house. If you remember, the basement was supposed to be off limits."

"Not for you. You found a secret entrance down there." Beth made it sound like an accusation.

"How did you know that?"

"Well, not because *you* told us."

"Seriously, Beth. Who—?"

Her thin shoulders lifted and fell. "I don't know. Everybody heard about it at school."

Liss glanced at Boxer. "Do *you* have any idea how people found out about the tunnel?"

Boxer grinned at her. "Maybe the ghosts spread the word."

"Oh, ha-ha. Here's the thing. Someone went inside the mansion *after* Halloween. They've been digging in the basement."

That got everyone's attention.

"Really?" Beth sounded thrilled. She glanced at Boxer.

Boxer pretended to be fascinated by a loose thread on the hem of his gray hoodie.

"The thinking is that they were looking for Blackie O'Hare's buried loot."

No one said anything.

"You wouldn't happen to know anything about that, would you?"

Slowly, Boxer lifted his head and met Liss's eyes.

For just a moment, he looked very young and vulnerable. Then his face hardened. His lips curled into a sneer. "Are you accusing me of something?"

"No, I'm not. But others might. If they do, I'd like to help you prove your innocence."

"He didn't do anything wrong!" Beth was on her feet, eyes blazing, hands fisted on her nonexistent hips.

Boxer rounded on the girl. "I don't need you to stand up for me!"

"Stand up for yourself, then," Liss challenged him. "Have you been out to the mansion since Halloween?"

"No."

"See," Beth said.

"Liss doesn't believe me." The boy sounded so forlorn that Liss wanted to pull him into her arms and hug him. The impulse didn't last long. Neither did Boxer's neediness. "I might as well be guilty. That's what everybody thinks anyway."

"Why?" Liss asked.

"Why?" He sent her an incredulous look. "I'm a Snipes."

"But have you ever actually *done* anything to merit being lumped with the rest of your family? Are you responsible for something *other* than digging in the basement? Something that dates back to the beginning of your work on the Halloween committee?"

She was looking for a confession that Boxer had taken her jacket, or borrowed the apple dookin tub and one of the manikins and then returned both. Those were the three items Ned would have had no use for and Boxer made a viable suspect. If he confessed to those "crimes," or to breaking in to dig for Blackie O'Hare's loot, she would make sure he didn't get into any trouble with the law, but once he *had* admitted to something, then she'd not only have solved one of the minor mysteries that had been plaguing her, but she'd also have an opening to ask him what else he'd seen while he was roaming around the mansion.

The sullen look on the boy's face did not bode well.

Liss waited, hoping silence might loosen his tongue, but he had no intention of spilling the beans. A minute passed. Two. Three. Even Liss was starting to get edgy. Another minute and *she'd* be confessing to digging those holes.

"I did it!" Samantha blurted out.

Liss stared at her niece in confusion. "What?"

"I did it. I broke it. Don't blame Boxer. He wasn't even here yet. And it wasn't Papelbon's fault, either." She sat in the straight-back chair, arms held stiffly at her sides. Her face worked, making Liss fear she would burst into tears at any moment.

Three long strides brought Liss to Samantha's side, everyone else in the room forgotten. She knelt next to the girl and seized her hands. They were ice cold and clenched into fists.

"Samantha? Sweetie, talk to me. What did you break?"

On a sob, she said, "The figurine."

"The fig—?" Liss struggled to understand what Samantha was talking about. She had a vague recollection of her niece looking at some of the knick-knacks in the living room on the day of their first committee meeting, but that had been *months* ago.

"I knew you'd miss it, but I hid it anyway. Papelbon didn't mean to jump on me. I didn't mean to drop it. And then it broke and it was in three big pieces and I didn't want you to see it, so I stuffed them into my backpack." She erupted into noisy sobs. Tears streamed down her cheeks as she buried her head in her hands.

Boxer came up beside them. "What's she talking about?"

"One of my—oh!" She gave Samantha's shoulders a little shake. "Honey? Was it a nineteenth-century lady in a long dress?"

Crying harder than before, Samantha managed a single nod.

Liss could visualize the scene with vivid clarity. Samantha examining the Royal Doulton figurine. Papelbon escaping from Sam and Dan, then bounding downstairs and into the living room, heading straight at his young mistress. "It was an accident, Samantha. No one blames you. Or the dog."

"But I stole the pieces. I took them home. I tried to stick them back together with super glue, but the lines all showed and it looked *awful.*"

"Do you still have the figurine?"

Samantha shook her head and looked even more miserable. "I threw it away in the Dumpster at school. I didn't want anybody to find out."

"Samantha, it's okay. Really. I'm not mad. Accidents happen." Samantha's behavior afterward, all those times when Liss had thought she looked guilty, finally had an explanation.

It took Liss a long time to convince Samantha she was forgiven, but finally the sobbing petered out and the tears dried. Beth and Boxer were long gone by then. And Liss, although she now knew what had happened to her missing figurine, was no closer to solving any of the mysteries that surrounded the old Chadwick mansion.

Chapter Ten

By the time February turned into March, Liss had begun to think that discovering the secret Samantha had been keeping would be the only "crime" she succeeded in solving. Then, halfway through the month, Gordon Tandy paid an unexpected visit to Moosetookalook Scottish Emporium.

"I have an appointment with your aunt," he said. "It might be a good idea if you joined us."

More bad news, Liss thought, and promptly hung out the CLOSED sign.

"How's she doing?" Gordon asked as they walked together toward the staircase that led up to Margaret's apartment.

Liss shrugged. "Better some days than others. She can go for a week, full tilt, accomplishing wonders in her job at the hotel. Then it's like she's hit a wall. She'll barely talk to people. Doesn't want to get out of bed in the morning. Calls in sick—when she remembers to—and then just holes up and sleeps."

The look of concern on Gordon's face softened Liss toward him. He really did care about Margaret.

It wasn't his fault that there hadn't been a break in the case.

"Has she seen a doctor?" he asked.

"She did back in November. He gave her medication for depression, but I don't think she's been taking it. And she hasn't gone back for a follow up."

If Gordon was thinking as Liss was, that Margaret might require an intervention, he kept his opinion to himself. Both knew the fastest way to restore her to her old self was to solve her son's murder.

"When are you going to release the contents of Ned's duffle bag?" Liss asked when they reached the top of the stairwell and paused in front of the apartment door.

"I'm not. It's evidence. But I have brought Margaret a list of what was in it. And an account number." He knocked.

"Account number?" Taken aback, Liss frowned. "You mean for a bank account?"

The door opened to reveal Margaret MacCrimmon Boyd, still in her nightgown and bathrobe at one in the afternoon. "Oh, hello," she said and turned away, leaving the door ajar to allow them to enter.

"Margaret, we need to talk," Gordon said.

"I suppose." Listlessly, she waved them into the living room. She made no offer of food or drink, an oversight that alarmed Liss as much as anything she'd seen to date. Margaret was nothing if not hospitable. The state of the apartment and Margaret's person gave her more cause for concern. Both had begun to smell a little ripe.

Gordon waited until Margaret sat down, then took the chair opposite her. He removed his hat and set it on the arm of the chair, but only unzipped his coat as if he didn't intend to stay long. Leaning forward, he took her hands in his. "Margaret, look at me."

Slowly, Margaret's head lifted. Her eyes met Gordon's. From her perch on the nearby sofa, Liss saw the moment when her aunt dared allow herself to hope that the news he had for her would bring closure. It faded as soon as he began to speak.

"Ned opened a bank account right after he was released. He didn't leave a will so, as his nearest relative, you inherit what was in it."

"I don't want—"

"Margaret, it's almost twenty thousand dollars."

Her expression stayed blank. Liss was quicker to catch on. "That's a lot of money for someone who just got out of prison."

"Yes, it is." Gordon shifted his steady regard to Liss. "How do you suppose he came by it?"

"I don't think I want to speculate." But her active imagination had already taken flight. "Did he open the account with that much?"

"No. There were three deposits."

"Almost as if someone was paying him off?"

Margaret's gasp jerked their attention back to her. She no longer sat slumped in the chair. Her back was straight and her shoulders squared. Her wide-eyed stare was fixed on Gordon's face. "You can't think Ned was blackmailing someone!"

"I'm afraid it looks that way."

"Who?" Liss asked.

"We're working on that. In the meantime, I've brought Margaret the account number. You can go ahead and claim the money, Margaret." He removed a slip of paper from his breast pocket and offered it to her.

She refused to take it. "If it's tainted money, I don't want anything to do with it."

"Donate it to charity, then." Gordon placed the paper on the end table.

"Why aren't you confiscating the money?" Liss asked.

"There's no proof that it was obtained illegally and no reason to keep it tied up indefinitely."

"Don't you need to keep the account intact as evidence? Assuming you ever catch Ned's killer, that is." Liss let just a hint of sarcasm creep into her voice.

Something—irritation?—flashed briefly in Gordon's dark brown eyes. "We have the bank records. That's enough. Unless either of you can tell me something more about this money?"

Abruptly, Liss's control snapped. Frustration had been building for months, side by side with worry about her aunt's mental health. "Is that why you came here? To badger us for information we don't have?" As she stood, her stance combative, Liss felt her temper rise, too.

Gordon could see how angry she was. He got hastily to his feet and reached for his hat. "We're continuing to work the case. That's all you need to know." His retreat was dignified, but he didn't waste any time moving closer to the door.

"Have you made any progress at all?" Liss demanded, stalking him. "Do you have a single suspect in mind?"

"I can't talk about that with you, Liss. You know that."

"Just move your head then. Up and down for yes. Side to side for no. Do you have a suspect?"

The fulminating look Gordon sent her way should have turned her to stone, but she had too much of a mad on to notice. She waited. He glared. Then he spun on his heel and stomped out of the apartment. No nod. No shake of the head.

"Damn! I was sure he'd give me a hint."

Behind her, Aunt Margaret spoke in a querulous voice. "What am I still doing in my robe? I've got to get dressed and go to work." She put a hand to her hair, which hung limply around her face. "Oh."

Struggling for self-control, Liss hurried back to her aunt's side. Her voice gentled. "You haven't been yourself lately. Why don't you take a shower while I make you something to eat and then tomorrow you can start fresh."

"What day is it?"

Liss told her.

Margaret frowned. "Do I still *have* a job?"

"I'm sure you do. You just needed to take a break. You used up some of your sick days."

Margaret's eyes narrowed. "Stop treating me like I'm three years old! I'm smart enough to know I haven't been entirely rational since Ned was murdered."

Liss straightened, offended and relieved at the same time. "You seem rational enough now! So do us both a favor and take that shower."

As soon as her aunt disappeared into the bathroom, Liss dug out the air freshener and started collecting unwashed dishes and dirty discarded clothing.

Thirty minutes later, bathed and dressed in slacks and a sweater, Margaret sat at a freshly scrubbed kitchen counter devouring a bowl of chunky soup. Liss wasn't sure the improvement would last, but she was grateful for the respite.

"It's obvious the state police are stymied," Margaret said after she set the empty bowl aside. "What about you, Liss? Any ideas?"

"Nothing. I had one suspect for some of the pranks played at the Chadwick mansion, but he denied it. Even if he'd confessed, I know he wasn't the one who murdered Ned."

Margaret's brow furrowed. "Who are you talking about?"

"You met him. That boy—Boxer Snipes. He's twelve years old. I know that's not too young to get into serious trouble, but his actions are fully accounted for on Halloween. He was taking tickets at the corn maze."

"Boxer," Margaret repeated as she carried her bowl to the sink and rinsed it out. "A nickname, I presume."

"His mother calls him Teddy." The clatter of a ceramic soup bowl as it slipped out of her aunt's hands had Liss on her feet again. "Are you okay?"

"Just clumsy. And I think I may be developing a touch of arthritis in my hands. Did Gordon leave that account number?"

"It's on the coffee table." Liss fetched it from the living room. She tried to hand it to Margaret, but her aunt waved it away.

"You keep it. Talk to the people at the bank for me. I'll write you a note authorizing you to act on my behalf. Someone there might remember something useful."

"Such as what? That Ned opened an account? I'm sure the state police have already asked everything I would." To be honest, Liss couldn't think of all that many questions to pose, whether she brought a note from Margaret or not.

Margaret drew in a steadying breath. "Please, Liss.

I need you to do this for me." She ran hot water into the sink and started to wash the dishes that had accumulated while she was in a funk.

"Are you *sure* you want to know what Ned was up to?" It would not be anything honest. Liss was certain of that much.

"I'm sure. Once I know all there is to know, I can deal with it. It's *not* knowing that's so difficult to handle."

"Then I'll see what I can find out."

First thing the next morning, Liss drove to Fallstown, the county seat, and introduced herself to the bank manager at the Fallstown Savings Bank. It was a small, local institution with an excellent rating. It also had the advantage of employing tellers who knew most of their regular customers by name. In spite of that fact, Liss didn't hold out much hope that anyone would remember her cousin.

"You're here about Edward Boyd?" The bank manager was a thin woman in her fifties. Behind the lenses of her rimless glasses, her eyes widened slightly as she repeated the name. "Perhaps you'd better come into my office," she suggested.

The wall separating it from the rest of the small branch bank—three teller windows, one of which also manned the drive-through—was glass. Liss sat with her back to it, but that was fine with her. She had no interest in anyone other than the woman across the desk from her, who looked as if she'd rather be anywhere but where she was. Her name plate identified her as Shirley Jacobson.

Liss cleared her throat.

With a start, Ms. Jacobson stopped worrying the

long, beaded necklace she wore. "Yes. Well. Edward Boyd." She glanced at the papers Liss had given her—a copy of Ned's death certificate; proof that his mother was his legal heir; and Aunt Margaret's notarized authorization for Liss to act on Margaret's behalf in making inquiries about the bank account. "I suppose you want to know how to transfer Mr. Boyd's balance to his mother's bank account."

Without waiting for an answer, she extracted several forms from a desk drawer. Liss barely glanced at them. She'd take them home to Aunt Margaret to be signed, but that wasn't her main concern.

"Do you remember opening Mr. Boyd's account?" Liss asked.

Ms. Jacobson didn't look up from her keyboard. "It isn't easy to forget someone who walks in with thousands of dollars in hundred dollar bills and asks to start a savings account."

"Hundred dollar—?"

Holding up one finger to signal Liss to wait, the bank manager continued to type numbers and commands. A moment later, paper began to spew out of a nearby printer. Ms. Jacobson collated and stapled and then handed everything over to Liss.

"Mr. Boyd opened this account six months ago, in September. There was activity in September and October. The police notified us of his death on Monday, the second of November. They had authorization to monitor any future activity, but there has been none."

"Which is no doubt why the state police finally gave the account number to my aunt and told her it was all right to claim her inheritance."

"You don't mind if I verify that?" She reached for

the phone. What was unmistakably one of Gordon Tandy's business cards was in her free hand.

"Of course not." Liss shifted her focus to the statements. There had been only three deposits, including the one with which Ned had opened the account. The second had been for the same amount, $6,000. The third had been $5,800. Liss's heart sank. No wonder Gordon suspected Ned of blackmailing someone. Those nearly identical amounts screamed *payoff!* But who had he extorted? And was that someone the same person who later killed him?

Ms. Jacobson looked marginally less stressed when she ended her phone call to Gordon. She tapped the bottom of one of the forms she'd supplied. "If you'll have Mrs. Boyd sign here and—"

"I have a few more questions," Liss interrupted.

Ms. Jacobson subsided into her chair. "There isn't much else I can tell you about the account."

"You can tell me if anyone here remembers seeing Ned when he made the other two deposits. Perhaps one of the tellers talked to him?"

"The police asked that, too," Ms. Jacobson admitted, "and they questioned the two tellers who handled those later deposits."

"*Did* either of them remember my cousin?"

The slightest of smiles skittered across Ms. Jacobson's face. "Both of them remembered the transactions, for the same reason I recollect my encounter with Mr. Boyd. Those deposits were also in cash— neat packets of hundred dollar bills."

"Didn't that raise a red flag?"

Ms. Jacobson shifted uncomfortably in her chair. It was very nearly a squirm. "If the amount had been higher. . . ."

As the woman's voice trailed off, Liss remembered reading somewhere that at $10,000, someone was automatically notified. The FDIC? The IRS? She had no idea and didn't really care.

"All hundreds," she repeated. "All cash. Surely that must be somewhat unusual in this day and age. Didn't you worry that Ned might be . . . oh, I don't know . . . a bookie or a loan shark . . . or a thief?"

The slightest hint of color came into Ms. Jacobson's face. "I did . . . express curiosity about that initial deposit. Mr. Boyd said he'd sold his car and been paid in cash. I had no reason to question that statement."

"And if he'd said he found the money stuffed in a mattress?"

"What do you think I should have done, Ms. Ruskin? We had no grounds to turn him away, and no reason to report him to the police."

"What about serial numbers? Did you check to see if the money was stolen? Or had been used to pay a ransom?"

Even before Ms. Jacobson spoke, the pained look on her face warned Liss that this concept, gleaned from detective fiction, wouldn't fly in the real world. "We don't have the ability to check random serial numbers. The only time those numbers come into play is when we've received an alert."

Checking serial numbers had seemed a reasonable action to Liss, but she had to accept the bank manager's explanation. Now that she thought about it, she supposed that some local businesses still dealt largely in cash. Customers at Moosetookalook Scottish Emporium preferred to use their credit cards, but there were exceptions. At a guess, places like fast food restaurants and arcades probably made large deposits on a daily basis.

"Was there anything else you wanted to know?" Ms. Jacobson's tone edged toward the frosty.

"Could you tell if the bills were . . . old? Maybe *really* old."

"I do not have that information," Ms. Jacobson said.

The possibility that Ned might have found Blackie O'Hare's loot, and that it had literally been a cache of cash, seemed remote, but any port in a storm. Or, as she'd once heard Boxer say, "any port-a-potty in a storm." Liss hid a smile and racked her brain for something else to ask.

"We are not in the business of questioning the form in which our customers make their deposits," Ms. Jacobson added, "or in gossiping about their transactions."

Liss could almost see the icicles depending from each word. The bank manager sat with her back ramrod straight and her hands primly folded on the desk blotter. It was a posture that warned Liss to be very careful what she said next.

"I'd appreciate it if you could tell me a bit more about the other two deposits," she said with a conciliatory smile.

Ms. Jacobson thawed slightly. "They were both left in the night drop. No one waited on your cousin in person."

"The last one was smaller than the previous two. Fifty-eight hundred instead of six thousand."

"Fifty-eight hundred dollars was the amount left in the night deposit drawer." A defensive tone came into Ms. Jacobson's voice.

Liss held up both hands, palms out. "Please. I'm

not accusing your teller of shorting the deposit. My cousin was probably paid six thousand dollars the third time, too, and kept two hundred dollars back for expenses."

He must have had some, even if he had saved on housing by squatting at the mansion. Food. Gas.

Liss frowned. Gas for what? Ned had gotten himself to Fallstown, but as far as she knew, he didn't own a car. He hadn't had one to sell for the initial $6,000 in cash and hadn't owned a second one to drive himself around in.

"Do you have a security camera aimed at the night deposit slot?" she asked.

The bank manager hesitated.

"I'm not asking to see your videotapes or film or digital images—whatever it is you record with these days. But if you gave what you had to the police, maybe you could just tell me what was on it?"

A considering expression on her pale, plain face, Ms. Jacobson relented. "I suppose it can't do any harm. The first of the night deposits was made just before midnight. Mr. Boyd pulled up alongside the night drop. He was visible in profile but he wore a hoodie, making it difficult to see his face."

"But you're sure it was him?" Liss had heard Sherri and Pete curse the ubiquitous hoodies often enough. They'd become the uniform of robbers, purse snatchers, and carjackers, as much of a cliché as dressing a cat burglar in unrelieved black.

Ms. Jacobson hesitated. "I certainly thought it was. And the state police officer viewing the image agreed with me."

"That would be Gordon Tandy?"

The other woman nodded. Satisfied, Liss accepted that Ned had made the deposit. She wasn't sure if Gordon had ever met Ned in person, but he'd certainly seen plenty of photos of her cousin.

"What kind of car was he driving?" she asked.

"An old Chevy. At least, that's what the officer said it was. I'm no good at identifying makes and models."

"And when he made the last deposit?"

"It was the same car." Again, Ms. Jacobson hesitated.

"But?"

"The person making the deposit was not Mr. Boyd, not that last time. It was a woman."

"You're sure?"

Ms. Jacobson's tone was dry. "I think I can tell the difference."

"Did Officer Tandy recognize her? Did you?"

"No. And no. Like Mr. Boyd, she took pains to avoid looking at the camera, and she wore a Red Sox ball cap, pulled low."

"Hair color?"

"At night, it's difficult to tell."

"Build?"

"She was in a car," Ms. Jacobson reminded her, "and she had on a bulky sweater. Still, I didn't get the impression that she was a big woman. Not fat, certainly." She shook her head. "The image isn't the best. I'm sure you've seen security camera footage on TV. The news programs run it every time someone robs a bank or a pharmacy."

The quality was universally poor. Liss wondered how much it could be improved in a crime lab. In TV shows, forensics worked wonders. In real life? Who knew?

She stared at the bank statement on the desk in front of her. Perhaps it had been the mystery woman who'd shorted the deposit by $200. *Pass GO. Collect $200?*

"What if there had been additional cash deposits?" she mused aloud. "What if they had continued for several months? For a year? At what point—?"

But Ms. Jacobson was no longer listening. She was staring through the glass wall. Liss glanced over her shoulder. The lines at each teller's station were three deep—a traffic jam in this part of the world.

"You'll have to excuse me, Ms. Ruskin."

"The point was moot anyway," Liss admitted as the other woman hurried out to lend a hand.

She gathered up the paperwork she'd been given and left the bank in a thoughtful frame of mind.

"Every time I think I'm going to find answers, I end up with more questions," Liss complained to Sherri the next day.

"I don't know what you think you're going to find out here," Sherri grumbled as the two of them entered the kitchen at the Chadwick mansion. "We've been keeping an eye on the place. There's been no indication that anyone has been out here since we investigated those holes dug in the basement floor."

"I'm sure you're right, but I still want to go through the place one last time." Liss placed the blueprints she'd brought with her on the dinette table and unrolled them. "Ned got that cash somewhere. Seventeen thousand eight hundred dollars all told. Maybe that's not much by today's standards, but it was a heck of a lot back in Blackie O'Hare's day."

"How can you be sure Ned didn't sell a car? That's

what he told the bank manager. Maybe it was the truth."

"Three times? One car for each deposit? I don't think so."

"All right, then. The next logical supposition is that he helped himself to some of the antiques scattered around this mausoleum and pawned them." Sherri sent a pointed look toward the door that led to the rest of the house. "I've said it before and I'll say it again—who'd miss a few?"

"It's possible Ned stole items from the mansion. Certainly more likely than Boxer having done so. But I'm positive that Ned did not own a car when he got out of jail. He had to sell the one he used to own, along with just about everything else of value, to pay his lawyer. Even so, Margaret ended up footing most of the bill."

"Yet he was driving a car in the bank's security footage. And it's unlikely that he walked all the way to Moosetookalook from the state lockup."

"You're not telling me anything I haven't already thought of. But you see what I mean about more questions? There's another one—did he hitchhike? Or did someone *know* he was getting out and pick him up?" Liss peeled off the floor plan for the attic. "I want to compare these blueprints to what's actually here. If there was one hidden room, there could be another. We stopped looking after we found the tunnel. Maybe we also stopped too soon once we located the room behind the linen closet."

With dragging feet, Sherri trailed after her up two flights of stairs. They investigated each room on the attic level. Liss looked in particular for loose floorboards that might conceal a space large enough to hide stacks of hundred dollar bills. She even climbed up to the room at the top of the tower to tap on floors and walls in search of a hollow hidey-hole.

They repeated the process on the second floor.

"We aren't going to find anything," Sherri said when they finished searching the last bedroom and came up empty again. "There are other ways Ned could have gotten that much money in cash. I'm still leaning toward fencing stolen antiques."

"I wonder if there's any way to tell what's supposed to be in the house. Did anyone ever make an inventory?" Liss frowned as her gaze ran over the furnishings. It seemed to her that some object *was* missing, but she couldn't put her finger on what that item might be.

"No idea," Sherri said, and sneezed. There was dust everywhere. "Then again, I'm not seeing a lot of bare spots. Maybe nothing has been taken after all." She sounded disappointed.

"If Ned didn't find a cache of cash and he didn't sell stolen antiques," Liss said as they headed back down to the first floor, "then that leaves blackmail."

"But who on earth could Ned have been blackmailing? He'd just gotten out of jail. He didn't have time to dig up any dirt on anyone."

"Any *new* dirt."

"If it was old dirt, then shouldn't he have been collecting hush money all along?"

"And again . . . more questions." Liss cast a wary eye toward the parlor door as she reached the bottom of the staircase. "We need to make sure there are no more secret panels or other hiding places." She jerked her head in the direction of the room where Ned had been murdered. "In there. And in the dining room, the library, the conservatory, and the kitchen."

"Don't forget the basement," Sherri muttered.

"Tell you what—if you'll take the parlor and dining room, I'll do the rest." Even the dank depths of a dirt-floored basement had more appeal than a return to the room where she'd found Ned's body.

Liss started in the conservatory. It still gave her the creeps. Grimacing each time, she lifted every single stuffed bird off its perch to check for a hollowed-out middle. She'd barely finished when Sherri joined her.

"Done already?"

Sherri shrugged, making Liss suspect her search had been cursory at best. She clearly thought the effort was a gigantic waste of time but, true friend that she was, she offered to do the library while Liss moved on into the kitchen.

Liss accepted. She couldn't do it all by herself and Sherri's help was better than nothing.

It didn't take long to check the obvious spots for a hidden "safe" in the kitchen. The cracked linoleum formed a solid barrier to hollowed out spaces in the floor. The pattern of the wallpaper likewise made a secret panel unlikely, although she took care to rap with her knuckles and listen for any difference that might indicate a hollow area behind the wallboard. Unfortunately, in an old house without much insulation, almost everywhere not only *sounded* hollow, it *was* hollow.

The cabinets, conveniently empty, showed no obvious difference in depth. Short of pulling all the appliances away from the walls, Liss could think of nowhere else to look for a secret compartment. She turned to eye the closed door to the basement. No one had gotten in since the last time she visited the mansion—hadn't Sherri just assured her of that? Before she could chicken out, Liss opened the door, turned on the lights, and went swiftly down the steps. At the bottom, she stopped short.

Everything was *not* as it had been when she'd last seen it. There was another hole, and it appeared to be much deeper than the previous ones.

Liss jumped at the sound of footsteps on the stairs behind her.

Sherri gave a low whistle when she spotted the new excavation and the abandoned shovel lying beside it. "So much for thinking we'd kept people out."

They looked toward the boarded-up tunnel entrance. The two-by-fours Dan had nailed across it had been ripped free.

Curiosity driving her, Liss left the stairwell to examine the new hole. She didn't expect to see anything out of the ordinary, but when she peered down into it, an empty eye socket stared back at her. She took an involuntary step back from the edge of the pit.

"Well hell," Sherri said, coming up beside her.

They stood there a moment longer. Liss averted her gaze from the partially exposed skeleton and found herself staring at the discarded shovel. It made her wonder if the person who'd been digging had tossed it aside in panic when he saw what he'd uncovered.

Sherri punched a single number into the cell phone she'd fished out of a pocket. When a faint voice answered—her boss, Moosetookalook Chief of Police Jeff Thibodeau—she identified herself and gave her location. "Better send for the state police," she told him. "Looks like our would-be treasure hunters have gone and dug up human remains."

Chapter Eleven

"Not him, then," Sherri was saying into the phone when Liss stopped by the PD a few days later. "And not this Lowell Danby character, either? Okay. Thanks."

"Who's Lowell Danby?" Liss asked, gingerly lowering herself into the uncomfortable red plastic visitor's chair.

Sherri waggled the paper she was about to stuff into a manila folder. "Guy on probation with Chase Forster who skipped out on him last year. I told you about him before, didn't I? Chase issued a warrant for his arrest, so all the local departments were alerted. I thought he might be our mysterious skeleton."

"I take it he isn't?"

"Nope. We don't have an ID yet on the bones we found, but it looks as if they are a lot older than that. Like maybe Blackie O'Hare really did plant him there."

"You sure it's a him? Not Blackie's wife? According to the stories I've heard—" Liss broke off, grinning when Sherri snarled at her. "Been getting a few calls, have you?"

"Like you wouldn't believe! Everybody and his brother seems to have an opinion on this one. I will be so glad when forensics identifies this guy. And yes, it is a guy. Maybe once we have an ID, things will settle down." As if to prove her point, the phone rang. Sherri answered, grimaced, and said, "No, Mrs. Westfall. It's not your husband we found in the Chadwick house, but thank you for calling."

Liss couldn't help smiling. Gerald Westfall had died of natural causes three years earlier. Despite the fact that she'd given him one of the biggest funerals Moosetookalook had ever seen, his wife had afterward convinced herself that he was still alive. Her theories varied. Sometimes, she insisted that he was a bigamist with a second family down to Three Cities. At others, she claimed he'd been abducted by aliens. The theory Liss liked best was the one where Gerald was a secret operative for the CIA. Fortunately, Mrs. Westfall lived with her son and daughter-in-law. Most of the time they managed to keep her away from the telephone.

Liss left the PD while Sherri was still on the phone. Her route to the front of the municipal building took her down the hall and past the town office.

"Hey Liss," Francine Noyes called out when she passed by.

It was only polite to stop in to say hello and stay to sample a bite of the coffee cake Francine had brought to work with her. She was trying out a new recipe. "Great," Liss told her, and meant it.

"Are you going to need the keys to the Chadwick mansion again?" Francine asked when they'd exchanged news of various family members and friends.

Liss barely repressed a shudder. "If I never go near that property again, it will be too soon."

Her comment got a laugh from the town clerk, but Liss wasn't joking. Still, the question made her curious.

"Does that offer mean the state police are through out there?" They'd been called in again to deal with the bones.

"I sure hope so. We've actually had a nibble from someone interested in buying the place."

"Jason Graye?"

"*Other* than him."

Liss tried to tell herself she wasn't interested, but she'd never been any good at self-deception. "Who, then?"

"Some woman named Greeley phoned. Wanted to know what the asking price was."

"Do you know who she is?" The surname sounded vaguely familiar, but Liss couldn't remember where she'd heard it before.

"No idea." Francine looked miffed about that. The petite brunette had been town clerk for as long as Liss could remember. She prided herself on knowing everybody in Moosetookalook.

It was a mild and spring-like March Sunday when Liss, Dan, Sherri, and Pete set off in Pete's car to catch a matinee performance at the movie theater in Fallstown. On the way out of town, they passed the gas station/convenience store owned by Sherri's father, Ernie Willett. There was only one car pulled up to the pump.

"You don't see too many of those old Novas

around anymore," Pete remarked, nodding his head in that direction.

Liss looked, then looked again. Hilary Snipes sat in the driver's seat, and although Liss caught only a quick glimpse of her through the car window, she did a double take at what Hilary was wearing. It was a lightweight, pale blue jacket, just like Liss's that had gone missing from the Chadwick mansion back in October.

Coincidence, Liss told herself. Her coat hadn't exactly been a designer original. If she remembered right, she'd bought it at the Renys in Fallstown. "Chez René" as the locals called it, was a department store that specialized in bargains and usually offered multiples of the same item in different sizes.

Still, it did seem peculiar. . . .

"Is the Nova a Chevy?" she asked.

Dan and Sherri turned startled stares her way. Pete kept his eyes on the road, but glanced at Liss in the rearview mirror.

"That car at the gas station," she reminded them. "You said it was a Nova, Pete."

"Oh, that. Yeah. Chevy Nova. Why?"

"Did you notice who was driving?"

"That's Hilary Snipes's car," Sherri said, "so it was probably Hilary. Boxer isn't old enough to have a license." At Liss's unspoken question, she added, "I've given her a few tickets over the years. Bad muffler. Headlight burned out. That sort of thing."

"What is it, Liss?" Dan asked. "Why are you so interested in Hilary Snipes's car?"

"Hilary was wearing a jacket just like that one of mine that disappeared from the Chadwick mansion last fall. The one Ned could have taken. I think Hilary could be the woman who made that last deposit to Ned's bank account." She'd told all three of them about her interview with Ms. Jacobson right after it took place. "The bank manager said the car was an old Chevy, first with Ned driving and then with a woman. If it *was* Hilary's car on the surveillance footage, then that means she knows something about how Ned spent his last days. Maybe she even knows where all that money came from."

"Turn the car around," Sherri told her husband.

"Hon, it's not your case."

"I want to talk to her."

"So do I," Liss said.

"It's police business." Three voices spoke in unison, making Liss wince.

"It's my jacket! That is, *maybe* it is. We won't know unless I take a closer look at it." She could identify it easily enough. She'd caught one pocket on a nail and mended the torn seam with thread that didn't quite match the blue of the original.

Sherri already had her cell phone out and was punching in another of her speed-dial numbers.

"Are you calling Jeff or Gordon?"

"Gordon. If you're right, he's the one who should handle this." The admission was grudging.

"Can't you hold off on contacting the state police until *after* we've talked to Hilary?"

"No."

Sherri's terse answer alone might not have discouraged Liss's attempts to persuade her to change her mind, but before she could say more, Gordon answered his phone. While Liss fumed, Sherri filled the state police officer in on their suspicions. She broke the connection a few minutes later.

"He'll check into it."

"Will he?"

Sherri shrugged. "He said he would." A wry smile tugged at the corners of her mouth. "He also gave me a message for you, Liss. He said to enjoy the movie."

Although Liss tried to follow Gordon's advice, she found it impossible to concentrate on the plot of the futuristic thriller Dan and Pete had picked for the afternoon's entertainment. Her thoughts kept straying back to Hilary, trying to work out scenarios that involved her with Ned.

The connection existed, but it was tenuous at best. Hilary was about the same age as Ned. That meant they'd known each other in school. Just about everybody in Moosetookalook knew just about everyone else, so that came as no surprise. The total population of the town was only slightly over a thousand.

More telling was the fact that, for a couple of years before he went to jail, Ned had rented an apartment above the High Street Market, the grocery store where Hilary worked. Still, try as she might, Liss could not remember a single instance when she'd seen Hilary and Ned together. She'd never heard any gossip about the two of them, either.

Maybe she'd been wrong about the jacket. And Hilary's Nova was certainly not the only old Chevy still on the road in Maine. Had she'd leapt to a foolish conclusion? By the time they returned to Moosetookalook, Liss was wishing she'd kept her mouth shut. She'd jumped the gun. She should have asked a few subtle questions first. She was sure someone in town would have been able to tell her if Ned and Hilary had ever been an item.

But, no. She'd had to share her suspicions. And then Sherri had gotten Gordon Tandy involved. Liss did not look forward to the inevitable phone call from the state trooper. He'd undoubtedly take her to task for meddling . . . again.

But when Gordon called her at home the next afternoon, it was not to complain. It was to thank her for the tip.

"You'll probably see it on the local news broadcasts tonight," he said. "We just arrested Hilary Snipes for your cousin's murder."

"What evidence do they have?" Margaret Boyd demanded. They were in her office at the hotel. After Gordon's phone call, Liss had driven straight to The Spruces to share his startling announcement with her aunt.

"He wouldn't say. Fingerprints at the scene, maybe? They probably didn't have hers to compare until they took her in for questioning."

Margaret busied herself at the coffee pot, pouring each of them a cup, then sat behind her desk. "I suppose they quarreled because she helped herself to some of the money he gave her to deposit for him."

"Two hundred dollars?"

"People have been killed for far less."

Liss picked up the coffee cup Margaret had placed in front of her and sipped but she barely tasted the dark, rich brew. Even though she'd suspected Hilary of being in cahoots with Ned, she was having difficulty picturing her as his murderer. Belatedly, another thought struck her.

"I wonder if Boxer knew who Ned was."

Margaret went very still. "Boxer," she repeated. "What will happen to the boy now?"

"I suppose one of his relatives will take him in.

Rhonda and Cracker have an extra bedroom. They sometimes rent it out."

Margaret drummed her fingers on the desk top. "That is not a home environment I'd wish on any youngster, let alone one whose mother is in serious trouble with the law."

"I don't see that he has any other option, unless the state puts him in foster care."

A pensive look came over Margaret's face. She stood staring at nothing for a few minutes, then glanced at her watch. "Shouldn't the school bus be dropping kids off about now?"

Liss consulted the wall clock. "It stops at the town square in ten minutes or so."

"You have just enough time. Go meet it. Take Boxer off. I have a spare room, too. He'll stay at my apartment until this business with his mother is sorted out."

Liss nearly spilled her coffee into her lap. "Margaret, you can't be serious!"

"I'm entirely serious. Hurry up. You don't want to miss him."

"It won't work. The authorities won't allow him to stay with a friend. It has to be family or foster—"

"But that's just it," Margaret interrupted. "Boxer *is* family."

Liss gaped at her. "He's . . . family?"

Margaret nodded. "I've had my suspicions for some time and you told me that his mother calls him Teddy. What's that short for?"

"Theodore?" Something in Margaret's tone of voice warned Liss she'd been on the wrong track with that one.

"Teddy and Ted *are* nicknames for Theodore," Margaret allowed, "but they are also diminutives of

Edward, just like Ed, Eddie . . . and Ned. There is a very good chance that *my* Ned was Boxer's father and if that boy is my grandson, then I intend to look out for him."

The school bus had been and gone by the time Liss reached the center of town. She drove out to Owl Road on autopilot, still trying to absorb the enormity of Margaret's bombshell. Boxer Snipes was Ned's son and Margaret's grandchild? The mind boggled.

It was possible, of course. More than possible. Now that Margaret had pointed out the obvious, Liss realized there had been something familiar about the kid from the first. Had she recognized Ned's features in Boxer's plain square face and his scowl? Was Boxer's reddish-brown hair a pale reflection of the fiery locks Margaret had been blessed with when she was younger?

Once she turned off onto the narrow secondary road, Liss kept her eyes peeled for what Sherri had described as a "beat-up old trailer." It wasn't hard to spot, although it was set well back from the road in a stand of trees. A state police cruiser was just pulling out of the unpaved driveway.

Liss didn't recognize the officer who was driving, but she followed him for a mile before using a convenient driveway, this one blacktopped, to turn around. Boxer wasn't in the police car, and if the trooper had spotted her in his rearview mirror, he'd never connect her with Hilary's place or feel obliged to turn back to check on her. He continued on his way in blissful ignorance while she backtracked.

At Hilary's trailer, Liss detected no sign of life.

She tried the door and was surprised to find it un-locked. "Boxer?" she called out. "It's just me. Liss. We need to talk."

She stepped inside, uncertain what to expect after the run-down appearance of the exterior. The first thing she noticed was how cold it was. Hilary appar-ently left the heat off when no one was at home, a frugal measure Liss approved of, at least in theory.

The furnishings were pitifully few and very old—except for the flat screen TV—but everything was clean and neat. Almost painfully so.

"Boxer?" Liss called again, encouraged when she spotted a backpack bulging with school books. It had been carelessly tossed onto the sagging sofa.

When she got no answer, she conducted a quick search to make sure he wasn't hiding on the premises. What was clearly the boy's room was far messier than the rest of the trailer, but still scrupulously clean. Re-turning to the kitchen area, Liss snooped in the cup-boards and found them well stocked with nutritious food. Hilary might look undernourished, but that did not appear to be due to her diet. That she worked so many hours to support herself and her son was a more likely reason.

Liss sat down at the small kitchen table, brooding and staring out the small window at the trees sur-rounding the trailer. A flicker of movement behind a pine caught her eye. Bird? Deer? More likely Boxer, she decided, waiting her out. She leaned across the table so she could turn the crank to open the win-dow. It screeched in protest and stuck an inch from the sill, but that was enough.

"I'm not going anywhere, Boxer," she called, pro-jecting her voice as she'd been taught during her theatrical career. "You may as well come in and talk to me." She waited a beat and added, "Better me than the police!"

Boxer stayed out of sight long enough to make her wonder if what she'd seen really had been a bird or a deer. He appeared without warning in the open doorway, startling Liss into sucking in her breath. He seemed pleased by her reaction, but made no effort to come the rest of the way inside.

"There's no one here but me."

"I knew that." He managed a bit of a swagger as he entered the trailer, as if to say, "You're on my turf now."

Liss studied him in the light of Margaret's revelation. There was something in the shape of the face and the hint of red in his hair. But the honest truth was that he more closely resembled his mother than he did Ned or Margaret.

Instead of taking the other chair when Liss resumed her seat at the table, Boxer propped one shoulder against the wall by the door. His arms were crossed in front of his narrow chest. His expression was rife with suspicion. "I know why the cops were here. Why are you?"

"How—? That is, why do you think they were looking for you?"

"They arrested my mother. But if they think they're going to stick me in foster care, they've got another think coming."

"You've been through this before?"

"Not me. My cousins."

"Which cousins? I know Rodney and Norman—"

"Not them." He attempted an evil leer, but it didn't quite come off. "I mean the two who are down to South Portland doing time."

"The same two who used the Chadwick house as a place to smoke and drink?"

"Yeah. Bobby and Woody. Back a while, Uncle George and Aunt Eloise got busted for growing pot and the boys got sent to this group home while their parents served their sentences. I'm not letting that happen to me. I'd rather live in the woods."

"Wouldn't Cracker and Rhonda—?"

A derisive snort cut short that suggestion. There was nothing phony about Boxer's reaction. He had neither fondness nor respect for his uncle and aunt.

"I may have an idea about where you can stay," Liss said, "but I don't know how much time we have before the state police come here looking for you again. I need you to answer some questions for me. Okay?"

He shrugged. She took that as a yes.

"Do you know why they arrested your mother?"

He hesitated, then shrugged. "She didn't say. Doesn't matter. She didn't do it. She's so clean she squeaks." A hint of pride crept into his voice.

"You talked to her?"

"Hey, she gets one phone call. Everybody knows that."

"And it's usually a good idea to use it to call a lawyer. Hilary has been accused of murder, Boxer. They think she killed Ned Boyd."

Boxer's jaw dropped. "Killed—? Naw. Not possible. She can't even stomp on a bug."

"Did Ned come here when he got out of jail? Did your mother let him borrow her car?"

A sullen silence answered Liss.

"Boxer, it's important. I'm trying to help."

"Yeah, okay. She went and picked him up. He

stayed here a couple of days. Then he left. No big deal."

Liss had more questions, but she was afraid he'd balk at answering. Besides, she wanted to get him away from Hilary's trailer before that state trooper reappeared. What Boxer had already told her was enough to convince her that Margaret might be right. Boxer *could* be Ned's son.

"The thing is, Boxer," Liss began, "the state won't let you stay here on your own. In fact, I'm surprised that a caseworker from the Maine Department of Health and Human Services didn't meet the school bus or come straight to the school after your mother's arrest and take you out of class."

"I'd like to see one try." This time the sneer was forced. Behind his brash façade, the kid was scared.

"Well, as it happens, there's another possibility—a place for you to live that doesn't involve foster care or any of the Snipes clan." She took a deep breath. "You remember my aunt, Margaret Boyd? She, uh, she'd like you to come stay with her." Knowing there was no easy way to break news of this nature, Liss just blurted it out. "Margaret may be your grandmother."

"Oh. Yeah." He shrugged. "Like I couldn't figure that one out."

"You already knew—?"

"Well, yeah. No big deal."

"But . . . *how* did you know?"

With a long-suffering sigh, Boxer shuffled back to his room and emerged again almost at once carrying a lockbox. He set it on the kitchen table and opened it with the key Hilary evidently left *in* the lock. He pawed through the papers inside until he found the one he wanted and handed it over to Liss.

It was his birth certificate. Under FATHER'S NAME it read *Edward MacCrimmon Boyd.*

"So, I guess this makes us cousins, huh?"

Boxer's lopsided grin tugged at her heart. Liss had to swallow hard before she could answer. "Yes, it does. I wish we'd known sooner, Boxer. Ned never told us about you."

"Mom never told me, either. Not until she brought him here last September."

But, somehow, Margaret had suspected.

Liss now had dozens of questions for both her newfound cousin and her aunt, but there would be time later to ask them. The priority at the moment was looking after Boxer. The birth certificate would go a long way toward securing Margaret's right to take responsibility for him.

"Okay, Boxer. Here are your choices. Come with me to Margaret's or wait around for the cops to pick you up and call in Child Protective Services. You'll probably have to talk to a caseworker at some point, but if we can postpone that interview until you're already settled at my aunt's apartment, then chances are good that they'll let you stay put. These days, unless the family is radically unstable, DHHS almost always leaves kids with relatives."

It didn't take Boxer long to pack clothes and books in a suitcase that was plainly his mother's—it was bright pink and at least twenty years old. He collected the lockbox and his school backpack, then gestured toward the flat-screen TV.

"I can't leave that here. Someone will walk off with it. Mom had to save up for a really long time to buy it for us."

"I guess we could take it with us," Liss said doubtfully. "I can store it in the stockroom at the Emporium."

Boxer unplugged the television and unhooked it from the cable box. It took both of them to wrestle it into Liss's hatchback.

"What about—?"

"We can come back later for more of your stuff," Liss interrupted. "Right now we need to get moving. Before that trooper shows up again," she added when a mutinous look came into his eyes.

Boxer got into the car without another word of protest.

Chapter Twelve

It didn't take long to settle Boxer into the guest room. His lip curled at the "girly" décor, but he dug into the hearty supper Margaret had waiting like the growing preteen he was. While he worked his way through a second helping, Liss slipped downstairs into the Emporium and phoned Gordon Tandy.

It was not a pleasant conversation, but it ended the way Liss wanted it to. She took another few minutes to phone home and give Dan the capsule version of the day's events before returning to her aunt's apartment.

"Officer Tandy will be here to talk to you in the morning," she told Boxer. "Margaret will stay with you during the interview, since you're a minor."

"What if I don't want to talk to the cops?"

"Then they're going to think you know more than you're saying. That won't help your mother. Besides, if they've arrested Hilary, they must already know something that makes them think she's guilty."

Liss glanced from Boxer to Margaret. Somehow,

she'd expected one or the other of them to be more ill at ease. After all, Boxer's mother had been accused of murdering Margaret's son. Remarkably, she saw no signs of tension between them. Margaret looked more relaxed than she had in months.

"What? You two bonded over chicken and dumplings?"

Margaret chuckled.

Boxer glanced up from the gigantic slice of chocolate cake on his dessert plate. "I told her Mom didn't do it. She believes me."

Hearing the challenge in his voice, Liss considered for a moment before she spoke. "I honestly don't know what to believe, Boxer. Why don't you tell me how, after all these years, Ned persuaded your mother to loan him her car and do his banking for him."

Someone had taught Boxer manners. He didn't try to talk with his mouth full. He swallowed before saying, "She said she owed him." He took a swig of milk and forked up more cake.

Liss thought that should have been the other way around, but given that Margaret was Ned's mother and Boxer was his son, she kept her opinion to herself.

"He phoned her and asked her to pick him up when he got out of jail." Boxer licked the last of the frosting off his fork and set it neatly atop the empty plate. "She brought him back to our place. Introduced us." He shrugged and shot an apologetic look at Margaret. "I wasn't real thrilled to have a father all of a sudden, but he didn't stay long."

"He moved into the Chadwick mansion," Liss said. "Why?"

Boxer's answer was another shrug, but he was paying way too much attention to the pattern on his plate. Liss didn't buy the nonchalant act.

"You knew he was living there, didn't you? And you must have guessed that he was responsible for the things that went missing. Did he give your mother my jacket?"

At that accusation, Boxer's head shot up. "He didn't . . . I didn't . . . I don't have to tell you anything. You're not the cops."

Margaret put her arm around the boy's thin shoulders. "Liss is only trying to help. She's good at finding things out. She'll help clear your mother of the charges against her if you tell her what she needs to know."

"At this point, I don't care who did what in the Chadwick house," Liss said, "so long as I can get it all straight in my head." She desperately needed to make a "who did what when" list. Never mind their motivations.

"I took the coat," Boxer mumbled.

"*You* did? Why?" Hearing the sharpness in her voice, Liss moderated her tone. "I'm not mad at you. I just need to understand the sequence of events. It could be important. Okay?"

Another shrug. Then the dam burst. "I took it because he was living there and I wanted him to get caught. I was pissed at him." He shot a sideways glance at Margaret. "I'm sorry, but I didn't like him much. We were doing just fine without him. I figured if he got caught hiding out at the mansion, they'd send him back to jail."

"It's all right," Margaret said. "Believe me, I am well aware of Ned's faults. Please go on."

"I thought Ned took the things that went missing." Liss settled in on the opposite side of the kitchen island from her newfound cousin, a spot from which she could watch his face and body language as they talked.

"Some of them. The lantern and the ladder and the hammer. But I took the wooden tub. I hid it in the woods. And I took that dressed-up dummy, too. I thought if you really looked for that stuff, you'd find *him*." The accusation was back in Boxer's voice.

"You might have dropped a hint about the location of the hidden room."

"I didn't know where it was. Not exactly." He sounded sulky.

"And the tunnel? Did you know about that?"

Boxer squirmed a bit before he confessed to following Ned when he'd moved out of Hilary's trailer. "He didn't say where he was going, but he told her he had this plan that was going to make him rich."

Him, Liss thought, *not them*. Was it any wonder Hilary was a suspect in his murder? Aloud, Liss said, "He already had plans to search the mansion for Blackie's loot *before* he got out of prison. That has to be the answer. It's the only thing that makes sense."

"Not *that* much sense," Margaret muttered.

"How about you, Boxer?" Liss asked. "Just why did you volunteer for the Halloween committee?"

The boy wouldn't meet her eyes. "Heard Beth talking about it. She was telling her friend Luanne how there was this great old haunted house in town, trying to talk Luanne into helping out with the plans for the festival. I figured she had to mean the Chadwick mansion."

"And Ned was already squatting there?"

Boxer nodded. "I thought that if I was on the committee, I could keep an eye on what he was up to. Maybe cause him some trouble, too."

"Did you see Ned again after he moved out of your trailer? Did Hilary?"

"Mom did. He borrowed her car a couple of times and once he had her go down to Fallstown for him."

"Was that, by chance, right before she bought that new TV?"

Boxer narrowed his eyes at her. "Maybe."

Liss considered keeping her theories to herself, but decided it would be better for Boxer to be forewarned. "Here's what I think made the police arrest your mother. Ned got Hilary to make a deposit for him at the bank in Fallstown. She took two hundred dollars of that money for herself. When he found out about what she'd done, they quarreled. The police will try to prove that their argument escalated into murder. Is there any chance she would have gone out to the mansion to meet him?" If she'd left fingerprints there, that would be even more reason to suspect her.

"I dunno," Boxer mumbled.

"Did she know he was living there?"

Another shrug.

Liss interpreted that to mean Boxer had been the one to tell Hilary where to find Ned. He looked so miserable she decided not to probe further in that direction. Instead, she asked, "How did your mother end up with my blue jacket?"

"Hey, that was an accident. I was going to return it to you, same way I put back the tub and the dummy."

"Manikin."

"Whatever. I took the coat home with me and hid it in my room, so it wouldn't get dirty. Mom found it when she was collecting the laundry. I couldn't tell her where I really got it, so I made up this story about buying it for five bucks at the lost-and-found auction at school. Once a year, they put all the unclaimed stuff up for bids."

"Did she believe you?"

"Oh, yeah. That was the problem. I mean, look at it. It's a girl color. What was she gonna think except that I got it as a present for her? She really liked it, too, and as soon as the weather got warm enough, she started wearing it all the time. That's how you caught on, isn't it? You saw her and recognized your stupid coat."

"I'm afraid so. I'm sorry, Boxer, but I mentioned it to Officer Campbell and she called the state police detective who's investigating Ned's murder. We thought your mother might know something about what Ned had been up to. That she might have killed him never crossed my mind."

"Well, good," Boxer said. "Because she didn't." He hopped down from his stool and began to prowl.

The apartment belonged to a woman in her mid-sixties. There wasn't much to interest a boy of twelve. Margaret hadn't even traded in her VCR for a DVD player. She was perfectly content to watch old videotapes, not that she had much time for them. Like Liss, she kept busy with work and activities within the community and when she had a spare moment to relax, she tended to spend it with her nose in a book.

"How long have you suspected Boxer was Ned's son?" Liss asked in a low voice as she and Margaret watched the boy explore the living room of his temporary home.

"Only since I met him," Margaret replied, her tone soft and sad. "Once I got a good look at him and found out who his mother is, I put two and two together. The first summer Ned was home from college, he was seeing Hilary."

"Why didn't I know that?" Liss asked.

"You'd left Moosetookalook by then."

Liss had been away for a decade before she returned for good. She supposed she'd missed quite a few tidbits of local gossip in the interim.

"Anyway," Margaret continued, "they didn't date for very long. They'd broken up by the time she realized she was pregnant. Ned was already seeing someone else—you remember Lois Patterson? He thought he was in love with Lois. He even talked about marrying her. It didn't work out, but at the time—"

"At the time," Liss finished for her, "Ned didn't want either you or Lois to know he'd fathered a child by someone else."

"By a Snipes, you mean." Although they'd been speaking quietly, Boxer had overheard. Liss couldn't blame him for sounding bitter.

"Her family didn't matter to me." Margaret caught Boxer's arm when he tried to escape down the hall to the guest room. She turned him to face her and looked him right in the eyes. "Not then and not now . . . but at the time I didn't think my son would lie to me. When I asked Ned about a rumor I'd heard—that he'd gotten Hilary pregnant—he insisted that he'd never slept with her. I believed him, Boxer. I'm very sorry now that I did. I'd have liked to have been a part of your life from the start."

When she hugged him, Boxer didn't pull away, but neither did he return the embrace.

Liss watched them in silence, fighting tears. Ned and Hilary couldn't have been more than nineteen or twenty at the time Boxer was conceived. Young.

Foolish. And, in Ned's case, careless of the conse-
quences of his behavior. He'd gone back to college,
leaving Hilary alone to bear his child.

Liss wondered if Ned had paid Hilary not to make
a fuss. Maybe he'd kept on paying her. Margaret had
been generous with his allowance. He'd been a
spoiled mama's boy. Until two years ago, when he'd
been arrested, Margaret had remained deliberately
blind to her son's many flaws.

"I swear I'll do everything I can to help your
mother." The vehemence behind Margaret's words
pulled Liss out of her reverie and focused her full attention on her aunt. "I just hope you'll let me be a
part of your life for this next little while," Margaret
continued.

"How long?" Boxer's voice was unsteady. He kept
his eyes lowered, making Liss suspect they were as
damp as her own. "How long do I have to stay here?"

Margaret's quick glance at her niece spoke volumes. "Until Liss finds out who really did kill your father."

"The problem," Liss confided to Sherri the next
day, "is that I'm not entirely convinced Hilary Snipes
is innocent. She wouldn't have been arrested if there
wasn't solid evidence against her."

Together they walked through the newly reno-
vated rooms in what had once been the second floor
of Liss's house. They now formed a cozy apartment
with two bedrooms, a small bath, a kitchen, and a
central living room, Sherri and Pete were set to move
in as soon as the smell of fresh paint cleared.

"You know as much as I do." Sherri poked her head
into a closet and came out smiling at the amount of

storage space it contained. "And that's only what's been in the news. Does she have a lawyer?"

"Margaret hired one for her—the same one who defended Ned."

"But this time the charge is murder. I don't think stabbing someone in the throat can be argued down to manslaughter."

"Self-defense?"

"Did Ned have a weapon? I don't think so."

"What am I supposed to do?" Liss plunked herself down on a built-in window seat/storage chest in the room that would soon be Adam's and let her head fall back against the panes. It wasn't like her to be indecisive, but for once she wasn't sure she *wanted* to discover the truth.

"Maybe you should talk to Hilary," Sherri suggested.

"And say what? Ask her if she killed Ned?"

"You've really got it in for her, don't you?"

"Of course not. I want her to be innocent. I just don't think she is."

"Because she's a Snipes?"

Liss winced. *Was* that it? In spite of all the times she'd railed at others for defaming Boxer, was she letting simple prejudice and a family's bad reputation push her into leaping to unfounded conclusions about his mother?

Two days later, having been screened for weapons and other contraband, Liss was shown into a small room at the county jail. A few minutes later, a corrections officer escorted Hilary in. The two women sat on opposite sides of a wooden table. The uniformed officer remained within shouting distance.

"Is Teddy okay?" The anxiety in Hilary's voice instantly softened Liss toward her.

"He's fine. You know he's staying with Margaret Boyd, right?"

Hilary nodded. "I guess she knows, huh?"

"Why didn't you tell her a long time ago? She would have helped you and . . . Teddy."

Hilary stiffened. "I take care of my own. Always have. I've never been on welfare and I don't take handouts."

"But you helped yourself to some of Ned's money, didn't you?"

Color stained Hilary's pale cheeks as she stared down at her clasped hands. "That was a mistake. I should have known better. Sticking up for myself never works out well."

Her muttered words reminded Liss of the altercation she'd observed between Hilary and her brother. Combined with what she'd seen of the way Cracker Snipes treated his sister and his wife, Liss was willing to bet that Hilary had been made to feel worthless from her earliest girlhood, first by her father and brothers and later, sad to say, by Ned. She'd been taught to expect to be taken advantage of by men . . . to the point where she'd simply accepted shabby behavior. Acts of rebellion, in Hilary's experience, weren't worth the effort.

"Hilary, Margaret believes in your innocence. So does your son. And I'm willing to be convinced. Will you let us help you?"

"How? What can *you* do?"

"Just talk to me, okay? For starters, I'd like to know why you helped Ned out in the first place. You certainly didn't owe him anything."

"Yeah, I did."

"Has he paid child support all these years?"

"Not exactly."

Liss waited.

"He gave me money when he could." Hilary sounded defensive.

"I thought he denied he was Teddy's father."

"He did. At first. But he sent me checks."

"Regularly?"

She shrugged, reminding Liss of Boxer. "On and off. And when he moved in above the market, sometimes I'd go up there."

"You slept with him? After what he—"

"I loved him!" For the first time, Hilary came to life. "You think I'm a tramp, but I'm not. There was never anybody else. Just Ned."

Stunned by this revelation, Liss needed a minute to regroup. She realized that she believed Hilary. "Did . . . did Ned—?"

"He was thinking about making things right. I know he was. Even before he went to jail. And while he was in prison he had a job and arranged for all the money he earned to come to me and Boxer. It wasn't much, but it helped."

"Did you visit Ned while he was locked up?"

Hilary shook her head. "He didn't want visitors. But he phoned me every few months."

And that, Liss thought, was why the police had zeroed in on Hilary so quickly. That she'd had Liss's jacket hadn't had all that much bearing on the investigation. By the time Gordon found out that detail, he must already have identified Boxer's mother as the woman on the bank's surveillance video.

"Did you ever go out to the Chadwick mansion?" she asked Hilary.

"Once."

"Touch anything?"

Hilary heaved a sigh. "I guess I must have left fingerprints, huh? I'm never going to get out of here, am I?" One tear rolled slowly down her cheek, followed by another.

"Hey, no crying!"

To her surprise, Hilary managed a watery grin and quoted Tom Hanks in *A League of Their Own.* " 'There's no crying in baseball.' "

"Good movie," Liss said.

"One of my favorites. Teddy likes it, too."

"Do you two spend a lot of time watching movies together?"

"A monthly cable bill is a lot cheaper than going out."

"So you were saving up to buy a better TV and the two hundred dollars you took out of Ned's bank deposit put you over the top."

Hilary nodded, confirming Liss's theory. "Teddy was so thrilled when we hooked that sucker up and turned it on."

And Teddy, Liss realized, had been so determined to take the TV with them because he knew how much it meant to his mother. Whatever else she might think of the two of them, they were devoted to each other.

"Do you have any idea who might have killed Ned?" Liss asked.

"I wish I did."

"Did he talk to you? Did he mention anything that was worrying him?" She got negative shakes of the head in answer to each question. "Do you know where he was getting the money he deposited in his bank account in Fallstown?"

"No. He never told me." Her hands clenched and

released, clenched and released, until Hilary realized Liss was staring at them and forced herself to hold still.

"Do you think Ned might have been blackmailing someone?"

One last clench made Hilary's knuckles stand out white against skin that was already unnaturally pale. "I . . . I don't know. I hadn't thought about it. Ned said to keep mum about his being in town, so I did. I didn't think anybody knew he was out of jail except me and Teddy."

"And his probation officer," Liss murmured. "What about his move to the Chadwick mansion? Did he tell you why he was living there?"

"I didn't even know that was where he'd gone until Teddy told me. It made sense, though. He used to go out to that old house all the time when we were kids."

"Treasure hunting?"

"Yeah. Blackie's gold. He used to talk about that all the time."

Gold? Liss let that pass without comment. She supposed that, if the hidden loot existed at all, it could as easily be gold as cash or jewels or rare stamps.

"Ned came by the trailer any time he needed me to do something for him," Hilary volunteered.

"How?" At her blank look, Liss clarified. "Did he have a car?"

"He borrowed mine sometimes."

"But he didn't keep your car out at the mansion. It would have been seen. Think, Hilary. Did he ever drive out to your place in another vehicle?"

She nodded.

"What kind of car was it?"

"I . . . I don't know. I didn't look, I just heard the engine when he left. I didn't think—"

Agitation had her twisting her hands together again. Liss touched her fingers to Hilary's to still them. The corrections officer, all but forgotten till then, cleared his throat.

Liss hastily withdrew her hand. "It's okay. Just knowing that he *had* a car, other than yours, could help." *Especially if he borrowed it from the person he was blackmailing.* "What did he want when he visited you at your trailer?"

Hilary blushed.

"*Besides* that."

"Mostly he wanted me to buy groceries for him. Or cook him a meal. And one time he made me promise to go to the bank down to Fallstown for him that same night. He was real particular that I go after dark." She sighed. "I don't know why I shorted him the cash. It was stupid, and I felt bad afterward. That's why I went out to the old Chadwick place to look for him. I figured I'd better tell him I'd kept some of the money for myself, before he found out on his own. Better that way, right? So I banged on the front door and called his name and after a long, long while, he came and let me in. We talked in the front room. I never saw any of the rest of the house."

"That was enough. That's where he was killed." Liss thought for a moment. "The, uh, weapon that killed him came from the dining room. Did you ever go into that room?"

"No. I told you. I was just in the one at the front of the house. I confessed to Ned about the money. He said some nasty things to me and then he yelled at me to get out, so I did. That was the last time I saw him. A couple of days later, he was dead."

A chill passed over Liss as a new thought struck her. "Did, uh, Teddy ever overhear Ned yelling at you?"

"I don't think so, but— Hey, wait a minute! You can't imagine that my son would kill his father. That didn't happen. No way!"

"Calm down."

But it was too late. Hilary was on her feet and the corrections officer was fast approaching the table.

"I want to go back to my cell," Hilary told him.

"I don't suspect Boxer of anything beyond a few pranks," Liss called after her.

She didn't think Hilary believed her.

Chapter Thirteen

That evening, Liss sat down at the desk in her attic office/library with a lined yellow tablet and started making lists. Now that she'd talked to Hilary, she was *almost* certain she could eliminate her as a suspect. She supposed the worm could turn, but in this case it seemed unlikely. Hilary was too accustomed to letting the men in her life walk all over her, everyone from her brothers to the customers at the grocery store. Added to that, she wasn't very bright. Liss didn't think she was smart enough to think of insisting she'd only gone into one room at the mansion, not if the truth was that she'd taken the two-pronged fork from the dining room into the parlor and stabbed Ned with it. She'd have been more likely to claim that she'd never visited the Chadwick mansion at all.

The first name Liss wrote down was Jason Graye's.

He wanted to buy the house. What if Ned had caught him trying to sabotage the furnace or the kitchen appliances in a sleazy attempt to lower the town's asking price? Would Ned then have been able to blackmail Graye into making three payments of $6000 each? And if he'd tried for more, could that have caused Graye to lose his temper and kill him?

"Oh, I wish," she murmured.

Unfortunately, she couldn't imagine Jason Graye coming at Ned with a two-tined fork. Come to think of it, she didn't see him agreeing to a payoff, either. She doubted Graye could *be* blackmailed, not once he realized that Ned was as much an intruder in the Chadwick mansion as he was. Graye would know he had a powerful threat to hold over Ned's head, one that packed more punch than what Ned had on him. One anonymous phone call and Ned would have been back in jail, serving the remainder of his original sentence. Given that Ned was a convicted felon, counter-charges that Graye was guilty of breaking and entering would have been easy for the authorities to dismiss. Graye would have fallen back on the old "your word against mine" defense and have pointed out that *Ned* was the one with a criminal record. Put the prominent local citizen up against the ex-con and Graye would have been believed . . . even though everyone in town knew what a crook he was.

Liss doodled on the page with her felt tip pen, trying to think who else might have had a reason to kill her cousin. What had the town clerk said about another potential buyer for the Chadwick mansion? Someone named Greeley had phoned. That was it.

The moment she wrote *Greeley* on the page, Liss remembered why the name had sounded familiar to her. Surely that was the last name of Gloria's Aunt Flo, the house guest no one in town had ever seen. Was she still staying with Gloria? Liss had no idea. In the months since Halloween, the only time she'd spoken to Gloria had been at MSBA meetings and their conversation had been the superficial kind that dealt with the weather, how tasty the muffins Patsy had brought were, and the ever-increasing price of home heating oil.

Liss crossed out *Greeley* and wrote *Florence Greeley*, after which she scribbled, *Gloria's great-aunt, plastic surgery after accident,* and *doesn't leave house?*

Then she wrote, *Gloria Weir, newcomer to town,* and *background unknown.*

If Ned had enjoyed a secret life with Hilary, maybe he'd been keeping other secrets. Was Gloria Weir one of them? Or some other woman? Liss wondered if she could find out whether or not Ned had authorized *anyone* to visit him while he was in prison. She was sure prison officials kept track of such things, and inmates' phone calls, too.

That train of thought led to another. Could Ned have been blackmailing someone he'd met while he was locked up? Was it too far-fetched to think that another convicted felon might eventually have gotten tired of paying Ned and killed him?

Another name tickled the back of her memory. Lowell Danby. She wrote it down and stared at it, unable for a moment to recall when or where she'd heard it before. Then it came to her. Sherri had told her about a warrant for the arrest of a man by that name. Danby had been released from prison and placed on probation with Chase Forster but, instead of reporting to Chase, he'd disappeared. Sherri had even wondered, briefly, if those were Danby's bones they'd found in the basement of the Chadwick mansion.

She reached for the phone and called her friend

at home. "This Lowell Danby character," she said when Sherri answered. "Is there any chance Ned could have met him in prison?"

"Depends on where Danby was held. Chances are they were both in the state prison in Warren for a while, but there are several facilities there. Where a prisoner is locked up depends on how much time is left in his sentence and how much of a security risk he's considered to be. Why?"

Liss explained her thinking. "You said this Danby character took off. Maybe Ned knew where he went."

"How? Ned got out of jail months after Danby did. Danby was long gone by then."

Liss drew a circle around Danby's name, reluctant to rule him out as a suspect. After all, he and Ned had both been assigned to Chase Forster. The connection implied that both were planning to live within Chase's jurisdiction. "Any idea what Danby looks like?"

"There's a physical description on the warrant, but no photo and I'd have to dig the paperwork out of the file at the office to know what it says."

"What? No wanted poster up on the wall?"

Sherri chuckled. "No one is actively looking for Lowell Danby. He could be anywhere by now. What's most likely to happen is that he'll be charged on this warrant *after* he's arrested for something else."

"That's depressing."

"Your justice system at work," Sherri quipped.

"People are still talking," Dan reported, shedding his coat as he entered their large, cozy, L-shaped kitchen through the back door. He'd been out early this Saturday morning and over to Patsy's for a newspaper and a listen. "Some profess to be astonished that the boy is really Edward Boyd, Jr. The rest claim to remember that Ned and Hilary were an item a dozen years ago and insist they knew who he was all along."

Less than a week had passed since Margaret had dropped her bombshell on Liss. Once Boxer had moved in with her, she'd made no secret of the reason. Human nature being what it was, the story of their newfound relationship had spread through Moosetookalook like wildfire.

Liss stopped folding laundry to glare at her husband. She'd taken one load out of the dryer and put another in, then brought the clothes out into the sun-filled room with its east-facing windows in an attempt to brighten her mood. "*The boy*, as you call him, is still Boxer Snipes, and I'm sick and tired of hearing him judged by what name he goes by. He's himself, whatever people call him." Liss knew she sounded waspish, but she couldn't help herself. "People should mind their own damned business," she added in an angry mutter.

"Crocuses are up," Dan said. "They're early this year."

"And don't try to change the subject!" She slammed the last neatly folded T-shirt into the basket.

"You want me to carry that upstairs for you?" Dan asked in a mild voice.

"Sorry. I'm just out of sorts. And *frustrated*!"

"Why?" He stood with one hip braced against the sink, the newspaper in his hand forgotten.

"Because I can't think of anything I can do to help. You know Margaret asked me to investigate." She'd been honest with him about that, even knowing he wouldn't like the idea.

He nodded. "I can understand why both of you want to prove Boxer's mother didn't kill Ned. For better or worse, we're all one family now."

"The thing is," Liss said, "I can't even decide what I think about Hilary's innocence or guilt. I keep waffling back and forth between believing her and thinking that the police have a pretty good case against her." She outlined her conclusions about the evidence pointing to Hilary Snipes. "That makes sense, you see. And it isn't as if we have any other viable suspects."

"You're overlooking the whole blackmail thing," Dan reminded her.

"No, I'm not. I made a list. It didn't help."

"Still, it seems to me that if the extortion angle is brought up at Hilary's trial, it will create that 'shadow of doubt' lawyers are always yammering about."

"Only if the jury believes it. What if they decide that the money came from finding Blackie O'Hare's loot or from selling antiques stolen from the Chadwick mansion?"

"Has anything turned up in pawn shops or at an auction? Any single item known to have come from that house?"

"I don't know. I don't know a *lot* of things!" She gave the laundry basket a kick to emphasize her irritation, sending it sliding halfway across the room. It struck the food and water dishes set out for the cats, both fortunately almost empty, but the sound woke Glenora, who had been napping on top of the refrigerator.

"That's one thing you may be able to check on," Dan said. "Who handled the estate? Maybe there's an inventory of the contents."

Liss thumped herself on the forehead with the heel of her hand. "I thought of that. Ages ago. Why didn't I pursue it?"

"A few other things on your mind, maybe?" He didn't add that it wasn't her job, but she could tell that the reminder was on the tip of his tongue.

"I'll ask around," she said quickly. "Maybe someone at the town office knows who handled Blackie O'Hare's inheritance from his wife. It'll probably be some snooty law firm from Boston." Liss stood to retrieve her laundry basket, stooping to pick it up just as Glenora, having quietly descended from her former perch, was about to leap into it. "Back off, cat."

Dan eased away from the sink and took the basket away from her.

She let him have it. Who was she to object to gallantry?

"Or you could talk to Jason Graye."

Side by side, they headed for the stairs. Glenora trailed along behind them.

"Why?" Liss asked as she climbed to the second floor.

"Simple. If he wants to buy the place, you can bet he's already done his research."

"You're assuming Graye didn't kill Ned."

"It shouldn't be too hard to find out if he has an alibi for the time of Ned's murder. And once you eliminate him as a suspect, even if you don't have another, you'll still be ahead of the game."

"I have to admit that's a good idea." Liss was a little embarrassed not to have thought of it herself. She took the laundry basket back once they entered their bedroom, but her mind was still on murder while she put clothing away in drawers, automatically getting everything in the right place. "And you're right. It shouldn't be difficult. There were lots of people around on Halloween. Surely someone can vouch for Jason Graye's whereabouts before he turned up at the haunted house and helped us keep the murder under wraps until the next day."

Liss had forgotten one thing. On Halloween, just about everyone had been wearing a costume.

"Jason was dressed as a vampire," Angie Hogencamp told her on Monday morning.

Liss had decided to make her first stop the apartment above the book store, knowing that Angie would be up early to get her kids off to school. In fact, she'd found Angie downstairs. The shop was closed, but she was already hard at work on book orders in her minuscule office at the back.

"So was I," Angie added. "So was Gloria Weir. There were vampires everywhere!"

"*Not* what I wanted to hear." Perched on a stool in Angie's closet-sized office, Liss tried for details, but Angie's memories of Halloween were vague and unhelpful.

"It was months ago," she protested. "I'm lucky to remember who I saw yesterday."

Liss sighed and stared out the postage-stamp-size window, seeking inspiration. Angie's Books was located on the northwest corner of the town square, on Main Street. Its front windows had a view along Ash Street, which actually dead-ended at that corner. But just to the west, Elm Street began, running north toward the health clinic and Dr. Sharon's office. Angie's side windows, including the one Liss was staring through, looked out across Elm. Angie could see the garage entrance into the former funeral home from the shop and, standing where she was now, looking directly across Elm Street, Liss had a clear view of what had once been Locke Insurance and was now Ye Olde Hobbie Shoppe.

"Have you ever caught a glimpse of Gloria's houseguest?" she asked abruptly.

"Nope. Never have." Angie didn't look up from her computer screen. "I'm not convinced she exists."

Liss stood and approached the small window. There was no snow left in Angie's small side yard or in front of Gloria's shop. "You can't see her back yard from here." Hadn't Gloria said that her aunt walked there for exercise? Or was it that the aunt *didn't* venture outdoors, not even that far? Liss couldn't remember.

"She doesn't have much land," Angie said. "The credit union is on the other side of her building and the paved area by their drive-up window comes within a couple yards of Gloria's place. Truth be told, I'm surprised she's still living above the store. She can afford to buy a separate residence."

"Can she?" Liss turned away from the window to find Angie watching her, her head cocked like a bird keeping its eye on a worm. "I didn't think Gloria was particularly wealthy. None of the obvious signs are there. No expensive jewelry. No designer clothing. On the surface, she doesn't appear to be any better off than anyone else in town."

"Looks can be deceiving, Then again, so can words, but she told me once that she's a trust fund baby." Angie shrugged. "Maybe she has to wait for the great aunt to kick the bucket before she comes into the really big bucks."

"If there *is* a great aunt," Liss muttered.

Angie chuckled. "What wild scenario are you dreaming up now?"

"What I'm thinking *is* pretty crazy," Liss admitted. "I was wondering if auntie is really a man."

"You think Gloria is having a hot love affair? Hiding a boy toy in her back bedroom?" Angie hooted with laughter.

"Not a lover. Maybe Flo is really her great-*uncle.*" Liss held up a hand to ward off further derisive laughter from Angie while she tried to work out what she *did* mean. "Say he was someone who'd been in prison until recently. Gloria told me that her aunt had plastic surgery after an accident. Maybe it was an *uncle* who had his face done, and he went under the knife so that he'd look radically different from the way he did back when he was committing crimes."

"And the point of that would be . . . ?" Angie had abandoned her paperwork and sat with both elbows propped up on a pile of publishers' catalogues, her hands fisted beneath her chin. She had the same bright-eyed, anticipatory look in her eyes that Liss had often seen on her daughter's face.

Unfortunately, even Liss's active imagination could not come up with a good answer. "Maybe the ex-criminal uncle came to town looking for Blackie O'Hare's treasure."

"Yeah, right. Assuming he really exists—which is a stretch—how would he even hear about it?"

"I guess there's only one way to find out. I need to talk to Gloria." Suiting action to words, Liss headed for the door.

At the hobby shop, as there was at the Emporium, an outside staircase led to the apartment on the second floor. Liss trotted up the steps and knocked.

Gloria flicked aside the curtain that covered the in-side of the small round window in the door. When she recognized Liss, she frowned. After a moment's hesitation, she opened up.

"Kind of early for a visit, isn't it?"

The kitchen smelled of bacon and burnt toast. Two plates, bits of egg still clinging to them, sat in the sink, but of Gloria's great-aunt, Liss saw no other sign.

"I wanted to catch you before you went out." Liss ignored Gloria's less-than-welcoming attitude. "I'm sure you've heard that Boxer's mother has been ar-rested for Ned's murder."

Gloria nodded. The wariness in her eyes ratch-eted up a fraction.

Liss suspected the aunt/uncle thing was probably no more than a flight of fancy on her part. On the other hand, everyone was a potential suspect, even Gloria.

She chose her next words carefully. "I promised Boxer I'd ask questions."

"Such as?"

"Such as, did you see Hilary Snipes the afternoon Ned Boyd was murdered?"

"I don't even know what she looks like."

"She's the skinny brunette who works at the High Street Market."

"The mousy-looking one?" At Liss's nod, Gloria shook her head. "I didn't notice her that day. Then again, it *was* Halloween. Everyone was in costume. You know—with masks."

Had Hilary dressed up? Liss wondered. Clearly, she hadn't provided the police with an alibi for the time of Ned's death. That meant she hadn't been at work. Even though the aisles of the grocery store had been empty the evening Liss had talked to Hilary there, it was rare that High Street Market didn't have at least one customer.

"She could have been one of the vampires," Gloria offered.

"I hear there were plenty of Dracula wannabes in town for the occasion."

Gloria relaxed enough to chuckle. "Isn't that the truth!"

"Here's the thing, Gloria. As a member of the committee, you must have been paying close attention to details that day."

"I was in charge of the costume parade," Gloria reminded her. "I was working with little kids."

"Damn." Liss had known that, but she'd forgotten, what with everything else that had been going on. "So I guess you don't remember seeing Jason Graye? He was dressed as a vampire, too."

Gloria huffed out an exasperated breath. "Oh, I remember him all right. That man is a huge pain in the butt. That day, at the last minute, he insisted on being one of the judges. He just wanted to get his picture in the paper. It was so *obvious*."

Gloria, Liss recalled, hadn't hesitated to hold a "press conference" on her own initiative after the murder. She bit back a snide comment about pots and kettles.

"So Graye was there all afternoon? In the town square?"

"I couldn't get rid of him," Gloria complained. "Not even after all the prizes had been handed out. It wasn't until it started to get dark that I had a brainstorm and told him to go out to the mansion and see if *you* needed any help. I was hoping that would get him out of my hair for a while." She sent a quick, apologetic look Liss's way.

"Was he reluctant to go?"

"Not at all. As things turned out, it was a good thing I sent him. To give credit where credit's due, he did some fast thinking when he saw all those police cars arriving on the scene. When the chief of police told him that somebody was dead inside the mansion, he came up with the idea of telling people there was an electrical problem. Let's face it, hearing that there was a real dead body in the haunted house would not have helped our fundraising effort."

The upshot was that Jason Graye had an alibi. He was off the hook for Ned's murder.

"Was there anything else you wanted?" Gloria looked impatient to be rid of her uninvited company.

That she'd not offered Liss coffee or other sustenance, or even a chair, had made that plain from the start, but seeing how antsy Gloria was only reinforced Liss's suspicions. The woman clearly had something to hide.

"I am curious about one other thing. Was it your great-aunt who phoned the town office to ask about buying the Chadwick mansion?"

"What? Of course not! Why would she?"

"I don't know. That's why I'm asking you. *Someone* named Greeley wanted to know the asking price."

Gloria started to speak, stopped, scowled, and abruptly excused herself to storm out of the kitchen. Liss hesitated only a moment before she followed. Her quarry had gone no farther than the adjacent living room.

One quick look at Flo Greeley convinced Liss that

her wild speculations had been way off base. The woman squaring off against Gloria, hands on generous hips and head tilted back in order to meet her niece's eyes, was short, squat, and stacked. A thin white scar bisected one cheek, coming perilously close to her left eye.

"What were you thinking?" Gloria demanded.

The older woman gave as good as she got. "We need a house. One away from the center of town. This apartment is too small. So is the lot it's built on. And, frankly, you're starting to get on my nerves!"

"Then move out. I like this place. It's convenient."

"That's exactly what I plan to do, with or without you. Why else have I been talking to real estate agents?"

"So you *were* the Greeley who phoned the town office?" Liss interrupted.

Two identical pairs of green eyes glared at her.

"Yes," Flo Greeley admitted after a beat. "What's it to you?"

"Just tying up a loose end," Liss assured her. Fierce as Gloria's Aunt Flo appeared to be, Liss could not imagine her stabbing Ned in the neck. For one thing, she'd have had to stand on top of the three-step stepladder just to reach that high.

Liss hoped to catch Jason Graye before he left for his office in Fallstown, but she was too late. The detached garage next to Graye's small Cape Cod cottage on the corner of Pine and Lowe, just a block distant from the town square, was open and empty.

She stood for a moment, studying Graye's lot.

The house and lawn were well cared for but some-how the property lacked character. Liss had been equally underwhelmed with the interior décor the one time she'd been invited inside. The furniture and accessories had been nice enough, and un-doubtedly expensive, but the house lacked the lived-in warmth that made a mere residence into a home.

The chairs hadn't been very comfortable, either.

By the time Liss returned to her own cozy do-main, she'd made a decision. Dan was right. It was a good bet that if an inventory of the contents of the Chadwick mansion existed, Graye had a copy. He was meticulous in his real estate dealings, even if he wasn't precisely honest. Besides, with a trip down to Falls-town, she could kill two birds with one stone. She had to do her weekly grocery shopping sometime, didn't she?

Less than an hour later, Liss parked in the small, secluded lot behind Graye's Real Estate. She gri-maced as she got out of the car and hit the button on her keychain to lock it. The last time she'd left a car there, it hadn't made it safely home with her. Her trusty old PT Cruiser had gone off the road and into the river, sinking to the bottom. She'd almost gone with it.

That, however, had not been Jason Graye's fault. She marched around to the front of the small build-ing and into the reception area.

It was much as she remembered it from her previ-ous visit more than two years earlier. The young woman sitting at the desk was different, but the hanging ferns and African violets looked the same. So did the computer, printer, and fax machine. Graye did not appear to have upgraded.

"Help you?" the receptionist drawled. Behind oversized glasses, her pale blue eyes were at half mast.

On a nearby table, a drip pot had yet to fill the waiting carafe with coffee, although the smell of it already pervaded the office. In Liss's opinion, that aroma made a nice change from the previous receptionist's pungent perfume. "My name is Liss Ruskin," she announced. "I'd like to speak to Mr. Graye about a house in Moosetookalook."

Now that she was there, details of her earlier dealings with the real estate broker came back to her. She remembered that he'd given her the card of an associate—an auctioneer specializing in the contents of old houses. Oh, yes, Liss thought. If Graye didn't have a copy of the Chadwick inventory, he'd definitely know how to lay hands on one.

"Liss!" A smarmy smile stretched Graye's thin lips wide. He'd obviously heard her speak and recognized her voice, because he hadn't given the young woman time to announce her. He stood in the door of the inner office, beaming at her in what he probably thought of as an avuncular manner.

"So," he said, waving her toward the chair in front of his desk, "what can I do for you this fine spring morning?"

It *was* spring, Liss realized with a start, and had been for over a week. In a few more days, five months would have passed since Ned's death.

Time to fish or cut bait.

She didn't sit down. "I only need a moment of your time. I—"

"Looking to sell out, are you? That house of yours will bring in a tidy sum now that the renovations are complete. Storefront on the first floor. Apartment on the second. I can offer you—"

She pointed to her mouth. "Read my lips. I'm not here to sell anything."

"Buying, then? I can—"

"I'm not here to buy, either."

He stopped smiling and took a step closer. Since he was only an inch or two taller than she was, this failed to intimidate Liss, but it did annoy her. He was invading her personal space. "Back off," she snapped.

Graye held his ground for a moment longer as if he needed to assert his ability to dominate the situation. Then he retreated behind his desk and settled into a well-padded swivel chair. He leaned back and once again gestured at the seating opposite him, a much less comfortable-looking piece of furniture.

"Why don't you sit down and tell me why you *are* here."

Liss was tempted to rest her palms on the desk and lean in until they were eye-to-eye but she caught herself in time. She'd come to ask a favor. That meant she had to play nice, no matter how big a jerk Jason Graye was. She sat down and crossed her legs at the knee. The smile she pasted on her face was every bit as phony as his.

"Are you still interested in buying the Chadwick mansion?" she asked.

He tented his fingers on his chest. "Possibly. If the price is right."

"Would I be correct in assuming that you've already checked into the property, and the contents of the house, fairly thoroughly?"

"If you're asking whether I've been able to examine everything for myself at my leisure, the answer is no. *You* thwarted my efforts before Halloween. Then the police put the place off limits. Twice. Since then, Thea Campbell has gone out of her way to be . . . difficult."

Good for Ms. Campbell, Liss thought. "That's too bad. But I know how thorough you are. You must have done a lot of research if you were considering buying the place. And you *were* a member of the board of selectmen when the town acquired the property."

"I was. If I hadn't been, the place would have been mine long before this. I've been through it once—the briefest of surveys—in company with the other selectmen. After that I was told it would be a conflict of interest for the town to sell it to me while I still held elected office."

"How fortunate for you that you were voted out."

Her thinly veiled sarcasm earned her a fulminating look, but Graye didn't pursue the point. "What exactly are you fishing for, Liss?"

"Information." Changing her mind, she rested her palms on the top of his desk. "There's been a suggestion made that my cousin was stealing antiques from the mansion before he was killed. I'd like to either prove or disprove that theory. To do so, I need to know what was in the mansion to start with. Was an inventory made when Blackie O'Hare's wife died?"

A flash of surprise crossed Graye's face and was quickly gone, replaced by a look Liss could only interpret as calculating. He swiveled slowly back and forth in his chair as if the movement aided his thought processes. "Well, well, well," he murmured after a few moments of silent contemplation. "It appears that I have something you want."

"My investigation could work to your advantage," Liss pointed out. "If there's stuff missing, the town might well lower their asking price."

"Let me make sure I'm clear on what you're offering. You want to take the inventory, go into the mansion, and compare what's there now with what the house is supposed to contain?"

"Exactly."

"You may have trouble getting permission from the board of selectmen. Thea won't want word getting out that they've been careless with the town's property."

"On the other hand, I'm offering to do the town a service. Free of charge."

"The work would go even more quickly if you had an assistant."

"You? Forget it." Thea would have a fit if she let Graye into the mansion.

"Too bad, since I *do* have an inventory." He picked up one of the papers on his desk and pretended to give it his full attention. "If that's all you wanted. . . ."

Liss studied him, thinking hard. She wouldn't beg, but she could bargain. "I may have some small influence with Ms. Campbell," she said, and left it to him to fill in the blanks.

Graye knew that Thea's son and daughter-in-law were among Liss's closest friends. If Pete urged his mother to okay the sale to Graye, she might just do it.

Or not.

Graye drummed his fingers on the blotter, considering Liss's admittedly vague promise. Was it enough to tip the balance? Would greed prompt him to take a chance?

He made her wait a full two minutes—she watched

the second hand on the wall clock go around twice—before he agreed.

Ten minutes later, feeling very pleased at her own cleverness, Liss walked out of Jason Graye's office with a copy of the Chatsworth inventory tucked into the canvas tote bag she'd brought along in anticipation of success. The contents of the carryall were heavy and of an awkward size. She paused on the front stoop to shift the weight to her shoulder. As she did so, the enormity of the task before her belatedly sank in, dampening her good mood. The "list" she'd been so anxious to obtain was almost two hundred pages long.

Chapter Fourteen

Liss had avoided collecting her mail for a full week. After Boxer moved in with Margaret, she'd let Dan pick it up. The moment she walked into the tiny post office on Monday afternoon, she remembered why she'd stayed away.

"Hey, Liss," Julie Simpson called out in her brassy New York voice. "What's this I hear about Ned Boyd having a secret baby?"

Liss winced. Every head in the minuscule lobby turned her way at the postmaster's question. There were three people present besides herself. Susie Farley had already removed the letters and bills from her box, but she lingered in the vestibule, ears stretched. Moose Mayfield, although he was nowhere near the gossip his wife the librarian was, showed a similar disinclination to leave. Belatedly, Liss recognized the man standing at Julie's window as the reclusive Homer Crane. He kept his head down as he waited for the postmaster to hand over a parcel wrapped in plain brown paper, but Liss suspected he was listening for her reply just as intently as the others.

"You've been reading too many romance novels, Julie," Liss said in a mild voice. The secret baby was a tried and true plot device in that genre. Ordinarily, Liss had no quarrel with it.

"Nuh-uh. That caseworker from Child Protective Services was as real as could be. She was trying to be subtle, but it was pretty clear she wanted to know if your aunt could give that boy—Margaret's *grandson*—a good home. I told her, sure. Margaret Boyd is the finest kind of people. So, you've got a new cousin now, huh?"

"Looks that way," Liss muttered.

Naturally, since she was anxious to escape the curiosity of her neighbors, the key fought turning in the lock of her post office box. When she finally got it to work, she grabbed her mail without looking at it and headed for the door. It was just closing behind her when she heard Moose speak.

"Dolores and me, we were saying just the other night how we remember when Hilary Snipes was sneaking around with Ned Boyd. Dolores was dead certain at the time that no good would come of it."

The door opened and closed again just as Liss reached the end of the short sidewalk. This time the voice was lower and sounded faintly apologetic.

"I'm sorry for your loss," Homer Crane said.

Liss stopped, turning to face the mystery man who'd moved into the old funeral home. The sun glinted off the rim of his glasses, drawing her gaze to a feature she hadn't noticed the only other time they'd met. How she'd missed it, even in the dim lighting of Crane's hallway, eluded her.

He had a long, thin nose that turned up at the end. In profile, it resembled nothing so much as a ski jump. She'd been wrong about something else, too. In the bright light of day, the hairline she'd pegged as receding was closer to nonexistent. A few tufts of wispy blond hair still clung to his scalp, but for all intents and purposes, Homer Crane was bald as an egg.

Trying not to stare, Liss thanked him for his sympathy.

"It's a terrible thing to lose someone to murder," Crane said. "A cousin, did I hear her say? Were you close?"

"In some ways."

His intense interest began to make her uncomfortable. Behind the thick spectacles, his eyes were a pale, watery blue. His steady stare shouldn't have been so unnerving.

"I, uh, need to get going."

The door of the post office opened again. It was almost five. Julie shooed her last two customers out and set about taking down the flag. Susie scurried away without delay, although she did send a curious look Liss's way.

"I'm sorry," Crane mumbled. "I didn't mean to delay you." He turned abruptly and walked rapidly homeward.

Moose Mayfield stared after him. "That the writer?"

"Why don't you ask him?" Liss suggested.

She felt no more than a flash of guilt when Moose trundled off in pursuit of Homer Crane. She doubted he'd catch up with Crane before the other man reached the sanctuary of his house and closed and locked the door behind him. In the meantime, Liss would have time to make her own way home in peace.

*   *   *

Bright and early Tuesday morning, Liss put a sign on the door of Moosetookalook Scottish Emporium to say she would be closed until 1:00 PM. It was the end of March—mud season—and a damp chill lingered in the air. She did not expect to lose any walk-in business in her absence.

At eight, she was standing on the far side of the long, high counter that separated the town clerk from the rest of the population of Moosetookalook. She had a clear view of the row of hooks along a nearby wall. Each held a set of keys. It was a simple matter to spot the ones that unlocked the Chadwick mansion, although the duplicate set was apparently being kept elsewhere.

"What can I do for you, Liss?" Francine asked.

"I need to borrow the keys to the Chadwick house again." Her hand was already out before she realized that Francine was shaking her head.

"Sorry. No can do. Besides, I thought you wouldn't be caught dead going back there."

Liss winced, remembering their last conversation on the subject, but she was more concerned about being refused access to the place. "What's up? I just have to check something out. I'm not going to steal anything."

"Not my call. You'll have to talk to Ms. Selectman Campbell."

"Thea Campbell doesn't want me to borrow the keys?"

"She doesn't want *anybody* going out there."

"Meaning Jason Graye," Liss murmured, belatedly catching on. "Okay. I'll go talk to Thea."

Pete's mother lived several blocks to the west along Main Street, not far enough away to make it worthwhile to get the car out and drive there. Prepared to walk the short distance from the town square, Liss zipped up the replacement jacket she'd bought after giving up on ever finding the light blue one Boxer had purloined. It was bright green, with a yellow stripe and, consequently, much harder to leave behind without noticing.

"You don't need to go anywhere," Francine called out before she reached the door.

Liss paused with one hand on the doorknob. "Why not?"

"Because Ms. Campbell is here, in the room where we keep records that aren't yet stored electronically."

Liss turned away from the door and headed to the records room. "Morning, Thea," she said a few minutes later.

Pete's mother glanced up from a musty old ledger and frowned. She shared her son's dark hair and chunky build, but there the resemblance stopped. No one would ever call Althea Briscetti Campbell easygoing. Tightly wound was more like it. And with each year into her long widowhood, she'd grown more conservative in her views on just about everything.

"What is it, Liss? I'm quite busy here."

"Apparently, I need your permission to borrow the keys to the Chadwick mansion."

"You want to go out there again? Why? Halloween is over."

Liss waged a brief debate with herself about how much to tell Thea. In the end she opted for full disclosure, although in a carefully edited version. "There's a possibility that someone may have stolen a few of the more easily portable antiques from the Chadwick mansion and sold them. It might have been my cousin. It might have been someone else. Either way, I'd like to find out if anything is missing. I have an inventory of the items that should be there. It's old. From when Alice O'Hare died, I think. But it—"

Thea stopped her with a preemptory gesture. She held out one long-fingered hand and waited. Liss sighed and reached into her tote bag. "You'll need both hands for this."

One glance at the inventory had Thea tut-tutting and shaking her head. "I won't ask where you got this, but you should know that it was actually compiled when the town took possession of the Chadwick property, not earlier. I have a copy of it myself. *All* the selectmen received one."

Liss neither confirmed nor denied Thea's assumption, but she was doubly glad she hadn't let Jason Graye talk her into taking him with her into the mansion. "It would be helpful to the town to know if anything has gone missing," she said instead. "So, if it's okay with you, I'd like to take a look around. All you need to do is authorize Francine to give me the keys."

"I think not." Thea placed Graye's copy of the inventory on the floor beside her, out of Liss's reach.

"But, Thea. If someone stole—"

"Then a proper investigation should be launched. Thank you for bringing this to my attention. I will have the police department look into the matter."

"But—"

"It's no longer your concern." Thea meant the words as a dismissal. She resumed her study of the old ledger, pointedly ignoring everything and everyone else.

Liss knew when she was beaten and left quietly.

* * *

The Emporium opened on time after all.

A few hours later, Liss phoned Sherri to ask if Thea had followed through with a request to check the inventory against the contents of the Chadwick house.

"Thanks loads," Sherri grumbled. "Do you have any idea how long it's going to take to go through all that stuff?"

"I offered to do it."

Sherri laughed. "I bet you did. Well, I'm stuck with it now. And, no, I can't ask for help from civilians. I'm hoping I might get some from the state police, but I'm not counting on it. Thea sent a copy of the inventory to Gordon Tandy."

With that food for thought, Liss went back to work. She had mail and e-mail orders to fill, but her mind kept circling back to all the questions about Ned's murder that still needed answers. By the time Boxer got home from school, she'd made a new list.

Boxer came straight to the Emporium, rather than going to Aunt Margaret's apartment, since she wouldn't be home from work for another hour or two. Margaret had made a point of asking him to check in with Liss as soon as the school bus dropped him off in the town square.

"I'm going out to the trailer." Boxer removed a backpack full of school books and homework and let it fall to the floor behind the sales counter with a thump.

"Now?"

"You got a problem with that?" His scowl told Liss that he didn't like having rules to follow. He wasn't accustomed to having to account for his whereabouts.

"I've got a responsibility to make sure the Child Protective Services caseworker can't find anything to complain about."

Boxer had already disappeared several times since he'd moved in with Margaret. On his return, he'd evaded her questions about where he'd been. Margaret had convinced herself that he'd been with friends. She didn't want to make him feel as if he was in jail, too. Liss was less easily mollified. She suspected that Boxer had returned to the Chadwick mansion and wondered if he'd managed to find another way to get inside.

Under her steady gaze, Boxer fell back on his patented nonchalant shrug. "I'm just gonna go get some more of my stuff. You said I could go back if I forgot anything."

Liss sighed. "Yes. I did. Although what I actually said was that *we* could go back. If you wait till I close, I'll drive you." She wanted to talk to the boy anyway. Some of the questions on her new list were for him.

"I don't see why I can't just *stay* out there," Boxer grumbled. "It shouldn't sit empty like that. Somebody might break in and rob us."

"We've already moved the TV to a safe location," Liss reminded him.

"I should get Mom's jewelry box."

Liss doubted that Hilary owned a fortune in gems, but Boxer's determination wore her down. "How about I close up now?" she suggested. "I'll drive you out to Owl Road and help you pack up anything you think may be at risk." A glance at him had her fighting a smile. "Oh, put away the suspicious face, will you! I'm not trying to invade your privacy or keep you on a leash. Don't you get it? You're family now. Your grandmother and I just want to help you."

"I don't need—"

"And we *care* about you."

"Funny, you never did *before* you found out who my father was."

"I liked you before that."

"Did not."

"Did too. You told me so yourself."

It didn't take long to shut down the shop, but by the time she flipped the OPEN sign to CLOSED and looked around for Boxer, he had disappeared.

Grumbling under her breath, Liss checked the stockroom. Then she dashed upstairs to Margaret's apartment. The boy was well and truly gone.

She drove slowly all the way to Owl Road, keeping her eyes peeled for Boxer, hoping to overtake him. She was relieved to find him already inside the trailer when she arrived. "What did you do?" she asked. "Cut through back yards and woods?"

His grin was quick and genuine. "I'm just faster than you. Faster than a speeding pullet."

Liss groaned at the malapropism. "Think you're clever, don't you?"

"Hey, I *know* I'm clever."

"You're right. You're a smart kid—which is why you're going to answer a few questions for me while we pack your stuff."

"Like what?"

They entered Hilary's room, which still smelled faintly of her perfume, so that Boxer could collect her jewelry box. It was a pretty little thing, wood decorated with flower decals—something a boy might give his mother for her birthday or Christmas.

"Like did Ned talk you into helping him remove antiques from the Chadwick mansion?"

She'd managed to take Boxer by surprise. "Fat

chance! He never even knew that I knew he was there."

"Are you sure about that? Once you started playing pranks he must have guessed someone else was in the house on the QT."

Boxer's brow creased into a frown. "Pretty sure. I never saw him."

"But you're certain he was there?"

"Yeah. Somewhere." Boxer moved into his own room, picking up CDs, books, and a small box he kept at the back of his sock drawer.

"So, you were aware of the hidden tunnel, but you didn't know there was a secret room?"

"I figured there *was* one. I just didn't know how to find it."

"You told us you *wanted* Ned to get caught. That's why you took the apple dookin tub and the manikin. I'm guessing you didn't like your father much."

"Why should I? He didn't give a tinker's dam about me."

Liss could sympathize. Ned had been thrust upon Boxer out of the blue. And given the boy's protective attitude toward his mother—

She cut off that train of thought before it could go any farther. Boxer had not killed Ned.

"Did you ever take anything from the mansion on your own? Other than the apple dookin tub, the manikin, and my jacket, I mean."

"I'm not a thief." He stooped to fish a pair of beat-up running shoes out from under the bed.

"Maybe no one is," Liss conceded. "Or maybe that's what got Ned killed."

Watching Boxer, she realized she should have talked to him one-on-one a long time ago. Sure, he was only a kid, but he'd already weathered more traumatic events than most adults had to face. And he was smart. Besides that, he was probably more familiar with the Chadwick mansion than any of them. Kids and treasure hunting? They went together like peanut butter and jelly.

Sitting down on the end of Boxer's bed, she filled him in on everything she'd been trying to discover about his father's activities from the time Ned got out of jail until his murder. "Ned got cash from somewhere," she concluded. "The only three sources I can think of are fencing antiques, blackmail, and Blackie's loot."

But Boxer was stuck on another aspect of the situation. "The police think my mother killed him because they argued over money?"

"I'm afraid so. I assume that they found her fingerprints in the parlor at the mansion and that placed her at the scene of the crime."

Boxer gave a vigorous negative shake of the head. "Never happened."

"Did you ever run into anyone else when you visited the mansion?"

He became very busy packing the remaining articles he wanted to take back to the apartment with him into a cardboard box. "I wasn't there all that much."

"No?" Rising, she picked up the nearest pile of CDs and headed for the living room. "Let's talk about those holes in the cellar of the Chadwick mansion, shall we?"

"Oh. Those." He avoided meeting her eyes.

"Yes. Those. Ned was dead by the time they were dug. You didn't need to sneak into the mansion to play tricks anymore, but I'm guessing you did anyway. Treasure hunting? Looking for the lost loot? The legendary cache of cash?"

He shrugged.

"Come on, Boxer. Give me a break here. I'm trying to help your mother. I can't put all the pieces together if some of them are missing."

He followed her out, carrying the carton and an armload of books. "Yeah. I dug the holes you found when you went back to the mansion. And let me tell you, that was hard work. That ground is petrified!"

"How did you get in? The tunnel had been blocked off."

"I broke a window. Okay? In the bird room."

That agreed with Sherri's report. "So, you lied to me the last time I asked about the holes."

"I was thinking about owning up, but then Samantha staged her big confession scene."

"Upstaged you, did she?" Liss fought a smile as she helped Boxer carry his possessions out to her car. "Never mind. Did you find anything?"

"No."

Once they were outside the trailer, Liss opened the hatchback and folded down the seats to make more room. Two more trips completed the loading. Having collected everything he'd come for, Boxer returned to the trailer only long enough to lock the door, then climbed in on the passenger side.

Liss took her place behind the wheel. "How did you get in the second time, when you dug up the skeleton?" When silence ensued, she started the engine, but she gave him a hard look before pulling out of the driveway. "You couldn't have opened the tunnel entrance from the outside."

"Blame it on the cops," he muttered.

"Okay. Blame *what* on the cops?"

Boxer was slouched as low on his spine as his seat-belt would allow. Liss fought the urge to tell him to sit up straight. From his posture, he was either embarrassed or feeling rebellious. Maybe a little of both.

"I went back out there after the local cops fixed the window and left. The back door was unlocked." He responded to Liss's skeptical sideways glance with another shrug. "*Somebody* got careless."

"So you just waltzed right in?" Liss's hands clenched on the steering wheel. "Boxer, there's a *murderer* on the loose. Didn't it occur to you that he might have—?"

"What? Returned to the scene of the crime? That only happens in books. Besides, how would anybody but the cops get in?"

"Maybe he picked the lock. How do I know? The point is, you took a foolish risk."

"There was nobody there, Liss."

"Are you sure?"

His silence spoke volumes.

"Let me see if I've got this straight. You broke a window, got in, did some digging in the basement, then had to stop because Sherri and I discovered the holes."

A nod.

"Then you went back and found the door unlocked, so you went in again and started digging again, only deeper?

"Well, first I opened up the tunnel, so I could get in and out. Then I made sure all the doors were locked. I didn't want anybody interrupting me while I was treasure hunting, did I? I was startled when I turned up bones instead of gold."

Liss pulled into the driveway beside Moose-tookalook Scottish Emporium and killed the engine. Then she folded her arms on the steering wheel and let her head fall forward on top of them. She felt like banging her forehead against the hard plastic.

"You okay?" The bewilderment in Boxer's voice was genuine.

Liss straightened and glowered at him. "Did you even look around first, to be sure there was no one in the house? Or did you just trot merrily down the cellar steps?"

"I never once ran into anyone else out there. Not when Ned was still alive and not afterward."

"Dumb luck, mister! You had no idea how that door came to be unlocked. You took a terrible risk."

Boxer paled as he thought back on that day. "I didn't hear anyone in the house."

"But you went straight down to the basement, right?"

He nodded. "I looked things over, and then I went looking for a crowbar. There are all kinds of old tools over in the corner by the furnace."

"So it was a while before you started ripping the boards off to unblock the tunnel entrance. Whoever was in the house must have left before you started making so much noise."

Boxer blew out a breath. "The door was already locked again when I went to check on it. I thought I'd thrown the dead bolt and just didn't remember doing it, but I guess. . . ."

"Yeah. I'm going to have nightmares about this," Liss added in a mutter.

She got out of the car and Boxer followed suit. She didn't ask him any more questions until they'd carried everything up to Margaret's apartment.

"Did you find the skeleton that same day?" Liss asked when she'd put the kettle on and had found two packets of instant hot chocolate in her aunt's kitchen cabinets.

Boxer's non-committal grunt was no answer.

"How many times, exactly, did you go out there after you discovered that unlocked door?"

"A couple. I told you how hard the ground was. But that spot looked a little different somehow. The dirt was off-color. Guess we know why now, but I was hoping for a pot of gold. I got out of there pretty quick after that skull turned up. I haven't been back since."

"You used the tunnel to get in and out?"

He nodded and thanked her when she handed him one of the steaming mugs. He blew on the hot liquid to cool it.

"Ever snoop around upstairs?"

"Not so you'd notice."

Liss had the feeling he was holding something back, but she couldn't imagine what it might be. "Anything else I ought to know?" she asked as she heard her aunt's footsteps on the stairs.

"Nope, but I've got a question for you."

"Let's hear it."

He grinned at her. "You got any cookies to go with this cocoa? I'm starving."

The Emporium was quiet the next morning. There wasn't a sound from the apartment above. Boxer was in school and Aunt Margaret had already left for work by the time Liss went through her usual routine of booting up the cash register and her laptop. She checked the website for new orders and, finding none, clicked on her favorite search engine.

Time for some research.

Trying to find out where the legend of Blackie O'Hare's "treasure" had originated was painstaking work, complicated by the fact that if she didn't enter the right search string, nothing relevant came up. Changing a single word could make a huge difference. She played with assorted combinations all morning without finding much in the way of solid information. She gave up by lunchtime.

Sherri phoned at one. "Nothing yet on missing antiques," she reported. "Jeff and I are going out to the Chadwick mansion this afternoon to start checking the contents against the inventory, but I thought you'd like to know that the bones from the basement turned out to be one of Blackie O'Hare's alleged victims."

"We assumed that. Didn't we?" That was part of the reason Liss had been surfing the Web. She'd wanted more information on the late mob hit man.

"Now we know. We also know that Blackie was here in Moosetookalook at least once after his wife died . . . to bury the body. But the important thing is that the remains were left in the cellar decades ago. They have no connection to Ned's murder."

Liss wasn't so sure about that.

Chapter Fifteen

When a second attempt also failed to find anything useful online, Liss broke down and returned to the library. She waved hello to Dolores and
headed directly to the file cabinets that contained
the folders full of clippings. She wasn't surprised
when the librarian followed her and watched with
blatant curiosity as Liss extracted the one labeled
with Blackie O'Hare's name.

"Something I can help you with, Liss?" Dolores
asked.

"I'm good for the moment, thanks."

She carried the file to the nearest table and sat
down, hoping Dolores would take the hint and go
away. She should have known better. Every time she
glanced up, it was to meet the librarian's avid gaze.

Ignore her, Liss told herself. *Skim through the material and get out.*

But skimming wasn't possible. The yellowed clippings in the file folder covered everything from
Blackie's marriage to the Chadwick heiress to his
trial and imprisonment, to his eventual murder

while still in jail. This last had taken place at about
the same time Liss started college. She was surprised,
initially, to realize that Blackie had died so long ago.
It had apparently taken several years to settle his estate and almost as many more for the town to go
through whatever legal maneuvers had been neces-
sary to seize the property for unpaid taxes.

The list of crimes Blackie had allegedly committed was long and chilling. Liss came across more
than one hint in the press that he had killed more
people than the police knew about. An involuntary
shiver racked her as she remembered the bones in
the cellar of the Chadwick mansion. It seemed that
Blackie had been very successful in his career as a hit
man for the mob.

Dolores had filed an entire page from one Massachusetts newspaper. Liss unfolded it and discovered
in-depth coverage of the investigation into Blackie's
death. The paper was published in the town where
the prison was located, which accounted for the local
interest.

Blackie had been stabbed, but although the other
prisoners had been subjected to repeated questioning
over a period of several months, prison authorities
had not been able to determine who had wielded the
fatal knife. Liss supposed that many people, especially
the families of Blackie's victims, felt he'd deserved his
fate. Some probably wanted to give a medal to the
person who removed Blackie from the earth. Liss
sighed as she refolded the page in quarters, once
more hiding the final chapter of Blackie's life on
the inside. Nothing was ever solved by more killing.

What had she expected to find? Liss had to admit
that she had no idea. It had seemed logical to look

into Blackie's history, since so much of what had happened seemed to revolve around the search for his "loot," but the only conclusion she'd come to was that there probably wasn't any treasure at all. Nowhere in anything she'd read had she found mention of missing money or jewels or gold . . . or anything else of value.

Blackie, for all his faults, had not been a bank robber or a cat burglar. He'd done one thing and done it well and had been well paid for it. He'd also spent a fortune on lawyers after his arrest.

More and more, as time went by, Liss felt certain that the only thing he'd buried in the basement of the house in Moosetookalook had been the body of one of his victims.

Abandoning her quest, she started to gather up the clippings and photocopies of articles about Blackie O'Hare. They were spread all over the surface of the library table.

"Those were in chronological order to start with," Dolores said.

Liss jumped. The librarian was standing right behind her. "For heaven's sake, Dolores! You scared me out of six years' growth."

"At your age, you should have stopped growing," came the tart reply. "I mean it. Put those back in the order you found them or let me do it. It's common courtesy to the next library patron who wants to look through that file."

Since Liss saw her point, she took the time to sort and rearrange, finishing up with the last item in the stack, the folded page from the Massachusetts paper. She was just tucking it back into the file folder when a name caught her eye.

Lowell Danby.

Liss frowned. Wasn't he the man Chase Forster was looking for on a probation violation?

Curiosity compelled her to read the entire piece, which was printed on the back of the page with the story about the investigation of Blackie's murder. It was short and to the point. Lowell Danby, age forty-three, had been released from prison because his conviction for armed robbery had been overthrown on appeal.

"What are the odds?" Liss murmured.

She didn't believe in coincidences and Lowell Danby was not a common name. It was a pretty good bet that the man who'd been in prison with Blackie O'Hare in Massachusetts was identical to the one who, a dozen years later, spent time incarcerated in a correctional facility in Maine with her cousin Ned. She wasn't sure what significance this conclusion had, but was certain it meant something.

With the clippings all neatly rearranged in chronological order, Liss returned the file folder to Dolores and headed back to work. She might have to return to search through the library's collection of Maine newspapers on microfilm, but first she intended to give the Internet another try . . . away from Dolores Mayfield's prying eyes.

At the Emporium there were no customers to distract her. Liss typed Danby's name into a search engine and grimaced at the number of hits it generated. She put the name in quotes and tried again, narrowing the field from thousands to mere hundreds. On impulse, she clicked on IMAGES and was instantly rewarded. Three JPEG files came up and only one of them showed a person.

The thumbnail was too tiny to see well. Liss clicked on it and was taken to a newspaper site that wanted her to sign up and pay a fee before she searched further. Liss tried SEE FULL-SIZED IMAGE instead, then enlarged what popped up on her screen by tinkering with the setting she usually left at 100% to view websites. Unfortunately, the only thing that increasing the size of the image accomplished was to make the photo of "Lowell Danby" blurrier. She could make out little more than a bushy head of light-colored hair above eyes and a nose.

Liss stared at the screen, trying to put her finger on why she felt there was something familiar about the man's face. Had she seen him in Moosetookalook? It was not impossible, but she could not recall. She let her gaze rove over the shelves and racks full of Scottish imports, not really seeing any of them, with the nagging sense that somewhere, sometime, she had met this man in person.

"Overactive imagination," she muttered. The figure in the photo could be anyone.

Still, if Danby had known both Blackie and Ned, then there was a possibility, however slight, that he could have been involved in Ned's death. It was a leap, and Liss had no facts to back her up, but if Ned had moved into the mansion to hunt for Blackie's treasure, why not Danby? Maybe they'd been working together. Maybe they'd found the cache of cash and quarreled over splitting the loot. Or maybe Ned had been blackmailing Danby, threatening to turn him in for probation violation and send him back to prison. If either guess was accurate, Lowell Danby would have had a reason to kill her cousin.

* * *

Liss wasted no time sharing her theory with Sherri Campbell, but it was nearly a week later before Sherri offered any update on the case to her civilian friend. Meanwhile, Hilary Snipes remained in jail, still charged with Ned's murder.

"It looks as if Ned did know Lowell Danby," Sherri said between sips of coffee. "They worked in the prison woodworking shop together."

"Woodworking? I thought prisoners made license plates."

"Some do. Some make furniture. Others make clothing. You should visit the prison store sometime. The prices are really good."

"Ah, Sherri—we're trying to open a storefront that sells custom woodworking products right next door. We don't need you to shill for the competition, thank you very much."

Sherri chuckled and helped herself to a slice of apple loaf, another specialty of Patsy's Coffee House. She and Liss were ensconced in the cozy corner of the Emporium. It was a Tuesday morning in April and they had the place to themselves.

"So," Liss summarized, ignoring her own coffee. "You're saying that Ned would have recognized Danby if he ran into him after they were both out of jail." That went along with her own thinking.

At Sherri's nod, Liss continued. "If Ned knew there was a warrant out for Danby—"

"But how would he know that?" Sherri interrupted.

"Wouldn't it be posted at the probation office?"

"Doubtful. Besides, Ned opened his bank account before he reported in to Chase Forster."

"Darn. I really liked the idea that Ned was blackmailing Danby with the threat to turn him in."

"It's still a possibility. Or maybe Ned knew something else about him. Or maybe, as you also suggested, they were in this together." Sherri shook her head as if amazed by her own credulity. "I'm as bad as you are when it comes to speculating, but it makes a crazy kind of sense that if Danby knew Blackie in Massachusetts he could have heard something about buried loot from him. The horse's mouth, so to speak. Years later, Danby met Ned, got to talking, discovered that Ned was from Moosetookalook and that he knew all about Blackie's house and the legend of hidden treasure. Sure would explain those holes dug in the cellar floor."

Liss covered her silence by sipping coffee. She had no intention of betraying Boxer's confidences. What harm did it do to let Sherri think Danby had been the one who'd uncovered the skeleton? That Danby *had* been in the house was all too chillingly possible. If he'd been the one who'd left the kitchen door unlocked, then Boxer had been lucky indeed not to have run into him.

"There is another possibility," Sherri said. "In fact, it's the real reason I came by today. We finished taking inventory at the Chadwick mansion."

"And?"

"There are several items missing—all valuable, all easily portable. Of course, we have no idea *when* they disappeared from the house. It could have been anytime in the last couple years."

"Since the town seized the property for back taxes."

"Right."

"Do you think Ned might have caught Danby robbing the place?"

Sherri gave a shrug that was eerily like Boxer's.

"Could be. It's equally possible there's another explanation that has nothing to do with either Ned or
Danby."

"And for all we know, Danby may have fled to
Canada or Mexico or Timbuktu months ago."

"Yup."

They drank more coffee.

"So, what's gone missing?" Liss asked after a short
silence.

Sherri pulled a list out of her pocket and handed
it over. Liss skimmed the items, stopping when she
came to *brown oil lamp from bedroom two.*

"Oil or owl?" she asked, showing Sherri the item.

"No idea. We were checking against the inventory
descriptions. Do you remember seeing an owl in one
of the bedrooms? Don't tell me it was another of
those creepy stuffed birds!"

"If it's what I'm thinking of, it's an owl-shaped
brown glass chimney on a small electric lamp. From
the early twentieth century, I think. I assumed it was
supposed to be used as a nightlight. The important
thing is that it was still there in late September when
Dan and I paid our first visit to the mansion."

"That will help." Sherri downed the last slug of
her coffee and got to her feet. "I'll tell Jeff. He's
sending descriptions of all the missing items out to
other PDs and to local auctioneers and pawn shop
owners. If we get lucky, one of them will recognize
one or more of them and contact us."

"That's it? That's all you're going to do?"

"That's about all we *can* do." Sherri looked as serious as Liss had ever seen her. "Tell me something—
are you absolutely certain that Boxer isn't the one
who took those things from the house? Because if
the seller can be identified and he leads us to that

boy, Boxer Snipes is headed straight to the youth center."

"He's a good kid, Sherri." But he was keeping *something* back. Liss wished she could be certain it wasn't the disappearance of small, valuable items from the mansion.

"Well, we'll keep investigating, although it's not high priority. My dear mother-in-law-the-selectman has changed her tune. She's lobbying to auction off the mansion's contents and sell the house for whatever the town can get."

"Even to Jason Graye?"

"Looks that way."

Three more days passed. Business picked up as spring advanced, but Liss still had plenty of time to wonder and worry. Hilary's trial date was creeping up on them.

On her way to work, Liss stopped at Patsy's, struck by a sudden craving for a sticky bun. Sherri was already there, sitting in one of the high-backed booths with the morning paper, a mug of coffee, and a muffin. Once Liss paid for her order, she joined her friend.

"We've got to stop meeting like this," she said as she slid in across the red vinyl seat.

"And I've got to stop drinking so much coffee," Sherri mumbled. "Especially since it doesn't seem to do a thing to wake me up."

"Rough night?"

"Adam's got a spring cold. He kept all of us awake with his coughing."

Liss made sympathetic noises before asking if there was any news on the stolen antiques.

"Some. We've got a really vague description of someone who sold a vase that appears to have come from the mansion."

If Sherri had been more alert, she might not have been so forthcoming. Liss took ruthless advantage. "How vague?"

"The owner of the pawn shop—old guy—said the seller had a nose like Bob Hope's."

It took Liss a moment to place the name. "The comedian?"

At Sherri's nod, she tried to remember what he'd looked like. He'd been dead for years, but he'd made a lot of movies, starting way back in the days when films were black and white. Her mother, Liss recalled, had owned the entire "Road to" series on video cassettes. Bob Hope had made five or six of those buddy pictures with Bing Crosby, the guy whose rendition of "White Christmas" was still played endlessly during the holidays.

But what *had* Bob Hope's nose looked like?

Liss munched on her sticky bun, dimly aware of other customers in the coffee shop. People called out greetings to one another. Liss waved back at Gloria, who was on her way out the door carrying a bulging bakery bag. Someone rocked the back of Liss's bench seat in the process of getting settled in the adjacent booth. The scent of cinnamon filled the air, driving every other thought away, as Patsy emerged from the kitchen with a fresh tray of hot-out-of-the-oven sticky buns.

"A nose like Bob Hope's," Sherri repeated, shaking her head. "When I asked him what he meant, he said I should picture a ski jump."

"What did you say?"

"Ski jump. You know, the thing that—"

"I know what a ski jump is."

Images flashed through Liss's mind in rapid succession—Bob Hope's trademark appendage; the face of the man in the blurry image online; and Homer Crane, standing in full sunlight in front of the post office.

"Oh, my God! Sherri, I know who he is! Or, at least, I know who he's pretending to be. He hasn't been using the name Lowell Danby since he's been in Moosetookalook. He calls himself Homer Crane. He's the guy who moved into the funeral home late last summer."

Sherri's eyes narrowed over the rim of her mug. "Are you sure?"

"You've never met him?"

She shook her head.

"The nose fits, Sherri. Lionel Danby has been right *under* our noses all along." Another thought struck her. "Good grief. Dolores was right. Homer Crane *was* using a pseudonym." No wonder he'd reacted so strongly to her words the day she'd gone to his house.

Sherri leaned forward across the table, lowering her voice as she caught Liss's forearm and squeezed. "Let's keep this to ourselves for the time being, okay? Let me see what I can find out about this Homer Crane before you go off half cocked and do something foolish like confront the man yourself."

"That's the last thing I'd do."

"Uh-huh."

Once again, the person in the booth behind Liss bumped against the back of the high seat, this time in the process of leaving. Liss didn't even look to see who it was. All her attention was fixed on Sherri.

"You've got to check into this as soon as possible. You can't leave a murderer running around loose."

"All we have on him at this point is the vague suspicion that he's a thief."

"He's dangerous or you wouldn't be warning me off. And we wouldn't be whispering. You've got to get moving on this."

"Agreed, but—"

"Bye, Dolores," Patsy sang out.

Liss met Sherri's eyes across the table, sharing the same alarming thought. Had it been Dolores Mayfield in the adjacent booth? And if it had been, how much had she overheard?

Sherri's head swiveled toward the door seconds after it closed behind the departing librarian. Liss craned her neck until she caught sight of Dolores through the café window. Her heart sank when she realized that Dolores was not heading toward the library. She passed the municipal building without stopping and continued on, her long, determined strides carrying her past Angie's Books in the direction of—

"Oh, damn. Come on. Dolores is going to the funeral home."

Sherri was already on her feet, but by the time they got outside the coffee shop, they were already too late. Across the width of the town square, Dolores mounted the steps of what had once been Preston's Mortuary and rapped on the door. A moment later, it opened and Dolores went inside.

"She must have heard us talking," Liss said as she and Sherri followed swiftly in Dolores's footsteps.

"She can't have overheard everything. Only the first part. After that we lowered our voices."

"What she heard was just enough to confirm her

own wacky theory. Dolores has been convinced for months that Crane is a famous novelist writing under a pseudonym. She didn't know what that pseudonym might be, but I've got a feeling that now, thanks to my big mouth, she *thinks* she does."

"Lowell Danby?" They'd reached the corner in front of Angie's Books. "That's crazy. There's no famous author named Lowell Danby."

"Since when has common sense made a dent in Dolores's thinking? We've got to get her out of there, Sherri. You've got that warrant for him. Go in there and arrest him."

"It doesn't work that way. The best I can do is knock on the door. You stay here."

Sherri started to cross Main Street but before she could take more than a few steps, Dolores emerged, unscathed, from their suspect's lair. She did a double take at seeing Sherri and Liss gaping at her, but then continued on her way. A smug little smile played around her mouth.

"A word with you, Dolores?" Sherri said, intercepting her. Liss fell into step on the librarian's other side.

"About what? I have to get to work."

"About someone named Lowell Danby."

When Dolores looked at Liss, her smile turned into a smirk. "I was right all along, wasn't I? He's written books under a pseudonym. And I bet he uses more than one nom de plume. All the best authors do, you know."

"What did you say to him?"

"I told him I was soliciting new library patrons. I just wanted to get a good look at him. What's the big deal?"

"You didn't mention the name Danby, did you?" Liss asked.

They reached the entrance to the municipal building and stopped. Dolores glanced back at the funeral home as if, belatedly, she sensed that something had been off key about her meeting with the "famous author."

"*Did* you?" Sherri asked, following the direction of Dolores's gaze.

Liss looked, too. The curtain at an upstairs window twitched. Danby was watching them. Suddenly uneasy, she remembered that he knew that Ned had been her cousin. And Sherri was in uniform. "Uh, ladies—maybe we should take this inside?"

Dolores flounced ahead, heading up the stairs to the library and leaving Liss and Sherri to follow. "I don't know what you're making such a fuss about. It's good for the town to have a real live celebrity living here, even if he is a bit of a recluse."

"Tell me you didn't come right out and ask him if he was Lowell Danby," Sherri said.

Dolores hoisted a pile of recently returned novels and headed for the fiction section to reshelve them. Liss and Sherri were only a few steps behind her.

"How else was I supposed to establish his identity?" Dolores grumbled.

"How did he respond?" Sherri asked through clenched teeth.

Dolores preened a little. "He was astonished that I'd figured it out."

"He didn't try to deny it?" Astonishment pretty well described Liss's feelings, too.

"Oh, no. He just wanted to know *how* I'd tumbled to his real name. So I told him."

"You . . . told him you overheard a member of the local police department talking about the fact that Lowell Danby and Homer Crane were the same person?" Sherri looked a trifle shell-shocked.

"That's right. He didn't know who you were, but he said he'd met Liss." Dolores sent her a sour look. "If you'll recall, you went over there and introduced yourself to him last fall . . . at *my* suggestion."

"I've run into him a couple of times since then, too," Liss admitted. "At the post office. But, Dolores—he's not a writer. He's a crook. Maybe worse."

"At the very least," Sherri put in, "he's wanted on a probation violation."

"He's a *felon?*" Appalled, Dolores abandoned the remainder of her armload of books on a convenient shelf and trotted over to the nearest window that had a view of the funeral home. "Then why aren't you down there arresting him?"

"I'm working on it. In fact, I'm going down to the PD right now and check on a couple things, after which I'll talk to our suspect. In the meantime, will you two please stay away from him?"

"Naturally. I would never interfere in police business." Dolores's gaze remained glued to Danby's corner of the town square. She didn't even look away from the window when Liss and Sherri left the library.

A few minutes later, back at the PD, Liss read the description on the papers Sherri had produced from a desk drawer. At the same time, she listened to her friend's side of a phone conversation with Chase Forster. After Sherri hung up, Liss handed back Chase's warrant.

"Five-foot-ten. Balding. Blue eyes. All that's right,

but this left out his most distinctive feature, that ski-jump nose. How long was Danby in prison here in Maine?"

"Nearly ten years. He's not a nice man, Liss. I want you to go home and stay out of this. If he is Lowell Danby, and it's looking more and more like he is, then he's dangerous."

"You aren't going to talk to him alone, are you?" If Liss wasn't to take any chances, Sherri shouldn't put herself at risk either.

"No, I'm not. I've notified his probation officer and I've asked for backup from the sheriff's department. They'll probably send Pete. When he gets here, we'll go over to the funeral home. If Homer Crane is Lowell Danby, then we'll arrest him and he'll go back to jail. Once he's safely behind bars, we can pursue his connection to the Chadwick mansion and to Ned."

Liss returned to the Emporium as ordered, but she couldn't settle. She paced, stopping in front of her display window at regular intervals to watch for the arrival of reinforcements. Belatedly, it occurred to her that they'd come in the back way, so that Danby wouldn't see them.

That thought led to another. The Moosetookalook Police Department wasn't the only place that had a back entrance. Liss abruptly left her window for the phone on the sales counter and punched in the number for Angie's Books.

"Can you do me a favor?" she asked when Angie answered. "Can you keep watch on the funeral home garage from your side window and tell me if you see anyone leave?"

Over the open connection Liss heard Angie's footfalls as she carried her phone across the shop.

"Huh," Angie said after a moment. "The garage door is open. That's unusual."

"Is his car gone?"

"I can't tell."

Liss thanked her, hung up, and punched in another number, glad she'd had occasion to memorize it during the time the Halloween committee had been working on their plans. Ye Olde Hobbie Shoppe had an even better view of the north side of the funeral home.

Gloria sounded annoyed at the interruption, but dutifully went to her window and looked out. "The garage is empty," she reported, "which makes sense, since I saw Mr. Crane take off in that black Toyota of his about fifteen minutes ago. Anything else I can do for you, because I—"

Liss disconnected and hit the speed dial.

"Pete just got here," Sherri said, having obviously read the caller ID before she picked up. "I can't talk now." She disconnected before Liss could explain why she was calling.

On the bright side, Liss thought, with Danby already gone, Sherri and Pete were in no danger. If what Dolores had told him hadn't been enough to sound an alarm, Danby had then seen a uniformed police officer talking to her and to Ned's cousin. It wouldn't have been too difficult for him to put two and two together. Danby had to know that he could be arrested for failing to report to his probation officer. Even if they couldn't make any other charges stick, he'd go back to prison to serve out the rest of his original sentence behind bars. Was it any surprise that he'd flown the coop?

Liss caught up with Sherri and Pete inside the funeral home garage just in time to hear Sherri state

the obvious. "The back door is wide open," she told
Pete. "I'm going inside to look for him."

"If his car's not here," Pete objected, "it's likely
he's long gone, too."

Liss started to confirm that fact, then held her
tongue. She wasn't sure what the law on searching a
house was, but perhaps it would be better if Sherri
didn't know for certain that Lowell Danby was no
longer inside.

"Mr. Crane?" Sherri called in a loud voice. "This is
Officer Campbell from the Moosetookalook Police
Department. I need to speak with you. I'm coming in."

Liss drew in a startled breath when Sherri drew
her gun and Pete followed suit. When they entered
the house, Liss stayed where she was. She doubted either Sherri or Pete would shoot her by mistake, but
she had sense enough not to take any chances. That
they'd gone in armed brought home to her just how
dangerous they believed Lowell Danby to be.

From inside the house, Liss heard Sherri shout
again. "Mr. Crane? We mean you no harm. Come out
and we'll talk this over."

Liss waited a beat, took a few more steps toward
the still open back door, and stopped. Although she
caught herself shifting her weight from foot to foot
like a nervous teenager, she managed to resist temptation.

After ten long minutes, Sherri and Pete emerged,
guns holstered. Spotting Liss, Sherri looked resigned. "I suppose you want an update?"

"Danby wasn't there." Liss relayed what Gloria
had told her. "Did you find any evidence against him
in the house?"

"We couldn't search for it. We don't have a search
warrant. All we could do under the law is walk

through to make sure Mr. Crane wasn't there. Unfortunately, he didn't leave anything suspicious lying around in plain sight. Even if he had, we wouldn't have been able to seize it. All that would allow us to do is back off the moment we spotted it."

"But then you'd have had grounds to get a search warrant, right?"

"Right."

"And since you don't?"

"The best we can do for now is keep an eye on the place, in case Mr. Crane returns."

"Mr. Danby," Liss corrected her.

"Maybe. We don't even have proof of that."

"Couldn't you dust the house for fingerprints?"

Pete had come up to stand beside them after checking the perimeter of the building. "Do the words *invasion of privacy* mean anything to you, Liss?"

She stuck her tongue out at him. Having been on the receiving end of a search warrant, she wouldn't wish that experience on anyone who was innocent. But Lowell Danby was another kettle of fish.

"Maybe you can get a picture of Danby from the prison and show it to that pawn shop owner," she suggested. "Meanwhile, you can put out an APB on Homer Crane. He's definitely gone missing."

Sherri and Pete exchanged an exasperated look.

"Come *on*, guys. He's dangerous! You have to do something!"

"He is dangerous, if he's Danby. That's why I'm calling in the state police." Suiting action to words, Sherri moved away from Liss to talk on her cell phone to Gordon Tandy.

"Well, what did he say?" Liss demanded the minute Sherri disconnected.

"I brought him up to speed. Then there was a

long silence. I was braced for a brush off, but he surprised me."

"How so?" Liss asked.

"He's headed for Moosetookalook even as we speak. He wants to talk to a few people." Sherri fixed Liss with a steely look. "You're one of them. He gave me another message to deliver to you. Stay where he can find you."

Chapter Sixteen

Gordon Tandy arrived in Moosetookalook less than an hour later. His first stop was the PD, his second the library, his third the post office, and his fourth the Emporium. Liss had just closed up for the day, but was still on the porch, key in hand. He greeted her with a curt nod and shoved a fax at her. "Is this the guy?"

It was a more recent photograph than the one she'd found online and looked even more like the man she knew as Homer Crane, although he still had hair in this shot. The odd little dip at the end of his nose was clearly visible.

"That's him. The man who bought the old funeral home. I talked to him in bright sunlight in front of the post office, standing as close to him as you and I are now. I'm certain of the identification."

"So were Dolores Mayfield and Julie Simpson. Okay, then."

"That's a picture of Lowell Danby, isn't it?"

"It is." Tandy nodded toward the door she'd just

locked. "Shall we go back inside? I'd like to hear how you think things went down."

Over Gordon's shoulder, Liss saw Dan's truck pull into their driveway. "We'll have to talk at the house. You're welcome to stay to supper if you like." Without waiting for an answer, she descended from the porch and crossed the street, leaving Gordon to follow.

He wasn't happy about the change of venue, or about Dan's presence, but knew better than to argue. He and Dan discussed the University of Maine Black Bears' performance in the Hockey East Tournament—must-see mid-March TV for most of the men Liss knew—while she fed the cats and then quickly assembled an eye round roast, potatoes, carrots, and an onion in her old reliable black enamel pan and stuck it in a 350 degree oven to roast for an hour. That, she hoped, would be long enough for Gordon to finish grilling her.

Accompanied by Lumpkin, Glenora having already deserted her for Dan's lap, Liss rejoined the two men. She brought one of her lined yellow tablets with her and handed it over to the state police officer ensconced in her living room. It had come with her from the Emporium in her tote bag. The top five pages were filled with her scribbled notes on the case.

"I've listed events chronologically," she said, referring to the writing on the top sheet.

"*Lowell Danby in same prison as Blackie O'Hare,*" Gordon read aloud. "*Hears story of Blackie's buried treasure.*" He shot Liss a skeptical look.

"Keep going." She didn't blame him for having doubts, but her theory made sense to her. If it wasn't right on the money, it wasn't far off. She sat on the sofa next to Dan and Glenora and scooped Lumpkin up to hug. For once, the big Maine Coon cat didn't fight her show of affection. He seemed to sense that she needed the comfort of holding and stroking him.

"Danby later in prison in Maine with Ned Boyd," Gordon read. *"Learns Ned is from same town Blackie mentioned and pumps him for information."*

"Why else would Danby have come here?" Liss asked. "Changing his name, buying that house—all that took time and careful planning. What he didn't count on was Ned getting out of jail early."

"Ned sees 'Homer Crane' in Moosetookalook and recognizes him as Lowell Danby," Gordon read. *"Demands cash to keep quiet about what he knows."*

"The money had to come from somewhere," Liss reminded him. "You haven't found any other source, have you?"

Instead of answering, Gordon asked a question of his own. "How did Ned come to see Danby? He was keeping a pretty low profile of his own. We've only found one person who saw him here in Moosetookalook."

"Where?"

"Out near Hilary Snipes's trailer, and that was only a *possible* sighting. The point is, if Ned didn't want to be recognized, it would have been stupid of him to come into the center of town, even in a car. That being so, how did he run into Danby?"

"He must have seen him out at the Chadwick mansion. In fact, that makes even better sense." Liss had considered the possibility already and didn't lose any time expanding on it. "Maybe he caught Danby picking the lock to get in, or actually found him inside the place. Danby probably never figured

out that Ned was *living* there." She remembered again
what Boxer had said about the unlocked kitchen
door and once more thanked God that Ned's son
had not crossed paths with Lowell Danby when he
was out at the mansion all alone.

Gordon, however, didn't look convinced. He went
on to the next item on the list. *"Danby and Ned quarrel and Danby stabs Ned."* Gordon cocked a brow at
her. "Only one problem, Liss. We didn't find Lowell
Danby's fingerprints at the scene."

"He's a career criminal. Maybe he was smart
enough to wear gloves."

"Smart isn't usually part of his MO. He's spent
most of his adult life in jail."

"His conviction was overturned in Massachusetts."

"On a technicality. That doesn't mean he wasn't
guilty. And it doesn't mean he was clever, just that he
was lucky enough to have a good lawyer."

"Why are you being so stubborn about this? You
know he's a better suspect than Hilary is."

"No, I don't know that at all."

Liss found his tone condescending. Annoyed, she
clutched Lumpkin too tightly and got a kick in the
solar plexus for her trouble. As the big yellow cat
took off at full speed for parts unknown, Liss was left
trying to catch her breath. The moment she recovered enough to do more than sputter indignantly,
she fully intended to give Gordon a piece of her
mind, starting with the words *pigheaded* and *narrow-
minded,* but when she looked his way again, something in his posture had changed. She realized that
he'd just read the last entry in her chronology.

*"Danby doesn't try to hide the body because leaving Ned
as he fell feeds his obsession with blood and gore.* Where
did you get an idea like that?"

"From Julie Simpson. The postmaster. She saw the contents of one of the packages he got. It was full of pictures, and the top one was a ghastly image of dead bodies, with lots of blood showing. He invented some foolishness about being an illustrator for graphic novels. You know—comic books. But that never quite sounded right to me."

"You haven't seen many graphic novels lately, have you?" Gordon muttered under his breath. In a louder voice, he asked, "How much did you see when you found Ned's body?"

"More than I wanted to."

"Do you need to get into that?" Dan interrupted. Dislodging Glenora, he reached for Liss's hand and gave it a reassuring squeeze.

"It's okay." Liss squeezed back and kept hold of his hand even as her attention returned to Gordon. "That afternoon is kind of a blur."

Were there details she'd missed? Details she really did *not* want to know about? Liss swallowed hard.

"Can you take me through what you do remember one more time?" Gordon asked.

"Tandy," Dan warned in a low, threatening voice.

Liss let go of her husband to rub her temples with both hands. She closed her eyes.

"The only light in the parlor was the one I'd rigged up—that spooky greenish glow. It made everything look unreal which, since it was Halloween, was the whole idea. I saw what I thought was one of the manikins from the dining room scene lying on the sofa. I was ticked off that someone had been messing with my set pieces and upset because the skeleton that was supposed to be there was nowhere in sight. I noticed the wound in Ned's neck, although I didn't yet realize that it *was* Ned, or even a real body. There was more blood staining the cushions and a pool of blood on the floor. It looked fake."

Her stomach roiled at the memory. She cleared her throat.

"Anyway, I started to look around for Napoleon Bony-Parts—that's what we called the skeleton we'd borrowed—and I'd just spotted it behind the sofa when I realized . . . when I saw . . . when—"

"Yeah. *When*. Okay. Try not to think about it anymore."

"Easy for you to say!" She'd had nightmares for weeks after discovering Ned's body. She had the feeling that she was in for still more bad nights.

Dan glared at Gordon as he slid one arm around Liss's shoulders, tugging her closer to him, silently offering encouragement and support. She was glad of the warmth of his touch, but she had more she needed to say. She'd come to a few conclusions in the course of the hour or so she'd spent making notes.

"That murder scene was staged, Gordon. The bones moved. The body arranged. Maybe Hilary Snipes could have killed Ned in the heat of anger or in self-defense, but she'd either have stabbed him and run or she'd have tried to stop the bleeding. If she tried to save him, she'd have ended up with blood all over her. She'd have called for help. She'd have been in shock. Never in a million years would she have been able to arrange him on that sofa and then walk away."

"You may be right," Gordon said.

"I may?" Astonished that he'd admit it, Liss fell silent. Had she really convinced him Hilary was innocent?

"*May*," he repeated. "Neither of us is qualified to

judge what Hilary Snipes might or might not be capable of in a desperate situation. Leave that to the shrinks. But I've had time to skim Lowell Danby's record. There are no previous charges of murder against him, but . . . well, let's just say that when he robbed somebody, he liked to leave his victim with a wound of some sort. A slash on the arm. A stab in the leg. A bloody nose."

A spurt of blood from the neck?

"Why stab him with the fork?" Dan asked. "Why not the knife?"

"What?"

"Why not use the carving knife from your Death by Poison scene?"

"Because the knife was a fake with a retractable blade. But the fork . . . the fork was real. It came from our kitchen. Whoever stabbed Ned knew just where to aim so Ned wouldn't have a prayer of surviving. He knew what he was doing."

"Cold-blooded bastard." Dan looked as shaken as Liss felt.

"He set the scene," she repeated in a whisper. Dan's arm tightened around her when she shuddered. "If anyone saw the blood on his clothing, they'd just think it was a Halloween costume. Maybe he was even dressed up as a ghoul or a zombie. How easy that would have made things for him! Go home. Shower. Destroy the blood-stained clothing. Then all he had to do was wait for someone else to be blamed."

It had been on a Friday that Lowell Danby fled, minutes ahead of the local police. By the following Tuesday, there was still no sign of him. His house had been searched and the state police had found enough evidence—Gordon refused to tell Liss *what* evidence—to prompt the Attorney General's office to drop all charges against Hilary Snipes.

On Tuesday morning, Sherri called to tell Liss that another pawn shop owner had identified Danby's photograph.

"We already knew he was the one selling things from the mansion."

"There's a difference this time. Danby sold this object—an antique brass spittoon—*before* Ned got out of jail. It looks as if he may have been in and out of the mansion from the moment he moved to Moosetookalook."

"There must have been days when that house resembled Grand Central Station," Liss muttered, looking up as the bell over the Emporium's front door jangled. Any further comment she might have made went right out of her head when she saw who'd walked into her shop. "Uh, I've got to go, Sherri. Talk to you later."

"Hello, Liss," said Hilary Snipes.

"Hilary." Liss stayed where she was behind the sales counter.

Hilary shoved a lock of mousy brown hair out of her face as she gave the Emporium's contents the once over. In contrast to the other times Liss had spoken to her, Hilary's eyes were sharp. Her manner was different, too. She'd spent only three weeks in jail, but in that time something fundamental seemed to have changed. Warily, Liss waited for the other woman to speak.

"I've come for my kid," Hilary said when she'd finished a cursory survey of the shop.

"He's in school."

"I'll wait. Meanwhile I want to pack up his things. And get my TV back."

"It's in the stockroom." Liss gestured toward that door. "Boxer didn't want to leave it out at the trailer for fear someone might walk off with it."

Hilary's lips twitched. "Always knew he was smart."

"If you haven't got room in your car for the TV, it will fit in the back of mine." Liss half expected Hilary to refuse the offer of help, but apparently she'd done some thinking since their last encounter.

"Appreciate it," she said. "Teddy's been living up-stairs, right?"

"Yes. With his grandmother. Let me give her a call at the hotel."

"Afraid to let me into her place alone? I promise I won't walk off with the silverware. Nothing like a couple weeks in the slammer to convince a girl to go straight for the rest of her life."

"I'm not questioning your honesty, but I am call-ing Margaret. I know she'll want to talk to you before you take Boxer away."

"Teddy. His name is Teddy."

Liss made her call and then, with Margaret's per-mission, led Hilary upstairs and into the room her son had been using during Hilary's incarceration in the county jail. In a relatively short time, he'd made it his own, adding movie posters to the walls and scat-tering his personal possessions over every available surface. The bed was neatly made, but one aban-doned running shoe stuck out from beneath the spread and a denim jacket had been carelessly flung atop the pillow. It was nearly the middle of April, one of the hardest times of year to predict what the day's temperature would be. Liss imagined that Boxer, or rather Teddy, had gone off to school that morning in shirtsleeves. She hadn't bothered with a sweater or jacket herself.

"Your suitcase is in the closet," Liss said. "The pink one. Teddy used it to pack his things in when he first came to us here."

"All this isn't going to fit now," Hilary observed as she lifted the bright pink case off the closet shelf. Every hanger held clothing. Every inch of floor space was likewise filled with Boxer's possessions.

"He made a few trips back for more."

"Yeah, but she's also been buying him stuff. Margaret. Probably trying to make him love her more than he does me."

"*Teddy's grandmother* has been feeding him, giving him a roof over his head, and getting to know him. Would you rather have seen him go into foster care?"

Hilary ignored the question and started filling the suitcase with Boxer's clothes.

"Look, Hilary, I'm glad you've been exonerated and I'm sorry you were ever suspected in the first place, but none of what happened was Margaret Boyd's fault. She didn't know Ned had a son. He told her the boy wasn't his and she believed him . . . until she actually met Boxer. Teddy."

"Well, then she knew different, didn't she?" Hilary slammed a pair of jeans into the already overflowing suitcase and tried to close the lid. She had to sit on it to get it fastened and she'd barely made a dent in the contents of the bedroom.

"You know, there's no rush about this. You've got all day. Why don't I make a pot of coffee and—"

"Don't you have a store to mind?" Hilary had returned to the closet. Her muffled voice sounded no less rude.

"I left the stairwell doors open, bottom and top. I should be able to hear the bell if anyone comes into the shop."

Emerging with her arms full of clothing, Hilary regarded Liss through narrowed eyes. "Not a lot of walk-in traffic, huh?"

"Not so you'd notice, no."

"Why do you bother to open up at all, then? I hear you do pretty well with the website and your catalog."

"Tradition, I suppose. The business has been in the MacCrimmon family since my grandfather's time."

"Huh. Got any trash bags?"

"What? Why?"

"So I can pack these." She nodded toward the garments she'd temporarily dumped on the bed.

"Oh. Look, Hilary. Leave that, will you. We need to talk. Lowell Danby's still on the loose, you know. We don't know where he is. Are you sure you want to move back out to Owl Road where you don't have any neighbors nearby?"

"This Danby guy doesn't know me from Adam." But Hilary made no move to collect more of Boxer's belongings and when Liss once again suggested coffee went along quietly into Margaret's kitchen.

"We don't know *what* Lowell Danby knows," Liss said as she measured Margaret's favorite blend into the pot, "or what he's thinking."

Hilary eased onto one of the stools drawn up to the central island, her alert brown eyes once again darting here and there to take in every detail of her surroundings.

"We do know he's dangerous. I, for one, won't rest easy until he's safely under arrest."

"He's not going to bother me or Teddy," Hilary insisted. "The cop asked me about him. Told me he's an ex-con and that he's been living in the old funeral home and calling himself Homer Crane. Harmless-looking little guy, I always thought."

"You met him as Crane?" Liss paused in the act of adding water to stare at Boxer's mother.

"Everybody in town comes into the High Street Market, Liss. Even you. So, yeah. I know who he is. But he doesn't know me, or that I had anything to do with Ned."

"Of course he does. The local grapevine aside, the report of your arrest was on the evening news. He couldn't have missed it."

"Even so, why would he bother me?"

"Did Gordon Tandy tell you anything else about Danby before you were released?"

She shrugged. "Mostly, he just asked more questions. I told him what I've been telling the cops right along. I don't know where the money Ned deposited came from. I don't know who was out at the Chadwick mansion besides Ned and the members of your Halloween committee."

"And your nephews," Liss said, turning to face her again while the coffee dripped.

Hilary laughed. "That was before Ned got out of jail. I don't think they count."

"I suppose not. They weren't, apparently, searching for Blackie O'Hare's treasure. Danby apparently was. And Ned. So was your son."

"What are you talking about?"

While Liss filled two mugs with coffee and set out creamer and sugar, she ratted Boxer out to his mother. She felt bad about that, but not sufficiently guilty to keep the information to herself. Hilary fumed silently, falling on her coffee and downing half of it in one gulp.

"He's promised not to go back," Liss added, "but you know boys. Until someone actually does find buried loot, the temptation to hunt for it will always be there."

"He won't set foot in the place again. We're starting fresh, Teddy and me. I had a lot of time to think while I was locked up. I want better than I've had for me and my son."

She might have said more, but at that moment Margaret bustled into the kitchen. She left the back door open, letting the warm spring air follow her inside. She went straight up to Hilary and hugged her.

"My dear girl. I am so glad you're out of that awful place. Welcome home."

For a moment, Hilary didn't seem to know what to do with her arms. Then, slowly, she let them curl around Margaret and return the hug. "Thank you," she murmured. Her face was flushed when Margaret finally released her.

Sipping her coffee, Liss studied the two women as Hilary asked questions about Boxer and Margaret answered. Hilary, it appeared, had reevaluated her life during the three weeks she'd been away. That was why she seemed more willing to stand up for herself. But was that new attitude just with other women, or would she be able to hold her own against aggressive men, as well? Liss sincerely hoped Hilary's brother was in for a rude awakening.

"Oh, no," Hilary said in answer to one of Margaret's questions. "I didn't have any problem getting my job at the High Street Market back. They knew I didn't kill Ned."

Margaret winced. "I had a few doubts at first," she admitted, "but not after I got to know your son. No one who could raise such a fine young man could possibly be a cold-blooded killer."

"I—uh, thank you."

It was clear to Liss that Hilary had mixed feelings about the fact that Boxer had stayed with Margaret all this time. She was anxious to take him home with her, even if her home wasn't much compared to Margaret's place.

"I wish I could invite you to stay with me, too, Hilary," Margaret said, "but I only have the one guest room."

"I couldn't accept anyway." Pride stiffened her spine as Hilary hopped down off the kitchen stool.

Liss was reminded, suddenly, of her interview with Hilary at the county jail. The other woman had told her then that she'd never even applied for low-income benefits she was entitled to—like food stamps, Liss supposed. That had been before the epiphany Hilary claimed to have experienced, which led Liss to wonder exactly what "starting fresh" entailed.

Would she now accept a little help, perhaps from Margaret, in spite of her determination to move back into that ancient, drafty trailer? Or did starting fresh mean that she'd be willing to accept a *lot* of help. Could Hilary's real plan involve taking advantage of Margaret Boyd's guilt over neglecting her grandson for so many years? Margaret wasn't wealthy, but with her help, Hilary and Boxer could certainly improve their standard of living.

Overactive imagination, Liss chided herself. *Totally unfounded suspicions! Get a grip.*

Ashamed of herself, Liss resolved to keep an open mind. When Margaret suggested she close up the shop and all three of them spend the rest of the day moving Boxer's possessions back to the trailer, she readily agreed.

They spent the entire afternoon on the project, adding Boxer's willing hands to the mix when he got home from school. At five, Margaret made a pizza run, and the four of them collapsed in front of the reinstalled flat screen TV to watch the local news. The first story banished Liss's aching muscles and perked up her appetite. A relentlessly cheerful Channel 6 reporter announced that the state police were convinced that suspected murderer Lowell Danby had fled Maine for points south. The black Toyota, last seen pulling out of the mortuary's garage on Friday, had been sighted on Monday in Rhode Island.

Chapter Seventeen

The next day, Jason Graye phoned Liss at the Emporium late in the afternoon. "Good. You're there," he said without preamble.

"Where else would I be?"

He ignored her question. "You need to come out to the Chadwick mansion as soon as you close up shop for the day."

"Why?"

Over the line she heard a deep, annoyed-sounding sigh. "To clear out the leftover Halloween trash. I've just bought the place. I can't begin renovations until all this clutter is removed."

Typical, Liss thought. *Graye expects me to drop everything just because he's in a hurry.* "There can't be that much," she said aloud. "The police already returned everything I remember leaving there."

"They missed a few things. Come and get them." With that, he disconnected.

Liss held the phone away from her ear, staring at it for a moment before hanging up. She had no idea what he was talking about, but had to admit that she hadn't gone anywhere near the front parlor or the dining room the last time she'd been inside the mansion.

"The pulley," she murmured. That had to be what Graye had found. She knew that the light and sound equipment was no longer there and that the manikins and Napoleon Bony-Parts had been returned to their rightful owners.

Liss glanced at her watch. It stayed light much later, now that the "spring forward" date had passed. She could close at the usual time, pick up her three-step stepladder from the house, run out to the mansion, dismantle the rig that had been designed to make the skeleton rise up from the sofa, and still be back home before dark. If that hadn't been possible, she doubted she'd have gone. She wasn't superstitious. She didn't believe in ghosts, or in vampires, either. But neither did she ever again intend to spend any time inside the Chadwick mansion after sunset.

"Out and back," she said aloud—to give herself courage? "A piece of cake."

She thought about phoning Sherri and asking her friend to come along, but Sherri was once again working the two-to-ten shift. Her job didn't include babysitting nervous friends. Besides, it wasn't as if she'd be out there alone. Jason Graye was already at the mansion. Liss went back to work on the orders she'd been processing before the phone rang.

At five o'clock, she locked up and headed home to pick up the ladder. Ten minutes later, she pulled into the small parking area in back of the Chadwick mansion. Graye's caddy was already there. She called out his name as she walked through the unlocked kitchen door.

"In here!" came a muffled shout from the direction of the parlor.

Steeling herself, Liss headed down the hall, lugging the stepladder with her. She told herself it wouldn't be too bad. She was certain the police had taken away the stained sofa and carpet. But the possibility that Ned's blood had seeped through to stain the bare floorboards unnerved her.

When she pushed open the door from the hallway into the parlor and entered the room, she found it in semidarkness. The dim lighting didn't surprise her. The borrowed generator had long since been returned to its owner. The only illumination came from daylight seeping in through cracks in the plywood and from the single battery-powered lantern Graye had placed on top of the parlor organ. He was seated in the deep shadows near the fireplace. She could just make out the vague shapes of straight-back chair and man.

"You can take the boards off the windows now that you own the place," Liss said as she set the ladder down and dusted her hands on the sides of her blue jeans.

Her gaze shifted to the corner of the molding where the pulley had been attached. She had to squint to find what remained of it. The sturdy metal wheel dangled loosely. Whoever had tugged the skeleton free of its wire had almost succeeded in bringing it down, too.

Graye said nothing, but at a strangled grunt from his direction, Liss glanced his way again, puzzled by the odd sound. Only then did she realize there was something unnatural about the way the realtor was sitting. She fumbled for the small flashlight she'd tucked into her pocket. The beam illuminated Graye's bruised and bloody face just as a voice spoke from behind her.

"You'll end up looking a lot like that," a man whispered, "if you don't tell me what you've done with Blackie O'Hare's loot."

Liss froze, her gaze riveted to Jason Graye in disbelief. He was tied to the chair. A gag had been stuffed into his mouth. One eye had swollen nearly shut. The other was open wide with fear and was fixed on the person who had spoken.

Slowly, Liss turned to play her flashlight over the features of the man standing a few feet behind her. Homer Crane, aka Lowell Danby, held a gun in one hand. It was pointed directly at her.

She had to swallow hard before she could speak. "I don't know what you're talking about."

He was Homer Crane and yet he was not. The nose was the same, and the nearly bald head, but the milquetoast demeanor was absent. The thick glasses were missing, too. Obviously they'd been part of his disguise. The eyes they'd hidden looked as hard and cold as blue diamonds.

"Oh, I think you do. Hands in the air so I can see them and turn around." He gestured with the gun.

Liss obeyed, one fist clenched around her little flashlight. It was the only potential weapon she had, and she was desperate to keep hold of it.

Danby covered the distance between them in seconds. He shoved her up against the nearest wall to conduct a thorough but mercifully swift pat down. She bit back a protest when he gave her left breast a totally uncalled-for squeeze.

"Just checking. You'd be amazed where some

women hide stuff." He laughed as, having found nothing more deadly in his search, he wrenched the flashlight out of her hand.

That laugh should have been an evil cackle. Or the wild, unrestrained mirth of a madman. Instead, it sounded perfectly ordinary, as if they were two friends who'd just shared an amusing story.

"What do you want from me?" Liss asked, frowning when she couldn't control the tremor in her voice.

"I already told you." Danby grabbed her roughly by the arm and spun her around to face him. His gun was nowhere in sight, but he was stronger than she was. Liss gave no more than a fleeting thought to trying to fight him off and run.

He aimed a flashlight—her flashlight—at the fireplace. A section of the decorative mantel jutted out, revealing a deep, hollow space behind it.

It figures, Liss thought. *Underground passage. Panic room. Now a secret hidey-hole.*

"I didn't suspect you at first," Danby said. "But then I didn't know you were Ned Boyd's cousin until after he was dead."

He'd overheard Julie Simpson's comments at the post office, Liss remembered. Her heart contracted with fear when she recalled that Julie had also mentioned Boxer. Liss could only hope Danby didn't know that the boy had been the one who'd dug up the basement. The possibility that he might go after Ned's son next, if he got no satisfaction from Liss, turned her blood to ice.

"There was never anything there," she blurted. "That's the truth, whether you believe it or not. There was never any treasure at all."

Danby hauled her closer, so she could see all the

way inside the opening. The faint smell of a cedar lining wafted out at her. Caught way at the back was a strip of the distinctive brown paper banks used to wrap bundles of bills.

"Blackie O'Hare himself told me there was money hidden in his house in Moosetookalook," Danby said.

He must have known Blackie pretty well in prison, Liss thought, and suddenly wondered if Ned had been the first man Danby had stabbed to death.

"There really was a cache of cash?"

"As if you didn't know!"

"The only cash I know about was what I thought Ned got from blackmailing someone."

Even in the dim light, Liss recognized Danby's expression as one of chagrin.

"I'm telling you the truth. There were three payments of six thousand dollars each. That money's in the bank, where neither you nor I can get at it."

Danby swore. "There was at least two hundred thousand dollars in Blackie's stash."

"And the eighteen thousand? Oh, wait—did that come from you?"

He backhanded her. She landed hard on her backside, head spinning, cheek throbbing. He hauled her upright again before she could catch her breath. "Yeah, that came from me. Your cousin was no choir boy. He put the squeeze on me and I let him . . . for a while. He figured that I didn't want anyone finding out my real name."

"So you paid to keep him quiet," Liss whispered. "That was smart."

"For a while," Danby repeated. He held her at arm's length, his fingers biting into her shoulders.

Liss's mind had shifted into hyperdrive. It had to

have been Hilary who'd identified Crane for Ned.
She'd said he used to shop at the High Street Market. Liss could almost picture the scene. Ned was
hanging around, keeping out of sight in the back
room, waiting for Hilary to close up for the night.
Then Crane came in for a few last-minute purchases.
Ned recognized him as Danby and, being Ned, remembered his interest in the Chadwick mansion and
Blackie O'Hare when they were both in prison.
Maybe he overheard Hilary address Danby as Crane
or maybe he asked her about him later. Either way,
Ned figured out what Danby was up to. The threat to
report him to their mutual probation officer had
been enough to extort money from his fellow excon. Ned would have gotten an extra charge out of
the fact that, in the hunt for Blackie's treasure, *he* secretly had the edge, since he was the one actually living in the mansion.

"If you know all about the money I gave your
cousin," Danby said, "I'm betting you know a lot
more. In fact, I'm thinking the two of you were in
this treasure hunt together from the first. All that
haunted house nonsense was just a cover, a way to
keep me away from here until after Halloween. I
should have caught on when you came to my door
pretending you'd heard I was a horror writer. You
just wanted to get a look at me, didn't you?"

Liss debated too long over trying to explain Dolores Mayfield to Danby.

He gave her a shake. "Do you think I'm stupid? It
was all a plot to keep me away from this house while
your cousin kept searching the place."

Keep him talking, Liss thought, *until I figure out how
to get away from him.* "You're not stupid. You invested
a lot of time, money, and effort into setting up a new

identity so you could take a crack at finding that two hundred thousand in cash."

He grinned. "Not so much. Fake papers are easy."

Modesty? Or did he want her to coax him into boasting about his own cleverness. She was game. It was better than the alternative.

"But you had to buy the old mortuary. That couldn't have been cheap."

"Didn't cost me a penny. I heard what happened to the former owner. Checked to find out where the wife went. She's long gone, so I just picked the lock and moved in."

Well, that explained why he hadn't bought the Chadwick mansion, instead. His pockets hadn't been deep enough. Liss tried to think of what else to say. It probably would not be wise to let on that she knew he'd broken into this house even before Ned got out of jail, or that he'd been helping himself to some of the more portable antiques. She wondered if that was where the money he'd given Ned had come from, but she didn't ask him that, either.

"What was in the U-Haul?"

He laughed. "Stuff I left in a storage locker under another name. Why?"

"You remember the librarian?"

He grimaced.

"She thought you unloaded office equipment. That's where she got the crazy idea you were a writer."

"Stupid cow."

"Let me guess—you packed your stuff in boxes from Staples or Office Max?"

"God, I hate small towns!" He peered more closely into Liss's face as if he couldn't quite figure her out. "You know I killed your cousin, right?"

Liss felt herself blanch.

"That's right. Me. Not his girlfriend. Good riddance to bad rubbish. He kept demanding more and more until I got sick of playing games and put a permanent stop to it."

Liss felt sick. No matter what Ned had done in his life, she could not be casual about his murder. Lowell Danby had killed her cousin. In cold blood. In this room. And unless a miracle happened, he was probably going to kill her, too.

Keep him talking, she told herself. "Ned always was too cocky for his own good."

"He was playing gracious host in the Chadwick mansion," Danby said with a sneer. "He tossed that skeleton over the back of the sofa so he could stretch out. Acted like he owned the place."

That was how the wires on the pulley had broken, Liss realized. She'd been wrong in her reconstruction of the scene, but with this new information she could picture her cousin as Danby described him, lounging there, so self-confident, so certain he was in control.

"I pretended to agree to another blackmail payment. Then I went away. Only I didn't leave. I just slipped into the dining room, grabbed that fork, and came back."

For a moment, the room swam before Liss's eyes. Her stomach lurched. There were times when she wished she didn't have such a vivid imagination. It was all too easy for her to envision Ned's last moments.

Jason Graye, still bound and gagged and tied to the chair, moaned in pain.

Danby's grip on Liss's arm tightened. "That guy's going the same way!" he hissed.

"What did he do?" Liss whispered.

"Nothing. That's just it. I thought he'd found it. Blackie's loot. Figured I'd persuade him to confess, but he didn't know anything to begin with. He never even got inside the house." Danby seemed to think this was a serious character flaw. "Tried to break in and couldn't do it. The only thing he accomplished was to get the cops checking the place out the next day. Damned nuisance!"

Danby eyed Liss up and down. "It'll go easier on you if you just tell me what I want to know."

She didn't buy that for a second. She knew with painful certainty that he meant to use her as a punching bag and kill her afterward, no matter what she said.

"I can't tell you what you want to hear." Liss hated it that her voice was so unsteady. "I can only tell you the truth. I don't know what happened to Blackie O'Hare's money. Did you ever consider that it could have been found years ago?"

"I don't believe it. He told me he hid his loot here."

"But the house has been searched countless times, starting back when Blackie was arrested. Maybe those police officers from Massachusetts found the mother lode and kept it for themselves."

Danby gave her another shake, this one so violent that it rattled her bones. "It was here. It was right *there*." He gestured toward the open panel. "You found it. Now you're going to tell me what you did with it."

Liss's voice rose to a shriek. "I—don't know where the—money is." She was sure Danby had already left bruises on her upper arms, but that would be nothing compared to what he might do to her next.

"M-Maybe we can figure out where it is!" She was so scared she was stammering. "Are y-you sure B-Blackie had only *one* hidey-hole?"

Danby kept shaking her, until she was certain she had whiplash.

"Have you checked the hidden room?" she blurted out.

The shaking abruptly stopped. "What hidden room?"

"Upstairs. Where Ned was hiding out while he lived here."

"He was *living* here?" Dumbstruck, Danby went very still. After a moment, he asked, "How did he find out about this hidden room?"

"He spent a lot of time here when he was a kid. Abandoned house. Rumors of buried treasure. He . . . broke in and explored."

She almost told him about the secret entrance, too, but caught herself in the nick of time. She might need to use the tunnel to escape, assuming she could get away from Danby in the first place. She hoped it hadn't been boarded up again.

"Hidden room," Danby repeated.

"I can show you where it is." If she could lure Danby upstairs, give him a shove, close the closet door on him . . .

"If you know where Ned Boyd was hiding, that proves you were in cahoots with him. Who else would that little shit trust but a relative?" Danby chuckled, another oh-so-ordinary sound that was scarier in its own way than the cry of a banshee. "It was a real rush to stab that son of a bitch. It'd been a long time since I had the pleasure of watching someone's lifeblood drain away."

The dim lighting in the parlor cast a demonic

glow over Danby's face. Another involuntary shudder wracked Liss's body. Seeing her fear, his smile grew wider. He wanted her to be terrified and he was doing a good job of getting her there.

There is something seriously wrong with this man.

Gordon had told her Danby liked to spill his opponents' blood. Julie had described the disturbing photographs he'd received in the mail. Liss knew with a cold certainty that if she didn't think of something fast, he was going to derive a great deal of sick pleasure adding two more murder victims to his tally.

"Did you kill Blackie O'Hare?" She hadn't meant to ask that question. It just burst out of her. Like Ned, Blackie had been stabbed.

Danby's smile broadened into a full-fledged grin that showed off a great many yellowed teeth. "I wish I had. But I did enjoy watching him die in the prison exercise yard. Funny thing," he added, sounding almost nostalgic. "I'd forgotten all about old Blackie until I ran into Ned Boyd. It was hearing where he was from that made me remember. It's a name that sticks with you—*Moosetookalook*. Just rolls off the tongue!"

We really *need to consider renaming this town,* Liss thought, and vowed to bring up the subject with the selectmen the first chance she got . . . if she lived that long.

Focus! Keep him talking!

"It was a mistake to kill Ned," she said. "You lost access to the mansion, what with the police likely to pop up at any moment. And you lost the one person who might have found Blackie's treasure, assuming it ever existed."

Danby glowered at her.

Keep him talking!

Liss didn't expect anyone to come riding to her rescue. No one knew where she was. But if she had enough time, surely she'd think of a way out of this mess. Her get-him-upstairs-and-shut-him-in-the-hidden-room plan didn't seem to be working. He showed no inclination to leave the parlor.

"The delay must have been very frustrating." She tried to sound sympathetic.

He responded by twisting her arm until she cried out in pain. He let her go then, leaving her to clutch the injured appendage to her chest and whimper. He liked seeing her cowed and rewarded her by answering her question.

"I had time. Or so I thought." He glared at Jason Graye, who appeared to have lapsed into unconsciousness. "Then this bozo came tromping in. I heard him talking on his cell phone about tearing the place down and putting up condos."

Without warning, he crossed to Graye's chair and gave the realtor's bound legs a vicious kick. Man and chair toppled to the floor. Liss flattened herself against the wall by the fireplace.

For just a few seconds, while their tormentor was distracted, she had an opportunity to scan the rest of the room. Her frantic gaze searched, found, and she quickly figured the odds.

Then Danby's lethal attention returned to her. He retrieved his gun from where he'd tucked it into his belt at the small of his back. His eyes narrowed as he paced toward her.

Liss swallowed convulsively. Her hands automatically shot up above her head, visibly shaking.

"I had to stay away from the mansion for a while," Danby said, "but you didn't. And when I started searching again after the police were done, there'd been holes dug down in the cellar."

Liss pressed her lips tightly together. Let him go ahead and think she'd been the one to dig in the basement. Danby had never caught a glimpse of Boxer. She prayed it wouldn't cross his mind that the twelve-year-old had been paying regular visits to the mansion.

"What possessed you to report finding that skeleton?" he demanded. "That was stupid. Real stupid . . . unless you'd already found the cash and were trying to throw up a smoke screen." He took a threatening step closer. "I'm only going to ask you nicely one more time. What did you do with the money?"

The truth hadn't done her any good so far. There was no point in outright denial. Liss glanced at the still open panel by the fireplace. She couldn't prove a negative, but maybe she could still stall.

"I . . . I didn't find money," she lied, going with the first idea that popped into her panic-stricken brain. "I mean, I did, but only the one stack of bills." There, that accounted for the paper strip in the hidey-hole! "What Blackie O'Hare hid in there was a fortune in uncut gems."

A look of disbelief crossed Danby's face. Liss lowered her arms, squared her shoulders, and shot defiance back at him. It took every ounce of her theatrical training not to let him see the sheer panic she was really feeling.

"Where are they?"

"I gave them to the police."

"I don't think so."

"Call the local PD and ask Officer Campbell. I've got her on speed dial if you want to use my cell." She reached for the side pocket of her jeans, where he'd felt the tiny phone during his pat down, but had not relieved her of it.

"Keep both hands where I can see them and turn around."

Again? Didn't we just do this? Warily, she obeyed, resting her palms against the wall. A moment later, she felt his hand insinuate itself into her pocket and close over the phone.

"Just press two. When she answers, hold the phone so I can speak into it. If I ask her about the gems, she'll give me an update on who has them now."

And Sherri would also catch on to the fact that Liss was in trouble. How much trouble was going to depend on how fast Sherri could figure out where her friend was calling from.

"Stay where you are," Danby ordered.

Liss heard him move closer to the window, probably trying for more bars. She risked a glance over her shoulder. Concentrating on the unfamiliar phone with its tiny keypad—he'd been in prison for the last ten years and missed a lot of developments in technology—Danby was no longer paying any attention to her.

Taking a deep breath to steady her nerves, Liss tensed the muscles in her legs, turned, and leaped, reaching for the pulley mechanism overhead. Her arm was on fire, but she caught the wheel in one hand, wrenching it the rest of the way free. Her follow through sent the heavy chunk of metal spinning toward the spot by the window where Danby stood.

The blow landed with considerable force against the back of his unprotected, nearly bald head. The gun flew from his right hand, the phone from his left. Both landed on the floor and skittered away. Danby dropped to his knees with a bellow of pain.

The words *Moosetookalook Police Department* floated through the air. They were barely audible, the phone having ended up under a chair, but they were loud enough for Liss to recognize Sherri's voice.

"Help!" she screamed. "Sherri! Come to the mansion!"

Danby flung himself at her. Strong, work-roughened hands closed around her throat. She hadn't managed to knock him unconscious. She'd only stunned him. And she'd made him mad.

They fell together to the floor, but he was stronger. One roll and he was on top, still trying to throttle her. Liss managed to get one arm between them and shove at his chest, momentarily pushing him far enough away to allow her to take in a precious gulp of air, but she didn't have the strength to repeat the maneuver.

Dark spots appeared before her eyes. The only sound she could manage was a gurgle. Blackness closed in fast when he began to bang her head against the hardwood floor.

The last thing she heard was a crash.

Chapter Eighteen

"**I**s she alive?"

"I think so."

Through the throbbing in her head, Liss struggled to think clearly. She began to cough, which made the pain worse. She had the terrible feeling she was about to throw up, but forced herself to open her eyes, anyway.

"What happened?" she asked.

Or, rather, that's what she tried to ask. Only a raspy croak emerged from her very sore throat. She brought one hand up to her neck and winced when she touched bruised and abraded skin.

She winced a second time at a loud noise, only belatedly identifying it as the sound of a rapidly approaching police car with its siren blaring.

"Liss? Are you okay?" The anxious voice belonged to Boxer Snipes.

She managed to nod. Mercifully, her stomach had settled enough to risk moving her head that much. She was afraid to risk doing more, but by shifting her gaze a little to the right, she recognized the other person bending over her as Jason Graye. He was a horrific sight. One look at his swollen lip and eye and broken and bloody nose shocked her into full consciousness.

Everything that had happened since her arrival at the Chadwick mansion to meet Graye came back to her in a rush. *Hey*, she thought, still in a dazed state that resembled the moments between waking up and her first cup of coffee, *that's good. If I didn't lose the last few minutes before I passed out, then I probably don't have a concussion.* She felt ridiculously grateful for small favors.

But what, exactly, had happened while she was unconscious?

Had Lowell Danby left her for dead?

How had Graye gotten loose?

And where had Boxer come from?

She couldn't voice a single one of those questions. Her throat was too raw. She sat on the floor, listening as the front door slammed open and someone shouted her name.

"We're in here!" Boxer yelled.

Sherri came through the door with her gun drawn. She lowered it as soon as she took in the scene, but didn't holster it. She glanced toward the three people huddled by the window, then headed to the opposite corner of the room.

For the first time, Liss realized there was another person in the parlor, someone who was gagged and hogtied in Jason Graye's place. Above the handkerchief stuffed in his mouth, Lowell Danby's beady blue eyes promised retribution if he ever had the power to deliver it.

After satisfying herself that the prisoner was securely bound, Sherri engaged in a low-voiced exchange over the police radio. Once she'd made sure reinforcements were en route, she returned to the survivors. She gave Graye's injuries a quick once over and then squatted down to study the rapidly rising bruises on Liss's face and throat.

"She might have a concussion," Boxer said. "He was banging her head on the floor."

"The EMTs are on their way," Sherri promised. "They'll take care of her. Someone want to tell me what the hell just happened here?"

"The boy saved our lives," Graye said, lisping a little through his split and swollen lip. "I couldn't see much, but I could hear everything. Go on. Tell her what you did."

"It wasn't all that much." Boxer's face turned a mottled shade of pink.

Liss fumbled for his hand and squeezed it. Poor Boxer—he'd inherited the MacCrimmon blush.

"I'd like to hear details," Sherri said. "And while you're at it, you can tell me what you were doing out here in the first place."

Pink flashed to red as Boxer automatically went on the defensive. "I didn't do nothing wrong."

"Yeah. Yeah. It was some other kid who looked just like you."

Liss swallowed painfully and jumped into the fray. "Danby was choking me. I blacked out."

"Liss—don't talk," Sherri ordered. "Boxer—spill it."

"I thought he'd killed her. I came in and saw him choking her and hitting her head on the floor and then she just went limp. I was scared she was dead." The words came out in a rush, the threat of tears beneath the words. Boxer had to clear his throat before he could continue and even then there was a hitch in his voice. "Then I spotted the gun. It was just lying there, next to the parlor organ."

Danby had dropped it, Liss remembered, when she hit him with the pulley.

"And?" Sherri prompted.

"And he fired a warning shot," Jason Graye cut in, unable to keep quiet any longer even though speaking made him wince in pain. "Scared the hell out of me," he added in a mumble.

"Me, too," Sherri muttered, reminding Liss that Sherri had been on the other end of an open phone connection at the time. "Boxer? I want to hear this from you."

In the distance, Liss heard more sirens. The ambulance. More police. She squeezed Boxer's hand a second time, silently encouraging him to finish the story before they arrived.

"The gun went off. He let go of Liss. The bullet went through the window." Boxer pointed.

Belatedly, Liss noticed a neat round hole in the glass and the plywood beyond. Had that been the crash she'd heard? She supposed it must have been.

"He was really mad," Boxer continued, "but I held the gun just like I've seen cops on TV do, with both hands real steady. I told him to go untie Mr. Graye, and he did."

He'd probably figured he could jump Boxer and take the gun away, Liss thought.

The kid had street smarts. He knew not to let Danby get close enough to make a move.

"Then I used the same ropes to tie *him* up," Jason Graye said with enough relish to temporarily overcome his injuries. "And I did a very good job of it, too. We were just checking on your condition, Liss, when Sherri showed up."

There was no time for more discussion after that. The cavalry had arrived to take Lowell Danby into custody and tend to the wounded.

Although she objected strenuously, Liss was kept overnight at the hospital in Fallstown for observation. The next morning, she was given a clean bill of health and released.

It took a little longer than that before she could speak normally again, and without pain, so she gave herself a few days of quiet contemplation before she asked her young cousin to stop in at Moosetook-alook Scottish Emporium after school. By then it was Tuesday. Almost a week had passed since her ordeal at the mansion.

"I'll drive you home after I close up," she told him when he arrived, "but I wanted a chance to thank you for saving my life. And to talk."

Naturally, since it was not a busy time of day or, for that matter, a busy time of year, a customer came in. Boxer retreated to the cozy corner with his homework until Liss was free. If he was nervous about answering the questions she had for him, he didn't show it.

Once she'd rung up the sale, she joined him there. He ignored her until she spoke to him.

"I was lucky you were there that day," Liss said.

He shrugged.

"Don't misunderstand. I'm grateful. But—"

"I followed you. Okay?"

"Want to tell me why?"

"I was hanging around town, waiting for Mom to get off work and I thought I'd see if Grandma Margaret was home. She wasn't, but I could see your drive-way from her place and you were loading that step-ladder into your car. When you drove off, I was pretty sure you were going out to the mansion and I had time to kill, so I thought I'd go see if I was right. It took me a while to get there, seeing as how I had to hoof it."

"Were you afraid I'd find evidence that you'd been in there again?"

Once again, his answer was a shrug.

How much, Liss wondered, *do I really want to know?*

"I'm glad you didn't just come rushing in. Danby might have caught you, too."

Killed you, too, she added silently.

Boxer snorted. "I saw the caddy parked in the dooryard. I knew you weren't alone. But I was curious, so I peeked in through a window where there's a crack in the plywood, and I saw what was going on."

She leaned toward him across the coffee table, trying to catch his eye, but he avoided meeting her gaze. "You should have gone for the police."

"If I had, you wouldn't have made it out of the mansion alive."

It was hard to argue with that logic. And impossible for Liss to demand an answer to the one question that remained—the nature of the secret she felt sure he was still keeping from her. He'd taken an awful risk for her sake, but he'd saved her life and Jason Graye's, too. His quick thinking and bold action meant that a sadistic killer would spend the rest of his natural life in prison where he belonged.

A quarter of an hour later, keeping her promise to take Boxer home, Liss turned off Owl Road into Hilary Snipes's driveway. She put the car in park. Then she just stared. The decrepit old trailer was gone. In its place was a brand new double-wide fancy enough to be called a modular home.

"Nice," Liss murmured.

"We think so." Boxer grinned at her, unrepentant, and slid out of the car. With a wave, he disappeared inside.

Liss was shaking her head as she drove away. When the Moosetookalook grapevine got wind of this, everyone would be speculating about where Hilary had gotten the money to upgrade. Aunt Margaret might have given Hilary and Boxer everything that had been in Ned's bank account. She certainly hadn't wanted it for herself. But the purchase price must have been much more than that . . . just about what was supposed to be in the cache of cash allegedly stashed in a certain hidey-hole next to the fireplace in the parlor of the Chadwick mansion.

It didn't really matter where the money had come from, Liss decided. After all they had been through, Boxer and his mother deserved a break.

She smiled to herself all the rest of the way home. Discovering the origin of their windfall was one mystery she was happy to leave unsolved.

Keep reading for an exciting sneak peek at
Ho Ho Homicide,
the next Liss MacCrimmon Scottish Mystery,
available November 2014!

Business is booming at the Scottish Emporium in Moose-
tookalook, Maine, and Liss MacCrimmon Ruskin couldn't
be happier—or busier. A romantic getaway at a rustic
Christmas tree farm is just what she needs. But the prop-
erty's mysterious past has her feeling less than merry . . .

Liss is surprised when an old friend from high school
asks her to spend a week at the Christmas tree farm
she recently inherited from a great-uncle. Realizing
it would be the perfect chance for her and her husband Dan to get away from work, Liss happily ac-
cepts the offer and packs her bags for the tiny town
of New Boston.

Upon their arrival, Liss and Dan are greeted by a
ramshackle farmhouse and unfriendly townsfolk. It's
hardly the idyllic vacation locale they'd hoped for, especially when needling neighbors start raising questions about the farm's dark history. Who was the man
whose body was found neatly netted in a shipment of
Scotch pine? Why did the owner vanish into thin air?
And why are the trees growing so close together,
forming a maze more twisted than a Celtic knot?

The rumors pile up faster than snowdrifts in a bliz-
zard, and as Liss starts unwrapping the truth, she
discovers something even more scandalous than murder hiding beneath the town's humdrum façade.
When a series of "accidents" strikes the farm, she'll
have to spring into action faster than a Highland
Fling to find the killer who's been lurking among the
pines—before she ends up in a pine box herself . . .

Chapter One

Liss MacCrimmon Ruskin emerged from the back room of Moosetookalook Scottish Emporium, where she'd been packing orders for shipment. A professional smile lit her face and the words "Good morning. How may I help you?" were on the tip of her tongue. They never made it out of her mouth.

"Gina?"

The last person Liss expected to see at ten o'clock on a Wednesday morning in early November was her BFF from high school, Gina Snowe. They'd long since drifted apart. Gina hadn't even come to Liss's wedding. In the nearly five and a half years since, their only regular contact had been an occasional Christmas card.

"The one and only," Gina said.

She was a walking advertisement for the successful, high profile businesswoman—power suit in a muted shade of red, perfectly manicured fingernails, exquisitely applied makeup, and light but expensive perfume. Liss didn't need to look down at Gina's feet to know she was wearing a designer brand of shoes with heels high enough to cause any ordinary woman to break an ankle. Not only could Gina walk in them, she thought they were comfortable!

In jeans and a loose pullover sweater, Liss felt decidedly underdressed.

They engaged in a brief hug. The gesture felt awkward, but it was a better alternative than air kissing. Liss retreated behind the sales counter as soon as Gina released her.

"This is a surprise."

"A good one, I hope. This place looks exactly as I remember it," Gina added as her gaze swept over the shop.

The shelves and tables were filled with Scottish-themed gift items, many of them imported from Scotland. Racks held ready-made kilts and tartan skirts. The walls were hung with colorful plaids and framed prints of heather-covered hills and rugged Highland peaks.

"It even smells the same."

"Lemon-scented furniture polish." Liss shoved a stray strand of dark brown hair behind her ear. "As the saying goes, if it ain't broke, don't fix it."

When Gina gave a toss of her head and laughed, Liss couldn't help but notice that her expertly styled black locks fell effortlessly back into place, not a single strand awry. Betsy Twining at the Clip and Curl, located in the back half of the building that housed the post office, couldn't have achieved such perfection if she'd had a month of Sundays in which to practice.

Liss eased herself onto the high wooden stool behind the sales counter and rested her elbows on its smooth, glossy surface. "What's up, Gina?"

"Up? Why should you think anything is *up*?"

"Oh, I don't know." Gina's "Little Miss Innocence" act didn't fool Liss for a second. The look in Gina's almond-shaped eyes was calculating rather than naïve. "Maybe because you're a hotshot lawyer in Chicago and I run what you'd probably call a mom-and-pop tourist trap in rural Maine? You didn't drop by to buy kilt hose or a thistle pin."

"We were good buddies once. Maybe I want to catch up with an old friend." Gina feigned interest in the small revolving display case on one end of the counter. It held an assortment of thistle jewelry, not only pins but also earrings, necklaces, and charms.

"That was half a lifetime ago," Liss reminded her. And even at seventeen, the two of them had never had a great deal in common. Just one thing, really. They'd each been deeply involved in extra-curricular activities that nobody else in their high school understood or appreciated.

Back in the day, Gina had claimed they broadened each other's horizons. While Liss had spent all her spare time at Scottish festivals entering, and usually winning, dance competitions, Gina had been on the beauty pageant circuit. She'd earned enough scholarship money to put herself through college and law school.

Gina batted the display case, setting it whirling. "Okay. Okay. I have an agenda. So, sue me!"

"I'm listening." With one hand, Liss stopped the spin, but she didn't take her eyes off Gina's face.

"I need a favor." The admission didn't sit well. Gina snapped out her next words, impatient and out of sorts. "Get something to write on. Knowing you, you'll want to take notes."

Liss's clipboard was on the open shelf beneath the sales counter. Without comment, she extracted it and fished a felt tip pen out of the cracked mug she used to hold pens, pencils, and markers. Holding it poised, she waited, curious to learn what had happened to shake the cool-as-a-cucumber composure of Ms. Gina Snowe.

"I'm here," Gina said, "to offer you and Dan an all-expenses-paid week's vacation in an idyllic location."

At the word vacation, Liss felt her interest quicken. She doodled a palm tree on the yellow, college-ruled page. "Define idyllic."

"Exactly your thing—rural, remote, and quiet."

Liss waved a hand toward the scene beyond the Emporium's display window. "Take a look outside. Moosetookalook already offers me all that and more." The village had a population of just over a thousand and was located in the scenic Western Maine mountains. It was close, but not *too* close, to several major ski areas.

Gina didn't bother to turn around. Instead she leaned in. "Here's the thing, Liss. I came to Maine to inspect a Christmas tree farm I inherited from a great uncle. The original plan was to stop by your place for a visit, maybe even try to persuade you and Dan to join me for a few days."

"Uh-huh." Liss took the part about the invitation with a grain of salt. It hadn't escaped her notice that the other woman hadn't once asked after Dan. For all Gina knew, Liss and Dan could have separated months ago. Or be encumbered by small children. Or have one on the way.

Still, the words "Christmas tree farm" struck a chord. Liss cherished fond memories of the annual pilgrimage to find the perfect Christmas tree. When she was a girl, she and her parents had tromped all over a local farmer's fields. When they finally agreed on one, her father had always let her help cut it down with a hand saw. Beside her first doodle, Liss drew a tiny Christmas tree.

"I no sooner arrived," Gina went on, "intending to stay for two weeks, than I was called back to Chicago. I'm needed there to handle a major criminal case. I don't know when I'm going to be able to return to Maine."

Gina's plight didn't spark Liss's sympathy, not when Gina was highly paid to be at her clients' beck and call. "I'm not sure I understand the problem. Reschedule your stay."

"One issue to do with the property is time-sensitive."

"Meaning?"

"It's a *Christmas* tree farm. I need to know if there's any chance to make money off the place this year. If you and Dan will spend a little time there in my stead—just a week—you can evaluate its potential for me."

"We don't know anything about trees." Liss's protest was automatic, but she had to admit that her curiosity was piqued.

"You know how to make a success of a small business."

"Sure—work ten-hour days, seven days a week. I don't have time to—"

Gina cut her off. "Some of the Christmas trees are Scotch pines. You can bring back as many boughs as you like to decorate the Emporium for the holidays."

"That's your best argument? You're slipping, counselor. And isn't Scotch pine the variety that stinks to high heaven?"

"You're thinking of white spruce," Gina shot back,

"and the branches only smell bad if you crush the needles."

"Been reading up on the subject, have you?" Quietly amused, Liss couldn't resist a bit more "needling."

"Come on, Liss—be a sport and help out an old pal."

With a sigh, Liss abandoned the clipboard, hopped off her stool, and headed for the stock room, leaving Gina to follow. "I wasn't kidding about the ten-hour days, Gina. The Emporium, especially the online and mail-order side of the business, keeps me plenty busy and Dan—"

Gina caught her arm. "I'll make it worth your while. I'll pay you for your time *and* pay the salary of someone to keep this place open while you're gone. Seems to me," she added as Liss turned to face her, "that if you two are working as hard as you say, you *need* a vacation."

"Gina, I can't take money for—"

"Call it a birthday present, then."

Liss winced. She'd celebrated her thirty-fourth a few weeks earlier. By her thirty-fifth, she had a pretty big decision to make, one she'd been brooding about lately.

As if she sensed Liss was wavering, Gina abruptly changed tactics. "Think of the romantic possibilities," she argued, drawing Liss back into the main room of the shop. "You and Dan all alone—no interruptions by family or friends. Face it, Liss. You live in a fishbowl here."

When she'd hauled Liss to the front window, Gina came to a stop. A passing neighbor—Stu Burroughs from Stu's Ski Shop on his way to the post office to pick up his mail—peered in at them and waved.

"Everybody in Moosetookalook knows everybody else's business. Wouldn't it be nice to get away for a bit to a place where *nobody* knows your name?"

There *were* some things she and Dan needed to talk about, Liss thought. And there was no question but that they could do with a short vacation. From one heartbeat to the next, she came to a decision. "What do you want us to do?"

Liss retrieved her clipboard from the counter and scribbled down details as fast as Gina could rattle them off. As she wrote, her mind worked even more furiously. An hour later, Gina was on her way to the airport and Liss had committed herself . . . and Dan . . . to spending a week on a Christmas tree farm.

Now all she had to do was convince her overworked husband that he needed a vacation.

Liss stood in the doorway of what had once been an old carriage house. She told herself she was planning her strategy, but the honest truth was that she was taking advantage of an opportunity to admire the man she'd married.

Dan Ruskin was not movie-star handsome, nor was he athlete muscular. But he had a certain strength, both of character and in his person. That was what had drawn Liss to him even before they fell in love. He was, in the simplest terms, a nice guy.

That was not to say that they always agreed. Or that he was never irritated with her. But he accepted her as she was. He didn't try to change her. And when she was a bit too impulsive and committed them to something without running it by him first, he usually went along with it.

Usually.

Dan had begun using the carriage house as a woodworking shop as soon as he bought the house behind which it was situated. When his custom woodwork started to sell well, he'd built onto the back, doubling the size of his work space. The long, narrow room contained nearly a dozen large pieces of equipment—saws, sanders, and who-knew-what-all. An elaborate filtration system kept down the amount of sawdust in the air and dissipated the fumes from varnish and other smelly substances. A propane-fueled heater warmed the place in winter.

Dan worked at the far end of the shop, securing Styrofoam corners onto one of his custom-made jigsaw-puzzle tables with stretch wrap and strapping tape. When a lock of sandy brown hair fell over his eyes as he worked, he absent-mindedly shoved it out of his way. Liss supposed she'd have to remind him to get a haircut. Dan never bothered with to-do lists of his own.

She must have made some small sound. She had no idea how he could hear it with stereo speakers blaring, but he glanced up, smiled when he saw her, reached over to flick a switch, and cut off Gordon Lightfoot just as the gales of November slashed the doomed freighter *Edmund Fitzgerald.* Sometimes Dan listened to folk music, sometimes hard rock, and some-times classical, but he never worked to the sound of skirling bagpipes. That was the one passion he and Liss did not share.

"Sorry to interrupt," Liss apologized when silence had descended.

"I'm almost finished for the day. All I have left to do is get this box ready for UPS to pick up in the morning."

Liss threaded her way through the shop until she was near enough to see his muscles flex beneath his sweatshirt as he wrestled the heavy wooden table and its equally well-wrapped detached legs into a reinforced cardboard carton for the trip to California or Florida or New Jersey. He'd dispatched jigsaw-puzzle tables to almost every state in the country and only the prohibitive cost of international shipping had discouraged potential buyers from as far away as England and Australia.

"I had a surprise visitor today," Liss began, plunging into a full confession of what she'd agreed to do.

She'd barely finished before Dan shook his head. "I can't take a week off. I've got six more orders waiting to be filled."

"You *always* have orders waiting to be filled. You made more than fifty jigsaw-puzzle tables last year."

Dan didn't look up from sealing the carton.

"You *know* you need a break. That's why you raised your prices six months ago. You were hoping that would result in fewer orders." The plan had backfired. Even *more* people had pre-ordered custom-made jigsaw-puzzle tables. "Dan, are you listening to me? The world will not come to an end if we go away for a few days of R&R."

"I can't just drop everything. Besides, what if Dad needs me? Or Sam?"

When they'd first been married, Dan had been working three jobs—at Ruskin Construction with his brother Sam, at The Spruces, the hotel his father owned, and as a woodworker, making boxes, clocks, and other small items in his spare time. Within a year of the wedding, he'd opened his retail storefront. Little had he known then that one of his offerings,

the jigsaw-puzzle table, would become so popular
that it would end up being his only product.

Both the credit and the blame for his success went
to Liss. She had been the one who'd designed his
webpage. Soon after, people from all over the U.S.
and Canada had started ordering his tables. He'd
stumbled upon a niche market lucrative enough to
allow him to earn a living supplying it . . . so long as
he was willing to work straight out seven days a week,
twelve months a year.

Hands on hips, Liss glared at her husband. "You
have an overdeveloped sense of responsibility, Dan
Ruskin. Right now, *I'm* the one who needs you."

At last she had his full attention. "You've *got* me,
babe," he said with a grin and a glint in his eyes.

When he reached for her, she danced away, holding one hand in front of her in the traditional "halt"
position. "Stop right there, mister. I'm trying to hold
a rational discussion here."

"Oh, come on. Use your womanly wiles to seduce
me into doing your bidding. Please?" This time he
caught her and tugged her close for a kiss.

Dan Ruskin was a seriously good kisser. He was
also six-foot-two to her five-foot-nine, broad shoul-
dered to her slender, and she was crazy about him.
For a brief interlude, Liss had a hard time remembering why she'd come looking for him.

"Rational," she repeated when they came up for
air. The firmest tone of voice she could manage
wouldn't have convinced a cat to roll in catnip, but
Dan released her anyway and went back to his packing.

"Give it your best shot," he invited her.

Liss leaned back against one of Dan's work tables,
arms crossed in front of her chest. "You and I have

both been working straight out ever since we got back from our honeymoon. No time off for good behavior. We *need* a vacation, and the timing is perfect. We're past leaf-peeper season and it's too early for the pre-Christmas rush. I can close up shop for a week without losing much in the way of walk-in business. If we both set up 'out of office' email responses, any new online customers will know when we'll be back and can plan accordingly. They'll still be able to send in orders."

"It's not a good idea to be unavailable. Customers expect fast service when they spend their hard-earned cash."

"Customers have to wait for the order to be filled anyway. Seriously, Dan. Give me one good reason why we can't take a week's vacation. It's not like I want to go to Hawaii or Australia or Sri Lanka. Gina's Christmas tree farm is in New Boston. We'll only be a couple of hours away from home. If there's an emergency, we can hop in the car and come straight back."

"What would constitute an emergency?"

She came close to answering with a flip "serious injury or death." In the nick of time, she realized that she might be tempting fate to joke about such a thing. It had been a long while since she'd last encountered sudden death—a little over five years, on a Halloween she'd never forget—but for several years before that she'd had an alarming tendency to stumble into murder investigations. She sincerely hoped she wouldn't have to deal with *any* sort of crime ever again.

"What if there's a crisis at the Emporium?" Dan asked.

"There won't be. I told you. I'll close it for the du-

ration." She'd already countered Gina's original
offer with the proposal that her old friend pay a cat-
and-house-sitter rather than a sales clerk. Liss had a
certain young relative in mind for the job, one who
was currently squirreling away every penny he could
earn into a college fund.

"My shop, then."

"*Your* shop?" Liss couldn't help but smile. Dan was
running out of excuses. "It's a co-op now. Or have
you forgotten?"

When he'd switched over to making nothing but
jigsaw-puzzle tables, Dan's inventory of hand-crafted
wooden objects had shrunk to almost nothing. He'd
solved the lack-of-stock problem by turning his storefront, Carrabassett County Wood Crafts, into a cooperative venture with other local craftspeople. They'd
pooled their resources as well as the products they
created and hired a full-time employee to run the
place.

"I haven't forgotten. But what if—?"

"If Maud can't handle anything that comes up,
she shouldn't be working for you." Maud Dennison,
the co-op's sales clerk and bookkeeper, was a retired
teacher who'd found she didn't like having so much
time on her hands. Since she'd capably managed ob-
streperous seventh graders for forty-plus years, Liss
knew she could handle anything that came along.

"I don't see how we can close up and go away without a care in the world," Dan grumbled as he walked
the heavy box onto a dolly and trundled it toward
the door. There was only one more step to go—print
a mailing label and assembly instructions and attach
those to the carton.

Liss trailed after him, gaining confidence with
every step. "It's easy. In my case, all I have to do is put

a sign on the door. It isn't as if the Emporium is ever swamped with customers."

"You get a lot more walk-ins than you used to. So does Carrabassett County Wood Crafts. So does everyone in town."

"Victims of our own success," Liss agreed.

Where once she and the other local business owners had taken every Sunday and Monday off, now they usually stayed open seven days a week. The Moosetookalook Small Business Association had become so adept at promoting the unique gift shops surrounding the village square as a shopping mecca that tour busses had them on their regular routes and groups of retirees booked blocks of rooms at The Spruces just to be able to enjoy the experience. Seasonal festivities drew good crowds, too, which meant that volunteering on behalf of the MSBA took up even more of Liss and Dan's dwindling supply of free time.

"I can't see how we'll manage, Liss," Dan said. "Tell Gina to hire someone to evaluate her property."

She threw her hands in the air. "She hired *me*. And she gave me a blank check to use to hire a cat sitter."

"Send it back." The box in position, he turned to face her.

Liss sent him her best exasperated glare. "If you really can't see your way clear to go, I'll take on the job without you. I gave my word to Gina that I'd evaluate the place for her. I don't break my promises."

Dan looked thoughtful. "How about this? You drive over there, take a quick look at the place, and come back the same day." He opened the door and gestured for her to exit first.

"I'm *going* for a week," she said as she swept past

him. "Even if you don't need a break from routine, I do. So, I'm leaving on Friday—two days from now." She looked back at him over her shoulder. "Are you coming with me or not?"

The challenge in her voice made him scowl. He locked up, then stood there, staring at the back of their house and what could be seen of the street between it and the building next door.

Progress, Liss thought. After a moment, she went back to him and eased herself in under his arm. She planted a quick kiss on his cheek.

Darkness came early at this time of year. The pale glow of streetlamps illuminated not only the sidewalk and street but also a section of the town square, where a bandstand and merry-go-round held pride of place, along with a monument to the Civil War dead. As Liss watched, a woman appeared on one of the paths that wound through the green. Liss recognized her as soon as the light struck her pale hair—Sherri Campbell on her way home, crossing from the police station in the municipal building to her apartment above Carrabassett County Wood Crafts.

Sherri must be on the two-to-ten shift, Liss thought, *and taking a supper break to spend a little time with Pete and the kids.* There were two of them, Sherri's teenaged son, Adam Willett, and the couple's four-year-old daughter, Amber.

Liss took a deep breath. "We could use an opportunity to talk about . . . things."

Dan said nothing, but she could feel his arm tense where it draped across her shoulders.

"I think I'll go look over what's in my closet." Liss slipped away from him. "I need to decide what to take with me. November weather is always tricky to pack for."

He waited until she reached the back door of the house before he spoke. "You'd best pick out clothes for me, too."

"Did you hear Liss and Dan are taking a vacation?" Sherri Campbell handed two heavy-laden plates to her husband and grabbed the other two herself. "They're leaving tomorrow."

"Yeah, Dan told me."

Pete deftly deposited his own supper on the table and slid the other plate into Sherri's place while she served Adam and Amber. The little girl's eyes lit up when she saw the mound of mashed potatoes. Sherri couldn't help but grin as she sat down and reached for the salt. Before their daughter ate a single bite, she would shape those spuds into the signature landscape from *Close Encounters of the Third Kind.* Young as Amber was, Sherri doubted she had understood much of the rest of that movie, but she definitely got the part with the potatoes.

"He's not exactly enthusiastic about it." As Pete settled into his chair, it creaked under his weight. He was built like a linebacker, solid and square, but what had been chunky when they met had begun to waver on the edge of overweight.

Sherri needed a moment to switch out of mommy mode. "Dan isn't? Why not?"

"Maybe he thinks Gina Snowe has a lot of nerve expecting them to drop everything to do her a favor."

"She always was something of a queen bee." Sherri ate mechanically, taking an occasional sip of Moxie, a beverage she'd only recently rediscovered. Her thoughts drifted back to the last time she'd run into

Liss's friend Gina. It had not been a pleasant encounter.

Why she'd decided to attend her tenth high school reunion, Sherri would never know. Maybe because she'd had Pete as her escort, and Liss and Dan were with them? She should have known better. Ten years hadn't been enough time for the cattier members of the class to sheath their claws. Gina Snowe wasn't the worst of the lot, but she'd been ready and willing to repeat what she knew about Sherri and the mistakes she'd made when she was younger. That most of what she'd said was true only made it worse. Sherri had dropped out of school and left town halfway through their senior year. She'd taken up with some pretty unsavory characters during her years away from Moosetookalook. She'd returned with Adam but without a husband, adding one more "sin" to the list.

That was all a long time ago, she reminded herself as she looked around the table at husband, son, and daughter. She'd built a new life for herself since then.

At the time of that tenth reunion, Sherri recalled, she'd barely taken the first steps toward a tentative friendship with Liss MacCrimmon. The bond between them had strengthened in the months and years that followed. These days, with Sherri married to Pete and Liss to Dan, Sherri was closer to Liss than Gina had ever been. While it might be petty to think in terms of a rivalry of BFFs, the truth of the matter was that it *did* make Sherri feel better to know that Liss thought highly of her.

And it wasn't only Liss who liked and respected her, either. Sherri was certain no one in their small town had forgotten her past, but she also knew that, in the present, she was well regarded by the community she served as chief of police of the Moosetookalook Police Department.

The subject of Dan and Liss's "vacation" didn't come up again that evening, but Sherri did find herself thinking about her friend while she watched Amber at play after supper. Once Adam had gone off to his own room to do homework, the little girl reveled in having her parents all to herself.

"Come on, pumpkin," Pete crooned. "Show me what you can do with that pencil." He was trying to teach her to print her name.

They sat side by side on the carpet, dark heads bent over the oversized drawing pad between them. Amber already resembled her father far more than her petite blond mother. Measurements taken by her pediatrician indicated she was going to be tall, close to Pete's five-foot-ten. She'd tower over Sherri by the time she finished growing, and probably end up being taller than Adam, too.

"She's only four, Pete."

"But she's the smartest little rug rat in the entire world. Look at that. That's an A."

It looked like three random lines to Sherri, but she hadn't the heart to burst Pete's bubble. Instead, from her perch on the sofa, she continued to watch the interaction between father and daughter.

There were a lot of smart little rug rats around, Sherri mused. She wondered if Liss and Dan were thinking of adding one of their own to the mix. Maybe there was more to their vacation than simply doing a favor for Gina Snowe.

Sherri was not the only one in their circle of friends and family to have been pregnant during the last few years. Sandy and Zara Kalishnakof, who owned and operated Dance Central, had two young children, both carrot-tops like Zara. And Mary Ruskin Winchester, Liss's sister-in-law, was currently expecting her sixth child. Liss, though, had never even hinted that she might want a child of her own.

Later, after Adam and Amber had been tucked into their beds, Sherri broached the subject with Pete. "Has Dan ever said anything to you about starting a family?"

"None of our business, hon." Pete avoided meeting her eyes by pretending to be fascinated by the late night news on TV.

Sherri wasn't buying it. He knew something. He just wasn't saying.

But he was also right. It was none of their business.

Frowning, Liss consulted the map Gina had drawn for her. "I can't make heads nor tails of this. We're going to have to stop in town and ask directions."

They had driven some hundred and forty miles, all the way from Moosetookalook to New Boston, the town in which the tree farm was located. Getting there had seemed simple enough at the outset but now that they were in the immediate vicinity the road signs and landmarks did not match up with Gina's squiggles.

Their truck did not come equipped with GPS. Dan considered these devices to be a waste of money and, in general, Liss agreed with him. None of them functioned well in rural areas and she'd heard that on long trips they tended to choose the route with the lowest mileage, ignoring the fact that it would inevitably take the driver into the center of every major city along the way. Paper maps worked much better when it came to avoiding traffic jams and other delays. Usually.

Dan grumbled, but eventually he complied with his wife's suggestion. He pulled into the parking lot of a small grocery store. He hailed the first shopper they saw, an elderly man loading overflowing reusable canvas shopping bags into the trunk of his car.

"We're looking for Simeon Snowe's place," Dan said. "Can you tell us how to find it?"

"Nobody lives there." The old-timer had a vague look in his pale, rheumy eyes. "Hasn't been a going concern for some time."

"Yes, we know," Liss called across the cab of the truck. She smiled encouragingly. "The new owner asked us to take a look at the place for her."

"Then she shoulda told you how to get there." He opened his driver's side door and eased himself into the car. Without so much as another glance in their direction, he started the engine and drove away.

"Taciturn old cuss," Dan muttered.

"At least he confirmed that the place exists," Liss said brightly. "We'll have to find someone else to tell us how to get there."

The grocery store—the New Boston Food City—was bigger than the High Street Market in Moosetookalook, but not by much. Of the three checkout lanes at the front, only one was open.

The clerk was a teenager with a ring through her nose. She'd never heard of Simeon Snowe. Her customer, a jeans-clad woman in her mid-twenties who was busily piling cans, bottles, and bags of frozen food on the counter, didn't recognize the name either, but she offered a practical suggestion—ask at the town office.

Following her directions, they drove to the New Boston municipal building, a one-story clapboard structure that looked as if it had originally been built for some other purpose. A real estate office, Liss thought. Or maybe—she sniffed the air as they entered the building—a take-out pizza place.

"Help you?" asked a sour-faced older woman seated at one of several desks separated from the entrance by a wide wooden counter.

"Can you tell us where to find the farm belonging to the late Simeon Snowe?" Liss asked.

The woman rose slowly, as if she suffered from arthritis, and shuffled up to her side of the barrier. She appeared to be well past the usual retirement age and stared at them through thick glasses. "What's your business there?" she demanded.

The rude manner in which she asked the question took Liss aback and left her momentarily speechless. Dan stepped up to fill the void.

"We're here on behalf of the new owner, Gina Snowe." He leaned in, as if intent upon sharing a confidence, and added his best smile. "Ms. Snowe paid a brief visit to the farm herself a few days ago, but she was unexpectedly called away on business. She asked us to finish up her evaluation of the place. She drew a map for my wife here, but we're having a little trouble finding the landmarks."

The attempt at boyish charm fell flat. The woman looked even more suspicious of their motives. "We don't generally give out that sort of information," she said in a snippy voice. "I'll have to fetch the town manager." With that, she stomped off toward the back of the building, now moving at a surprisingly fast clip for someone who, only moments earlier, had looked as if she needed a cane.

Liss glanced down at herself. She'd worn jeans and a bulky sweater for the drive. Dan was similarly dressed. "Do we *look* like people who are planning to break in and rob the place?"

"She's right to be cautious. After all, we're strangers in town."

"Most folks aren't so stand-offish."

"That old guy at the grocery story wasn't inclined to be helpful," he reminded her.

The New Boston town manager, a middle-aged man in shirtsleeves and an unknotted tie, emerged from the rear of the town office before Liss could reply. He smiled at them in that particularly insincere way politicians have perfected and shook hands with Dan in a hearty manner.

"Steve Wilton," he said. "Call me Steve. Bea here tells me you're looking for the Snowe Christmas tree farm. Imagine that! Am I to gather that the estate has finally been settled?"

"Apparently." Dan's tone was dry as he introduced himself and Liss. He explained again about the map.

"A map, you say? Let's have a look."

Liss handed it over. It was proof, she supposed, that they had the right to request directions to the farm.

Ten minutes later, they were back in the truck and headed west. It turned out that their destination was some seven miles distant from the center of New Boston, just short of the town line. Curious, Liss dug out the most recent edition of *The Maine Atlas and Gazetteer*. New Boston had a population of four thousand nine hundred and eighty. That was almost five

times the size of Moosetookalook. Even so, the
Snowe farm was well away from any neighboring
houses.

It started to spit snow the moment Dan turned off
a two-lane country road into a long winding driveway. Sunset was at least an hour away, but the sky had
already turned an ominous gray that made everything look dark and dreary. To make matters worse,
overgrown rows of evergreens planted on either side
of the narrow way formed a high, nearly impenetra-
ble hedge.

Liss began to feel uneasy as she peered at the
thickly intertwined branches. "All we need are a few
thorns and I'll be wondering if we're about to stumble onto Sleeping Beauty's castle," she muttered
under her breath.

"Hold on!"

That was all the warning she had before Dan
slammed on the brakes.

Liss's seatbelt tightened, pressing hard against
her chest and lap. Fortunately, Dan had not been
going very fast. They didn't hit anything and the
airbags did not deploy.

When she looked out through the windshield,
Liss half expected to see a deer blocking their way,
but what had caused their precipitous stop was not
an animal. A heavy chain had been stretched across
the driveway. Dan opened his door and got out of
the truck. While he unhooked the barrier, Liss squinted
to read the words on the sign attached to the links.

The message was *not* WELCOME TO VACATION-
LAND.

It said: PRIVATE PROPERTY. TRESPASSERS
WILL BE SHOT.